Thank You PTSA

for generously purchasing this book!

BY MARIE RUTKOSKI

The Cabinet of Wonders
The Celestial Globe
The Jewel of the Kalderash
The Shadow Society
The Winner's Curse
The Winner's Crime

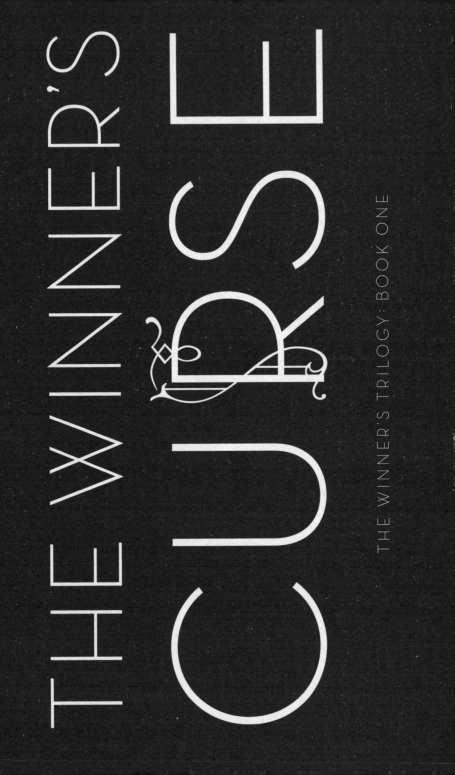

THE WINNER'S CURSE

THE WINNER'S TRILOGY · BOOK ONE

A NOVEL BY

MARIE RUTKOSKI

FARRAR STRAUS GIROUX · NEW YORK

SQUARE
FISH

SQUARE
FISH

An Imprint of Macmillan
175 Fifth Avenue
New York, NY 10010
macteenbooks.com

Square Fish books may be purchased for business or promotional use. For information on bulk
purchases, please contact the Macmillan Corporate and Premium Sales Department at
(800) 221-7945 x5442 or by e-mail at specialmarkets@macmillan.com.

Library of Congress Cataloging-in-Publication Data

Rutkoski, Marie.
The winner's curse / Marie Rutkoski.
pages cm — (The winner's trilogy ; book 1)
Summary: An aristocratic girl who is a member of a warmongering and enslaving
empire purchases a slave, an act that sets in motion a rebellion that might overthrow
her world as well as her heart.
ISBN 978-1-250-05697-9 (paperback)
[1. Slavery—Fiction.   2. Love—Fiction.]   I. Title.
PZ7.R935Wi 2014   [Fic]—dc23   2013000312

Originally published in the United States by Farrar Straus Giroux
First Square Fish Edition: 2015
Book designed by Elizabeth H. Clark
Square Fish logo designed by Filomena Tuosto

3 5 7 9 10 8 6 4 2

AR: 5.3 / LEXILE: 680L

Again, for Thomas

THE FROZEN WASTES

PLATEAU

THE PLAINS

Queen's City
(TARATANIR)

DACRA

TEMPLE
ISLAND

N

EQUATOR

W

E

S

SHE SHOULDN'T HAVE BEEN TEMPTED.

This is what Kestrel thought as she swept the sailors' silver off the impromptu gaming table set up in a corner of the market.

"Don't go," said one sailor.

"Stay," said another, but Kestrel cinched her wrist-strap velvet purse shut. The sun had lowered, and caramelized the color of things, which meant that she had played cards long enough to be noticed by someone who mattered.

Someone who would tell her father.

Cards wasn't even her favorite game. The silver wouldn't begin to pay for her silk dress, snagged from the splintery crate she had used as a stool. But sailors were much better adversaries than the average aristocrat. They flipped cards with feral tricks, swore when they lost, swore when they won, would gouge the last silver keystone coin out of a friend. And they cheated. Kestrel especially liked it when they cheated. It made beating them not quite so easy.

She smiled and left them. Then her smile faded. This

hour of thrilling risk was going to cost her. It wasn't the gambling that would infuriate her father, or the company she had kept. No, General Trajan was going to want to know why his daughter was in the city market alone.

Other people wondered, too. She saw it in their eyes as she threaded through market stalls offering open sacks of spice, the scents mingling with salty air that wafted from the nearby port. Kestrel guessed the words people didn't dare whisper as she passed. Of course they didn't speak. They knew who she was. And she knew what they would say.

Where was Lady Kestrel's escort?

And if she had no friend or family available to escort her to the market, where was her slave?

Well, as for a slave, they had been left at her villa. Kestrel did not need them.

As for the whereabouts of her escort, she was wondering the same thing.

Jess had wandered off to look at the wares. Kestrel last saw her weaving like a flower-drunk bee through the stalls, her pale blond hair almost white in the summer sun. Technically, Jess could get in as much trouble as Kestrel. It wasn't allowed for a young Valorian girl who wasn't a member of the military to walk alone. But Jess's parents doted on her, and they hardly had the same notion of discipline as the highest-ranking general in the Valorian army.

Kestrel scanned the stalls for her friend, and finally caught the gleam of blond braids styled in the latest fashion. Jess was talking to a jewelry seller who dangled a pair of earrings. The translucent gold droplets caught the light.

Kestrel drew closer.

"Topaz," the elderly woman was saying to Jess. "To brighten your lovely brown eyes. Only ten keystones."

There was a hard set to the jewelry seller's mouth. Kestrel met the woman's gray eyes and noticed that her wrinkled skin was browned from years of working outdoors. She was Herrani, but a brand on her wrist proved that she was free. Kestrel wondered how she had earned that freedom. Slaves freed by their masters were rare.

Jess glanced up. "Oh, Kestrel," she breathed. "Aren't these earrings perfect?"

Maybe if the weight of silver in Kestrel's purse hadn't dragged at her wrist she would have said nothing. Maybe if that drag at her wrist hadn't also dragged at her heart with dread, Kestrel would have thought before she spoke. But instead she blurted what was the obvious truth. "They're not topaz. They're glass."

There was a sudden bubble of silence. It expanded, grew thin and sheer. People around them were listening. The earrings trembled in midair.

Because the jewelry seller's bony fingers were trembling.

Because Kestrel had just accused her of trying to cheat a Valorian.

And what would happen next? What would happen to any Herrani in this woman's position? What would the crowd witness?

An officer of the city guard called to the scene. A plea of innocence, ignored. Old hands bound to the whipping post. Lashes until blood darkened the market dirt.

"Let me see," Kestrel said, her voice imperious, because she was very good at being imperious. She reached for the earrings and pretended to examine them. "Ah. It seems I was mistaken. Indeed they *are* topaz."

"Take them," whispered the jewelry seller.

"We are not poor. We have no need of a gift from someone such as you." Kestrel set coins on the woman's table. The bubble of silence broke, and shoppers returned to discussing whatever ware had caught their fancy.

Kestrel gave the earrings to Jess and led her away.

As they walked, Jess studied one earring, letting it swing like a tiny bell. "So they *are* real?"

"No."

"How can you tell?"

"They're completely unclouded," Kestrel said. "No flaws. Ten keystones was too cheap a price for topaz of that quality."

Jess might have commented that ten keystones was too great a price for glass. But she said only, "The Herrani would say that the god of lies must love you, you see things so clearly."

Kestrel remembered the woman's stricken gray eyes. "The Herrani tell too many stories." They had been dreamers. Her father always said that this was why they had been easy to conquer.

"Everyone loves stories," Jess said.

Kestrel stopped to take the earrings from Jess and slip them into her friend's ears. "Then wear these to the next society dinner. Tell everyone you paid an outrageous sum, and they will believe they're true jewels. Isn't that what stories do, make real things fake, and fake things real?"

Jess smiled, turning her head from side to side so that the earrings glittered. "Well? Am I beautiful?"

"Silly. You know you are."

Jess led the way now, slipping past a table with brass bowls holding powdered dye. "It's my turn to buy something for you," she said.

"I have everything I need."

"You sound like an old woman! One would think you're seventy, not seventeen."

The crowd was thicker now, filled with the golden features of Valorians, hair and skin and eyes ranging from honey tones to light brown. The occasional dark heads belonged to well-dressed house slaves, who had come with their masters and stayed close to their sides.

"Don't look so troubled," Jess said. "Come, I will find something to make you happy. A bracelet?"

But that reminded Kestrel of the jewelry seller. "We should go home."

"Sheet music?"

Kestrel hesitated.

"Aha," said Jess. She seized Kestrel's hand. "Don't let go."

This was an old game. Kestrel closed her eyes and was tugged blindly after Jess, who laughed, and then Kestrel laughed, too, as she had years ago when they first met.

The general had been impatient with his daughter's mourning. "Your mother's been dead half a year," he had said. "That is long enough." Finally, he had had a senator in a nearby villa bring his daughter, also eight years old, to visit. The men went inside Kestrel's house. The girls were told to stay outside. "Play," the general had ordered.

Jess had chattered at Kestrel, who ignored her. Finally, Jess stopped. "Close your eyes," she said.

Curious, Kestrel did.

Jess had grabbed her hand. "Don't let go!" They tore over the general's grassy grounds, slipping and tumbling and laughing.

It was like that now, except for the press of people around them.

Jess slowed. Then she stopped and said, "Oh."

Kestrel opened her eyes.

The girls had come to a waist-high wooden barrier that overlooked a pit below. "You brought me *here*?"

"I didn't mean to," said Jess. "I got distracted by a woman's hat—did *you* know hats are in fashion?—and was following to get a better look, and . . ."

"And brought us to the slave market." The crowd had congealed behind them, noisy with restless anticipation. There would be an auction soon.

Kestrel stepped back. She heard a smothered oath when her heel met someone's toes.

"We'll never get out now," Jess said. "We might as well stay until the auction's over."

Hundreds of Valorians were gathered before the barrier, which curved in a wide semicircle. Everyone in the crowd was dressed in silks, each with a dagger strapped to the hip, though some—like Jess—wore it more as an ornamental toy than a weapon.

The pit below was empty, save for a large wooden auction block.

"At least we have a good view." Jess shrugged.

Kestrel knew that Jess understood why her friend had claimed loudly that the glass earrings were topaz. Jess understood why they had been purchased. But the girl's shrug reminded Kestrel that there were certain things they couldn't discuss.

"Ah," said a pointy-chinned woman at Kestrel's side. "At last." Her eyes narrowed on the pit and the stocky man walking into its center. He was Herrani, with the typical black hair, though his skin was pale from an easy life, no doubt due to the same favoritism that had gotten him this job. This was someone who had learned how to please his Valorian conquerors.

The auctioneer stood in front of the block.

"Show us a girl first," called the woman at Kestrel's side, her voice both loud and languid.

Many voices were shouting now, each calling for what they wanted to see. Kestrel found it hard to breathe.

"A girl!" yelled the pointy-chinned woman, this time more loudly.

The auctioneer, who had been sweeping his hands toward him as if gathering the cries and excitement, paused when the woman's shout cut through the noise. He glanced at her, then at Kestrel. A flicker of surprise seemed to show on his face. She thought that she must have imagined it, for he skipped on to Jess, then peered in a full semicircle at all the Valorians against the barrier above and around him.

He raised a hand. Silence fell. "I have something very special for you."

The acoustics of the pit were made to carry a whisper, and the auctioneer knew his trade. His soft voice made everyone lean closer.

His hand shifted to beckon toward the open, yet roofed and shadowed structure built low and small at the back of the pit. He twitched his fingers once, then twice, and something stirred in the holding pen.

A young man stepped out.

The crowd murmured. Bewilderment grew as the slave slowly paced across the yellow sand. He stepped onto the auction block.

This was nothing special.

"Nineteen years old, and in fine condition." The auctioneer clapped the slave on the back. "This one," he said, "would be perfect for the house."

Laughter rushed through the crowd. Valorians nudged each other and praised the auctioneer. He knew how to entertain.

The slave was bad goods. He looked, Kestrel thought, like a brute. A deep bruise on the slave's cheek was evidence of a fight and a promise that he would be difficult to control. His bare arms were muscular, which likely only confirmed the crowd's belief that he would be best working for someone with a whip in hand. Perhaps in another life he could have been groomed for a house; his hair was brown, light enough to please some Valorians, and while his features couldn't be discerned from Kestrel's distance, there was a proud line in the way he stood. But his skin was bronzed from outdoor labor, and surely it was to such work that he would return. He might be purchased by someone who needed a dockworker or a builder of walls.

Yet the auctioneer kept up his joke. "He could serve at your table."

More laughter.

"Or be your valet."

Valorians held their sides and fluttered their fingers, begging the auctioneer to stop, stop, he was too funny.

"I want to leave," Kestrel told Jess, who pretended not to hear.

"All right, all right." The auctioneer grinned. "The lad does have some real skills. On my honor," he added, laying a hand over his heart, and the crowd chuckled again, for it was common knowledge that there was no such thing as Herrani honor. "This slave has been trained as a blacksmith. He would be perfect for any soldier, especially for an officer with a guard of his own and weapons to maintain."

There was a murmur of interest. Herrani blacksmiths were rare. If Kestrel's father were here, he would probably bid. His guard had long complained about the quality of the city blacksmith's work.

"Shall we start the bidding?" said the auctioneer. "Five pilasters. Do I hear five bronze pilasters for the boy? Ladies and gentlemen, you could not *hire* a blacksmith for so little."

"Five," someone called.

"Six."

And the bidding began in earnest.

The bodies at Kestrel's back might as well have been stone. She couldn't move. She couldn't look at the expressions of her people. She couldn't catch the attention of Jess, or stare into the too-bright sky. These were all the reasons, she decided, why it was impossible to gaze anywhere else but at the slave.

"Oh, come now," said the auctioneer. "He's worth at least ten."

The slave's shoulders stiffened. The bidding continued.

Kestrel closed her eyes. When the price reached twenty-five pilasters, Jess said, "Kestrel, are you ill?"

"Yes."

"We'll leave as soon as it's over. It won't be long now."

There was a lull in the bidding. It appeared the slave would go for twenty-five pilasters, a pitiful price, yet as much as anyone was willing to pay for a person who would soon be worked into uselessness.

"My dear Valorians," said the auctioneer. "I have forgotten one thing. Are you sure he wouldn't make a fine house slave? Because this lad can sing."

Kestrel opened her eyes.

"Imagine music during dinner, how charmed your guests will be." The auctioneer glanced up at the slave, who stood tall on his block. "Go on. Sing for them."

Only then did the slave shift position. It was a slight movement and quickly stilled, but Jess sucked in her breath as if she, like Kestrel, expected a fight to break out in the pit below.

The auctioneer hissed at the slave in rapid Herrani, too quietly for Kestrel to understand.

The slave answered in his language. His voice was low: "No."

Perhaps he didn't know the acoustics of the pit. Perhaps he didn't care, or worry that any Valorian knew at least enough Herrani to understand him. No matter. The auction was over now. No one would want him. Probably the person who had offered twenty-five pilasters was already regretting a bid for someone so intractable that he wouldn't obey even his own kind.

But his refusal touched Kestrel. The stony set of the slave's shoulders reminded her of herself, when her father demanded something that she couldn't give.

The auctioneer was furious. He should have closed the sale or at least made a show of asking for a higher price, but he simply stood there, fists at his sides, likely trying to figure out how he could punish the young man before passing him on to the misery of cutting rock, or the heat of the forge.

Kestrel's hand moved on its own. "A keystone," she called.

The auctioneer turned. He sought the crowd. When he found Kestrel a smile sparked his expression into cunning delight. "Ah," he said, "*there* is someone who knows worth."

"Kestrel." Jess plucked at her sleeve. "What are you doing?"

The auctioneer's voice boomed: "Going once, going twice—"

"Twelve keystones!" called a man leaning against the barrier across from Kestrel, on the other side of its semicircle.

The auctioneer's jaw dropped. "Twelve?"

"Thirteen!" came another cry.

Kestrel inwardly winced. If she had to bid anything— and why, why had she?—it shouldn't have been so high. Everyone thronged around the pit was looking at her: the general's daughter, a high society bird who flitted from one respectable house to the next. They thought—

"Fourteen!"

They thought that if *she* wanted the slave, he must merit the price. There must be a reason to want him, too.

"Fifteen!"

And the delicious mystery of *why* made one bid top the next.

The slave was staring at her now, and no wonder, since it was she who had ignited this insanity. Kestrel felt something within her swing on the hinge of fate and choice.

She lifted her hand. "I bid twenty keystones."

"Good heavens, girl," said the pointy-chinned woman to her left. "Drop out. Why bid on *him*? Because he's a singer? A singer of dirty Herrani drinking songs, if anything."

Kestrel didn't glance at her, or at Jess, though she sensed the girl was twisting her fingers. Kestrel's gaze didn't waver from the slave's.

"Twenty-five!" shouted a woman from behind.

The price was now more than Kestrel had in her purse. The auctioneer looked like he barely knew what to do with himself. The bidding spiraled higher, each voice spurring the next until it seemed that a roped arrow was shooting through the members of the crowd, binding them together, drawing them tight with excitement.

Kestrel's voice came out flat: "Fifty keystones."

The sudden, stunned quiet hurt her ears. Jess gasped.

"Sold!" cried the auctioneer. His face was wild with joy. "To Lady Kestrel, for fifty keystones!" He tugged the slave off the block, and it was only then that the youth's gaze broke away from Kestrel's. He looked at the sand, so intently that he could have been reading his future there, until the auctioneer prodded him toward the pen.

Kestrel drew in a shaky breath. Her bones felt watery. What had she done?

Jess slipped a supporting hand under her elbow. "You *are* sick."

"And rather light of purse, I'd say." The pointy-chinned woman snickered. "Looks like someone's suffering the Winner's Curse."

Kestrel turned to her. "What do you mean?"

"You don't come to auctions often, do you? The Winner's Curse is when you come out on top of the bid, but only by paying a steep price."

The crowd was thinning. Already the auctioneer was bringing out someone else, but the rope of excitement that had bound the Valorians to the pit had disintegrated. The show was over. The path was now clear for Kestrel to leave, yet she couldn't move.

"I don't understand," said Jess.

Neither did Kestrel. What had she been thinking? What had she been trying to prove?

Nothing, she told herself. Her back to the pit, she made her foot take the first step away from what she had done.

Nothing at all.

THE WAITING ROOM OF THE HOLDING PEN WAS open to the air and faced the street. It smelled of unwashed flesh. Jess stayed close, eyeing the iron door set into the far wall. Kestrel tried not to do the same. It was her first time here. House slaves were usually purchased by her father or the family steward, who supervised them.

The auctioneer was waiting near soft chairs arranged for Valorian customers. "Ah." He beamed when he saw Kestrel. "The winner! I hoped to be here before you arrived. I left the pit as soon as I could."

"Do you always greet your customers personally?" She was surprised at his eagerness.

"Yes, the good ones."

Kestrel wondered how much could be heard through the tiny barred window of the iron door.

"Otherwise," the auctioneer continued, "I leave the final transaction in the hands of my assistant. She's in the pit now, trying to unload twins." He rolled his eyes at the difficulty of keeping family together. "Well"—he shrugged—"someone might want a matched set."

Two Valorians entered the waiting room, a husband and wife. The auctioneer smiled, asked if they would mind taking a seat, and said he would be with them shortly. Jess whispered in Kestrel's ear, saying that the couple settling into the low chairs in a far corner were friends of her parents. Did Kestrel mind if she went to greet them?

"No," said Kestrel, "I don't." She couldn't blame Jess for feeling uncomfortable with the gritty details of purchasing people, even if the fact of it shaped every hour of her life, from the moment a slave drew her morning bath to when another unbraided her hair for bed.

After Jess had joined the husband and wife, Kestrel looked meaningfully at the auctioneer. He nodded. He pulled a thick key from his pocket, went to unlock the door, and stepped inside. "You," Kestrel heard him say in Herrani. "Time to leave."

There was a rustle and the auctioneer returned. The slave walked behind.

He lifted his gaze to meet Kestrel's. His eyes were a clear, cool gray.

They startled her. Yet she should have expected to see this color in a Herrani, and Kestrel thought it must be the livid bruise on his cheek that made the expression in his eyes so uncanny. Still, she grew uncomfortable under his gaze. Then his lashes fell. He looked at the ground, letting long hair obscure his face. One side was still swollen from the fight, or beating.

He seemed perfectly indifferent to anything around him. Kestrel didn't exist, or the auctioneer, or even himself.

The auctioneer locked the iron door. "Now." He clasped his hands together in a single clap. "The small matter of payment."

She handed the auctioneer her purse. "I have twenty-four keystones."

The auctioneer paused, uncertain. "Twenty-four is not fifty, my lady."

"I will send my steward with the rest later today."

"Ah, but what if he loses his way?"

"I am General Trajan's daughter."

He smiled. "I know."

"The full amount is no difficulty for us," Kestrel continued. "I simply chose not to carry fifty keystones with me today. My word is good."

"I'm sure." He didn't mention that Kestrel could return at another time to collect her purchase and pay in full, and Kestrel said nothing of the rage she had seen in his face when the slave defied him, or of her suspicion that the auctioneer would take revenge. The likelihood of it rose with every moment the slave remained here.

Kestrel watched the auctioneer think. He could insist she return later, risk offending her, and lose the entire sum. Or he could pocket not even half of fifty keystones now and perhaps never obtain the rest.

But he was clever. "May I escort you home with your purchase? I would like to see Smith settled in safely. Your steward can take care of the cost then."

She glanced at the slave. He had blinked at his name, but didn't lift his face. "Fine," she told the auctioneer.

She crossed the waiting room to Jess and asked the husband and wife if they would escort the girl home.

"Of course," said the husband—Senator Nicon, Kestrel remembered. "But what of you?"

She nodded at the two men over her shoulder. "They will come with me."

Jess knew a Herrani auctioneer and a rebellious slave were not the ideal escort. Kestrel knew it, too, but a flash of resentment at her situation—at the situation she had created—made her sick with all the rules that governed her world.

Jess said, "Are you sure?"

"Yes."

The couple raised eyebrows, yet clearly decided that the situation was none of their business except as a piece of gossip to spread.

Kestrel left the slave market, the auctioneer and Smith trailing behind her.

She walked quickly through the neighborhoods that separated this dingy part of town from the Garden District. The cross-hatching of streets was ordered, right-angled, Valorian-designed. She knew the way, yet had the odd sense of being lost. Today, everything seemed foreign. When she passed through the Warriors' Quarter, whose dense barracks she had run through as a child, she imagined soldiers rising against her.

Though of course any of these armed men and women would die to protect her, and expected her to become one of their own. Kestrel had only to obey her father's wishes and enlist.

When the streets began to change, to twist in irrational directions and bend like water, Kestrel was relieved. Trees leafed into a green canopy overhead. She could hear fountains behind high stone walls.

She came to a massive iron door. One of her father's guards peered through its window and swung the door open.

Kestrel said nothing to him or the other guards, and they said nothing to her. She led the way across the grounds. The auctioneer and slave followed.

She was home. But the footfalls behind her on the flagstone path reminded Kestrel that this had not always been her home. This estate, and the entire Garden District, had been made by the Herrani, who had called it by another name when it had been theirs.

She stepped onto the lawn. So did the men, their footsteps now hushed by grass.

A yellow bird trilled and swooped through the trees. Kestrel listened until the song dwindled. She continued toward the villa.

The sound of her sandals on the marble floor of the entryway echoed gently against walls painted with leaping creatures, flowers, and gods she didn't know. Her footfalls blurred into the whisper of water bubbling up from a shallow pool set into the floor.

"A beautiful home," said the auctioneer.

She glanced at him sharply, though she heard nothing

bitter in his voice. She searched him for some sign that he recognized the house, that he had visited it—as an honored guest, friend, or even family member—before the Herran War. But that was a foolish notion. The villas in the Garden District had belonged to aristocratic Herrani, and if the auctioneer had been one of those, he wouldn't have ended up in his line of work. He would have become a house slave, perhaps a tutor for Valorian children. If the auctioneer *did* know her house, it was because he had delivered slaves here for her father.

She hesitated to look at Smith. When she did, he refused to look back.

The housekeeper came toward her down the long hall that stretched beyond the fountain. Kestrel sent her away again with the order to fetch the steward and ask him to return with twenty-six keystones. When the steward arrived, his blond brows were drawn together and the hands holding a small coffer were tight. Harman's hands became tighter still when he noticed the auctioneer and slave.

Kestrel opened the coffer and counted money into the auctioneer's outstretched hand. He pocketed the silver, then emptied her purse, which he had carried with him. With a slight bow, he returned the flat bag to her. "Such a pleasure to have your business." He turned to go.

She said, "There had better not be a fresh mark on him."

The auctioneer's eyes flicked to the slave and traced his rags, his dirty, scarred arms. "You're welcome to inspect, my lady," the auctioneer drawled.

Kestrel frowned, unsettled by the idea of inspecting any

person, let alone *this* person. But before she could form a response, the auctioneer had left.

"How much?" Harman demanded. "How much, total, did this cost?"

She told him.

He drew in a long breath. "Your father—"

"I will tell my father."

"Well, what am I supposed to do with *him*?"

Kestrel looked at the slave. He hadn't moved, but remained standing on the same black tile as if still on the auction block. He had ignored the entire conversation, tuning out the Valorian he probably didn't fully understand. His eyes were raised, resting on a painted nightingale that graced a far wall. "This is Smith," Kestrel told the steward.

Harman's anxiety eased somewhat. "A blacksmith?" Slaves were sometimes named by masters for their work. "We could use that. I'll send him to the forge."

"Wait. I'm not sure that's where I want him." She spoke to Smith in Herrani: "Do you sing?"

He looked at her then, and Kestrel saw the same expression she had seen earlier in the waiting room. His gray eyes were icy. "No."

Smith had answered in her language, and his accent was light.

He turned away. Dark hair fell forward. It curtained his profile.

Kestrel's nails bit into her palms. "See to it that he has a bath," she told Harman in a voice she hoped was brisk rather than frustrated. "Give him appropriate clothes."

She started to walk down the hallway, then stopped. The words flashed out of her mouth: "And cut his hair."

Kestrel felt the chill of Smith's gaze on her back as she retreated. It was easy, now, to name that expression in his eyes.

Contempt.

2

KESTREL DIDN'T KNOW WHAT TO SAY.

Her father, fresh from a bath after a hot day of training soldiers, watered his wine. The third course was served: small hens stuffed with spiced raisins and crushed almonds. It tasted dry to her.

"Did you practice?" he asked.

"No."

His large hands paused in their movements.

"I will," she said. "Later." She drank from her cup, then ran a thumb over its surface. The glass was smoky green and finely blown. It had come with the house. "How are the new recruits?"

"Wet behind the ears, but not a bad lot." He shrugged. "We need them."

Kestrel nodded. The Valorians had always faced barbarian invasions on the fringes of their territories, and as the empire had grown in the past five years, attacks became more frequent. They didn't threaten the Herran peninsula, but General Trajan often trained battalions that would be sent to the empire's outer reaches.

He prodded a glazed carrot with his fork. Kestrel looked at the silver utensil, its tines shining sharply in the candle-light. It was a Herrani invention, one that had been absorbed into her culture so long ago it was easy to forget Valorians had ever eaten with their fingers.

"I thought you were going to the market this afternoon with Jess," he said. "Why didn't she join us for dinner?"

"She didn't accompany me home."

He set down his fork. "Then who did?"

"Father, I spent fifty keystones today."

He waved a hand to indicate that the sum was irrele-vant. His voice was deceptively calm: "If you walked through the city alone, *again*—"

"I didn't." She told him who had come home with her, and why.

The general rubbed his brow and squeezed his eyes shut. "*That* was your escort?"

"I don't need an escort."

"You certainly wouldn't, if you enlisted."

And there they were, pressing the sore spot of an old argument. "I will never be a soldier," she said.

"You've made that clear."

"If a woman can fight and die for the empire, why can't a woman walk alone?"

"That's the point. A woman *soldier* has proved her strength, and so doesn't need protection."

"Neither do I."

The general flattened his hands against the table. When a girl came to clear away the plates, he barked at her to leave.

"You honestly don't believe that *Jess* could offer me any protection," Kestrel said.

"Women who are not soldiers don't walk alone. It's custom."

"Our customs are absurd. Valorians take pride in being able to survive on little food if we must, but an evening meal is an insult if it's not at least seven courses. I can fight well enough, but if I'm not a soldier it's as if years of training don't exist."

Her father gave her a level look. "Your military strength has never been in combat."

Which was another way of saying that she was a poor fighter.

More gently, he said, "You're a strategist."

Kestrel shrugged.

Her father said, "Who suggested I draw the Dacran barbarians into the mountains when they attacked the empire's eastern border?"

All she had done then was point out the obvious. The barbarians' overreliance on cavalry had been clear. So, too, had been the fact that the dry eastern mountains would starve horses of water. If anyone was a strategist, it was her father. He was strategizing that very moment, using flattery to get what he wanted.

"Imagine how the empire would benefit if you truly worked with me," he said, "and used that talent to secure its territories, instead of pulling apart the logic of customs that order our society."

"Our customs are lies." Kestrel's fingers clenched the fragile stem of her glass.

Her father's gaze fell to her tight hand. He reached for it. Quietly, firmly, he said, "These are not my rules. They are the empire's. Fight for it, and have your independence. Don't, and accept your constraints. Either way, you live by our laws." He raised one finger. "And you don't complain."

Then she wouldn't say anything at all, Kestrel decided. She snatched her hand away and stood. She remembered how the slave had used his silence as a weapon. He had been haggled over, pushed, led, peered at. He would be cleaned, shorn, dressed. Yet he had refused to give up everything.

Kestrel knew strength when she encountered it.

So did her father. His light brown eyes narrowed at her.

She left the dining hall. She stalked down the northern wing of the villa until she reached a set of double doors. She threw them open and felt her way through the dark interior for a small silver box and an oil lamp. Her fingers were familiar with this ritual. It was no trouble to light the lamp blind. She could play blind, too, but didn't want to risk missing a note. Not tonight, not when today she had done little but fumble and err.

She skirted the piano in the center of the room, skimming a palm across its flat, polished surface. The instrument was one of the few things her family had brought from the capital. It had been her mother's.

Kestrel opened several glass doors that led into the garden. She breathed in the night, letting its air pool inside her lungs.

But she smelled jasmine. She imagined its tiny flower

blooming in the dark, each petal stiff and pointed and perfect. She thought again of the slave, and didn't know why.

She looked at her traitor of a hand, the one that had lifted to catch the eye of the auctioneer.

Kestrel shook her head. She wouldn't think about the slave anymore.

She sat in front of the instrument's row of black and white keys, nearly a hundred of them.

This wasn't the kind of practice her father had had in mind. He had meant her daily sessions with the captain of his guard. Well, she didn't want to train at Needles, or anything else her father thought she should learn.

Her fingers rested on the keys. She pressed slightly, not quite hard enough for the hammers inside to strike the loom of metallic cords.

She took a deep breath and began to play.

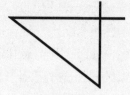

SHE HAD FORGOTTEN HIM.

Three days passed, and the lady of the house seemed entirely oblivious to the fact that she had purchased a slave to add to the general's collection of forty-eight.

The slave wasn't sure he felt relieved.

The first two days had been blissful. He couldn't remember the last time he had been allowed to be lazy. The bath had been amazingly hot, and the soap made him stare through the steam. The lather was richer than he'd had in years. It smelled like memories.

It left his skin feeling new, and though he'd held his head rigid while another Herrani slave cut his hair, and though he kept lifting his hand to sweep aside locks that were gone, on the second day he found that he didn't mind so much. It gave him a clear view of his world.

On the third day, the steward came for him.

The slave, having no orders, had been wandering the grounds. The house was off-limits, but he was content to consider it from the outside. He counted its many windows and doors. He lay on the grass, letting its warm green static tickle his palms, glad that his hands weren't too calloused to feel it. The yellow ocher of the villa walls glowed in the light, then faded. He listed in his mind which rooms of the house grew dark at which time of the day. He gazed up at orange trees. Sometimes, he slept.

The other slaves did their best to ignore him. At first, they shot him looks that varied from resentment to confusion to longing. He couldn't bring himself to care. As soon as he'd been directed to the slaves' quarters, housed in a building that looked almost exactly like the stables, he caught on to the pecking order of the general's Herrani. He was last.

He ate his bread like the rest of them, and shrugged whenever asked why he hadn't been assigned to a task. He answered direct questions. Mostly, though, he listened.

On the third day, he was making a mental map of the outbuildings: the slaves' quarters, the stables, the barracks for the general's private guard, the forge, small sheds for storage, a little cottage near the garden. The estate, particularly for being still part of the city, was large. The slave felt lucky that he had so many free hours to study it.

He was sitting on a gentle hill near the orchard, at a height that let him see the steward striding toward him from the villa long before the Valorian arrived. This pleased the slave. It confirmed what he had come to suspect: that General Trajan's home would not be easy to defend if attacked in the right way. The estate had probably been given to the general because it was the largest and finest in the city, and ideal for maintaining a personal guard and horses, but the tree-covered slopes surrounding the house would have advantages for an unfriendly force. The slave wondered if the general truly didn't see this. Then again, Valorians didn't know what it was like to be attacked at home.

The slave stopped his thoughts. They threatened to plow up his past. He willed his mind to be frosted earth: hard and barren.

He focused on the sight of the steward huffing up the hill. The steward was one of the few Valorian servants, like the housekeeper, whose positions were too important to be assigned to Herrani. The slave assumed that the steward was well paid. He was certainly well dressed, in the gold-shot fabrics Valorians favored. The man's thin yellow hair flew in the breeze. As he came closer, the slave heard him muttering in Valorian, and knew himself to be the target of the man's irritation.

"You," the steward said in heavily accented Herrani. "There you be, lazy good-for-nothing."

The slave remembered the man's name—Harman—but didn't use it. He didn't say anything, just let Harman vent his anger. It amused him to hear the man butcher his language. The steward's accent was laughable, his grammar worse. His only skill was a rich vocabulary of insults.

"You come." Harman jerked a hand to indicate that he should be followed.

The slave quickly realized he was being led to the forge.

Another Herrani was waiting outside. He recognized her, though he saw her only for meals and at night. Her name was Lirah, and she worked in the house. She was pretty; younger than him, probably too young to remember the war.

Harman began talking at her in Valorian. The slave tried to be patient as Lirah translated.

"Lady Kestrel can't be bothered to place you, so I"—she blushed—"I mean, *he*"—she nodded at Harman—"has decided to set you to work. Usually the general's guard see to their own weapon repair, and a Valorian blacksmith from the city is hired on a regular basis to forge new weapons."

The slave nodded. There were good reasons why the Valorians trained few Herrani blacksmiths. One had only to look around the forge to understand. Anyone could see the heavy tools and guess the strength it would take to manipulate them.

"You will do this from now on," Lirah continued, "so long as you prove to be competent."

Harman took the silence that followed as an invitation to speak again. Lirah translated. "Today you will make horseshoes."

"Horseshoes?" That was too easy.

Lirah gave him a sympathetic smile. When she spoke, it was in her own voice, not the stilted repeating of Harman's. "It's a test. You're supposed to make as many as you can before sunset. Can you shoe a horse, too?"

"Yes."

Lirah seemed to regret this answer on his behalf. She told the steward, who said, "That's what he'll be doing tomorrow, then. Every horse in the stable needs to be shod." He snorted. "We'll see how this animal gets along with the other ones."

Before the war, Valorians had admired, even envied— yes, envied—the Herrani. After, it was as if the spell had been broken or a new one had been cast. The slave never could quite believe it. Somehow, "animal" had become possible. Somehow, the word named *him*. This was a discovery ten years old and yet remade every day. It should have been dulled by repetition. Instead, he was sore from its constant cut of surprise. He was sour with swallowed anger.

The pleasant, trained expression on Lirah's face hadn't faltered. She pointed to the coal bin, kindling, and heaps of raw and used iron. The steward set a box of matches on the anvil. Then they left.

The slave looked around the forge and debated whether he should pass the test or fail.

He sighed, and lit a fire.

His holiday was over. On his first day in the forge, the slave made more than fifty horseshoes—enough to appear dedicated and skilled, but not so much that he drew attention. The following day, he shod all the horses, even those whose shoes were new. The groom warned that some of the animals could be dangerous to handle, especially the general's stallions, but the slave had no trouble. He made sure, however, that the task took the whole day. He liked listening to the horses' low whickers and feeling their gentle, warm breath. Also, the stables were a decent place to hear news—or they would have been, if a soldier had come to exercise a horse.

Or if the girl had.

The slave was judged to be a good buy. Lady Kestrel had a fine eye, Harman said grudgingly, and the slave was given several weapons to repair, as well as orders for new ones.

Every dusk, when the slave walked across the grounds from the forge to his quarters, the villa blazed with light. It was curfew and bedtime for slaves, but the restless Valorians would stay up for a long while yet. They trained to get by on very little sleep, perhaps six hours a night—less, if necessary. It was one of the things that had helped them win the war.

The slave was the first to stretch out on his pallet. Each night, he tried to sift through the events of the day and glean useful information from them, but all he had experienced was hard work.

Weary, he shut his eyes. He wondered if those two days of idyll would turn out to have been a stroke of bad fortune. That time had let him forget who he was. It played tricks with his mind.

Sometimes, at the edge of sleep, he thought he heard music.

USUALLY, KESTREL THOUGHT OF HER HOUSE AS
an echoing place, one filled with mostly uninhabited, if
lovely, rooms. The grounds, too, were quiet, the noises small:
the scratch of a hoe in the garden, the faint thud of horse
hooves from the paddock set far back from the house, the
sigh of trees. Usually, Kestrel enjoyed how the space and
quiet made her senses more awake.

Lately, however, she had no peace at home. She seques-
tered herself with her music, but found that she played only
difficult pieces, with notes clustered thickly together, her
fingers chasing each other across the keys. Her sessions left
her worn. The stiffness was minor and in localized spots—
her wrists, the small of her back—but when she wasn't playing she couldn't ignore the twinges. Each morning she would
swear to herself that she would go gently on the piano. Yet
at dusk, after hours of feeling suffocated—no, as if she were
hiding in her own home—she would again wrest something
demanding from the music.

One afternoon, perhaps eight days after the auction, a

note came from Jess. Kestrel eagerly opened it, glad for the distraction. Jess, in her typical swirly writing and short, eager sentences, asked why Kestrel was hiding from her. Would she please pay Jess a visit today? Kestrel's advice on what to wear to Lady Faris's picnic was needed. Jess added a post-script: a sentence in smaller writing, the letters bunched and hurried, signaling that she couldn't resist dropping an obvious hint even at the same time she worried it would bother Kestrel: *By the way, my brother has been asking about you.*

Kestrel reached for her riding boots.

As she wound through the rooms of her suite, she caught a glimpse in a window of the thatched cottage near the garden.

Kestrel paused, the leather boots in her hand tapping against her thigh. The cottage was not so far away from the slaves' quarters, which loomed at the border of the window's view. She felt a tug of discomfort.

Of course she did. Kestrel glanced away from the slaves' quarters and focused on Enai's cottage. She hadn't been to see her old nurse in several days. No wonder the view troubled her, when it showed the sweet little house Kestrel had had built for the woman who had raised her. Well, she would visit Enai on her way to the stables.

But by the time she had finished lacing her boots and gone downstairs, the steward had already discovered through the almost instantaneous gossip of the household that Kestrel was leaving. Harman ambushed her by the parlor door.

"Going for a ride, my lady?"

She pulled on a glove. "As you see."

"No need to ask for an escort." He snapped his fingers at an older Herrani man scrubbing the floor. "This one will do."

Kestrel let out a slow breath. "I am *riding* to Jess's house."

"I'm sure he can ride," Harman said, though they both knew full well this wasn't likely. Riding was not taught to slaves. Either they had the skill from before the war or never would. "If not," Harman said, "you can take the carriage together. The general would gladly spare the use of two horses for the carriage to make sure you're properly escorted."

Kestrel nodded, just barely. She turned to leave.

"My lady, one more thing . . ."

Kestrel knew what that one more thing would be, but couldn't stop him, for to do so would have been to admit that she knew and wished she didn't.

"A week has passed since your purchase of that young slave," the steward said. "You've given no instructions for his employment."

"I forgot," Kestrel lied.

"Of course. You have more important things to deal with. Still, I was certain you had no intention of him lazing around, doing nothing, so I assigned him to the forge and to serve as a farrier for the horses. He has done well. My compliments, Lady Kestrel. You are an excellent judge of the Herrani market."

She looked at him.

Defensively, he said, "I only put him to work in the forge because he was suited to it."

She faced the door. When she opened it, she'd see

nothing but trees. There was no view from this part of the house that could unsettle her. "You made the right choice," she said. "Do with him as you see fit."

Kestrel stepped outside, her escort wordlessly following.

She didn't stop by the cottage after all. She walked straight to the stables. The old Herrani groom was there, as always. There was no one else. Kestrel went to stroke the nose of her horse, a big-boned animal bred for war and chosen for her by the general.

When she heard footsteps behind her, the sound of someone new entering the stables, she turned. Two soldiers walked up to the groom and ordered that their horses be saddled. Kestrel looked beyond them and saw the Herrani slave Harman had selected as her escort waiting patiently by the door.

She had no wish to waste time finding out if he could ride. She wanted to leave now. When they reached Jess's house she would send him to the kitchens so she wouldn't have to see him until the return home.

"Ready my carriage first," she told the groom, giving the soldiers a look that dared them to argue. They didn't, but were visibly irritated. She didn't care. She had to leave, the sooner the better.

"This one?"

Kestrel looked up from where she sat on a low divan strewn with dresses.

"Kestrel," said Jess, "pay attention."

Kestrel blinked. A black-haired girl, Jess's slave, was tying a sash around her mistress's waist, drawing in the flowery skirts so that they belled at the hips. Kestrel said to Jess, "Didn't you already try on that dress?"

"No." Jess snatched the sash out of the slave's hands and threw it onto the silken pile next to Kestrel. "You hate it, don't you?"

"No," said Kestrel, but Jess was already struggling out of the dress while her slave anxiously tried to undo its buttons before they popped. Pink skirts landed on Kestrel's lap.

"What are you going to wear?" Jess stood there in her slip. "Lady Faris's picnic is *the* event of the summer season. You can't look less than stunning."

"That will pose no problem for Kestrel," said a trim, stylishly dressed man lounging against the jamb of the door he had opened without their hearing. Jess's brother smiled at Kestrel.

Kestrel smiled back at Ronan, but in a crooked way that showed that she knew his exaggerated brand of flirtation was all the rage among young Valorian men these days and not to be taken seriously. She also knew that this—this dress-up session, Ronan's safe compliments—was what she had come for, in the hopes her mind would become too cluttered to think for itself.

He crossed the room, pushed dresses off the divan and onto the floor, and sat next to Kestrel. The black-haired slave, looking besieged, bent to collect the delicate fabrics.

Kestrel felt a sudden impulse to say something sharp, but wasn't sure to whom. Then the strains of music drifting in from the corridor saved her from embarrassing everyone in the room, including herself.

"The Senest nocturne," she said, recognizing the piece.

Ronan tilted his blond head against the ornately carved wood that edged the divan. He slunk against its soft back, stretching out his booted legs, and gazed up at Kestrel. "I told Olen to play," he said, referring to their Herrani musician. "I know it's one of your favorites."

Kestrel listened. The notes were careful, but oddly paced. She tensed at the arrival of a tricky passage and wasn't surprised to hear it flubbed.

"I could play," she offered.

Brother and sister exchanged a look. "Another time," Ronan said. "Our parents are home."

"They won't notice."

"You're too talented." He rested a hand on hers. "They will."

Kestrel slipped her hand away. Unbothered, Ronan reached for a stray ribbon between them and toyed with the strip of fabric, weaving it around his pale fingers. "So," he said, "what's this I hear about your extravagant purchase at the auction? Everyone's talking about it."

"Or they were," said Jess, "until a duel between the Trenex cousins."

"To the death?" said Kestrel. Duels had been banned by the emperor, but they were too entrenched a custom to be easily rooted out. They were usually overlooked by the authorities so long as there was no loss of life, and even then the only punishment was a levied fine.

"No," said Jess excitedly, "but blood was drawn."

"Tell me everything."

Jess inhaled, ready to spill her gossip, but Ronan raised

one ribboned finger and pointed it at Kestrel. "You," he said, "are changing the subject. Go on. Explain the mystery that cost you fifty keystones."

"There is no mystery." She decided to give a sensible reason that had nothing to do with why she had bought him.

And why *had* she?

Pity, perhaps. That strange sense of affinity.

Or had it been nothing more than simple, shameful possession?

"The slave is a blacksmith," Kestrel said. "My father keeps a personal guard. We needed someone to maintain weapons."

"That's what the auctioneer advertised," Jess said, stepping into another dress. "The slave was a perfect fit for Kestrel's household."

Ronan raised his brows. "To the tune of fifty keystones?"

"What do I care?" Kestrel wanted to end this conversation. "I am wealthy enough." She touched Ronan's sleeve. "And how much"—she rubbed the silk between her fingers—"did this cost?"

Ronan, whose deftly embroidered shirt was easily the same price the slave had been, allowed that a point had been made.

"He will last longer than this shirt." Kestrel let go of the cloth. "I'd say I got a bargain."

"True enough," said Ronan, looking disappointed, though whether because she had pulled away or because her mystery had turned out to be not so mysterious, Kestrel couldn't say. She preferred the latter. She wanted to forget the slave, and for everyone else to do the same.

"Speaking of clothes," said Jess, "we still haven't settled on what I am to wear."

"What about this?" Kestrel stood, glad for an excuse to leave the divan, and crossed the dressing room to lift out a dress whose sleeve peeked from an open wardrobe. She held it, gazing at the extremely light shade of lilac. She ran a hand under the sleeve and let it fall, admiring its shimmer. It was silvery. "The fabric is lovely."

"Kestrel, are you mad?" Jess's eyes were wide. Ronan laughed, and Kestrel realized it was because he thought she had made a joke.

"I don't know why I even own that dress," Jess said. "The color is so unfashionable. Why, it's practically gray!"

Kestrel shot Jess a startled look, but didn't see her friend's face. She saw only the memory of the slave's bitter, beautiful eyes.

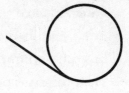

THE SLAVE PULLED A STRIP OF RED-HOT METAL from the fire and laid it on the anvil's face. Still gripping the metal with tongs, he used a hammer to beat it flat and even. Quickly, before it could cool, he set the strip against the horn of the anvil and rang at it until half of it curved. He reminded himself that he needed to bend, too. He needed to take the shape that was expected of him here at the general's house or he would never achieve what he wanted.

When he was finished, he packed the shoes into a wooden crate. He considered the last one, running a finger along the line of holes where nails would be driven into a horse's hoof. The horseshoe was, in its own way, perfect. Resilient.

And once nailed to the horse, rarely seen.

He brought the shoes to the stables. The girl was there.

She was fussing over one of the war horses. She had returned with the carriage but looked as if she intended to ride on the grounds; she was wearing boots. The slave kept his distance, stacking the horseshoes among the rest of the tack. Yet she approached, leading the horse.

She hesitated, though he could see no reason why. "I'm worried Javelin is throwing a shoe," she said in Herrani. "Please check him."

Her tone was polite, but the "please" grated. It was a lie, a pretense that her words were not an order. It was a slick coat of paint on a prison.

And he didn't like to hear her voice, for she spoke his language too well. She sounded mother-taught. It unnerved him. He focused on the one Valorian word. "Javelin," he said, rolling the horse's name around in his mouth.

"It's a weapon," she said. "Like a spear."

"I know," he said, then regretted it. No one—especially her or the general—should discover he understood anything of the Valorian language.

But she hadn't noticed. She was too busy rubbing the horse's neck.

After all, why would she notice anything a slave had said?

The horse leaned against her like an overgrown kitten. "I named him when I was young," she murmured.

He glanced at her. "You *are* young."

"Young enough to want to impress my father." There was a wistfulness in her face.

He lifted one shoulder in a shrug. He replied in a way that showed no awareness that she had shared something that sounded like a secret. "The name suits him," he said, even though the big beast was far too affectionate with her for that to be entirely true.

She looked away from the horse and straight at him. "Yours doesn't suit *you*. Smith."

Perhaps it was the surprise. Or the trick of her flawless

accent. Later, he would tell himself that it was because he was sure her next step would be to rename him, as Valorians sometimes did with their slaves, and if that happened he would surely do or say something stupid, and then all his plans would be in ruin.

But to be honest, he didn't know why he said it. "Smith is what my first slaver called me," he told her. "It's not my name. It's Arin."

THE GENERAL WAS A BUSY MAN, BUT NOT SO
busy that he wouldn't find out if Kestrel flouted his wishes.
Since the day of the auction, Kestrel felt watched. She was
careful to attend her training sessions with Rax, the captain
of her father's guard.

Not that Rax would mind if she didn't turn up in the
practice room adjoining the guards' barracks. When she had
been a child and ferocious in her need to prove herself, Rax
had been, in his own way, kind. He did little more than
observe that she had no natural talent for fighting. He smiled
at her efforts and saw to it that she was adequate at all weapons a soldier needed to wield.

But as years passed, so did his patience. She became careless. She would drop her guard in fencing. Her eyes wouldn't
stop dreaming, even when he shouted. She let arrows go wide,
head tilted as if listening to something he couldn't hear.

Kestrel remembered his mounting suspicion. The warn-
ings he had given her to stop trying to protect her hands.
She held her practice sword too gingerly, shrank back if it

seemed possible Rax's attack could endanger her fingers, and took body blows that would have killed her had his sword been steel and not wood.

One day when she was fifteen, he wrenched her shield away and smashed the flat of his sword against her exposed fingers. She dropped to her knees. She felt her face go white with pain and fear, and knew she shouldn't have wept, shouldn't have cradled her fingers to her, shouldn't have hunched her body to hide her hands from further assault. She should not have confirmed what Rax already knew.

He went to the general and told him that if he wanted a musician, he could buy one at the market.

Kestrel's father forbade her to play. But one of her few true military skills was going without sleep. In this, she rivaled the general. So when the swelling in her left hand had gone down and Enai had unwound the stiff wrapping that had held her fingers rigid, Kestrel began to play at night.

She was caught.

She remembered running after her father, pulling on his arms, his elbow, his clothes as he strode to the barracks in the middle of the night for a mace. He ignored her begging.

He would have easily destroyed the piano. It was too big, and she too small, for her to stand in the mace's way. If she had blocked the keys, he would have broken the case. He would have crushed its hammers, snapped its strings.

"I hate you," she had told him, "and my mother would, too."

It wasn't her wretched voice, Kestrel later thought. It wasn't the tears. He had seen grown men and women weep over worse. That wasn't what made him drop the mace.

But even now, Kestrel didn't know whether he had spared the instrument for love of her or love of the dead.

"What's it to be today?" Rax drawled from his bench at the other end of the practice room. He ran a hand over his grizzled head, then over his face as if he could wipe away the obvious boredom.

Kestrel meant to answer him but found herself looking at the paintings along the walls, though she knew them well. They showed girls and boys leaping over the backs of bulls. The paintings were Valorian, just as this particular building was Valorian-built. Blond, reddish, even chestnut hair streamed in banners behind the painted youths as they vaulted over the bulls' horns, planted palms on the beasts' backs, and flipped over the hindquarters. This was a rite of passage, and before it had been banned by the same law that forbade dueling, it was something all Valorians had had to do when they turned fourteen. Kestrel had done it. She remembered that day well. Her father had been proud of her. He had offered any birthday gift she desired.

Kestrel wondered if the slave—if Arin—had seen the paintings, and what he might think of them.

Rax sighed. "You don't need to practice standing and staring. You're good at that already."

"Needles." She pushed thoughts of the slave from her mind. "Let's work on Needles."

"What a surprise." He didn't say that they had done that yesterday, and the day before, and the day before that. Needles was the one technique he could reasonably bear to see her try to hone.

Rax hefted a broadsword as she strapped the small knives

to her calves, waist, and forearms. Each blunted practice blade could fit easily in her palm. Needles were the only weapons that let her forget they were weapons.

Rax lazily blocked the first one that spun from her fingers across the room. His blade knocked hers out of the air. But she had more. And when it came to close hand-to-hand fighting, as Rax always made sure it did, she might actually be able to beat him.

She didn't. Kestrel limped across the grass to Enai's house.

On her fourteenth birthday, Kestrel had asked her father for the woman's freedom. By law slaves belonged to the head of a household. Enai was Kestrel's nurse, but she was the general's property.

He had not been pleased at the request. Yet he had promised Kestrel anything.

And although Kestrel was now grateful Enai had chosen to remain at the villa, that she would be there today when Kestrel knocked on her door, sweaty and disheartened, she remembered how her happiness had dissolved when she had told Enai about her birthday gift, and the Herrani had stared at her.

"Free?" Enai had touched her own wrist, where the brand would be.

"Yes. Aren't you . . . glad? I thought you would want this."

Enai's hands fell to her lap. "Where would I go?"

Kestrel saw, then, what Enai did: the difficulties of an old Herrani woman alone—however free—in her occupied country. Where would she sleep? How would she earn enough to eat, and who would employ her when Herrani couldn't employ anyone and Valorians had slaves?

Kestrel used some of the inheritance settled on her after her mother's death to have the cottage built.

Today, Enai scowled when she opened the door. "Where have you been? I must be nothing to you, that you should ignore me for so long."

"I'm sorry."

Enai softened, tucking a scraggly lock of Kestrel's hair back into place. "You certainly are a sorry sight. Come inside, child."

A small cooking fire chittered on the hearth. Kestrel sank into a chair before it, and when Enai asked if she was hungry and was told no, the Herrani gave Kestrel a searching look. "What's wrong? Surely by now you're used to being beaten by Rax."

"There is something I am afraid to tell you."

Enai waved this away as nonsense. "Haven't I always kept your secrets?"

"It's not a secret. Practically everyone knows." What she said next sounded small for something that felt so big. "I went to the market with Jess more than a week ago. I went to an auction."

Enai's expression grew wary.

"Oh, Enai," Kestrel said. "I've made a mistake."

ARIN WAS SATISFIED. HE WAS GIVEN MORE orders for weapons and repair, and took the absence of complaints from the guard to mean his work was valued. Though the steward frequently demanded more horseshoes than could possibly be necessary, even for stables so large as the general's, Arin didn't mind that rote and easy labor. It was mind numbing. He imagined his head was filled with snow.

As his newness to the general's slaves wore away, they spoke more with him during meals, grew less cautious with their words. He became such a common feature in the stables that he was soon ignored by the soldiers. He overheard accounts of training sessions outside the city walls. He listened, knuckles whitened as they gripped a horse's bridle, to awed tales of ten years ago, of how the general, then a lieutenant, had razed a path of destruction from this peninsula's mountains to its port city and brought an end to the Herran war.

Arin unclenched his fingers, one by one, and went about his business.

Once, at dinner, Lirah sat next to him. She was shy, sending sidelong looks of curiosity his way well before she asked, "What were you, before the war?"

He lifted a brow. "What were *you*?"

Lirah's face clouded. "I don't remember."

Arin lied, too. "Neither do I."

He broke no rules.

Other slaves might have been tempted, during the walk through the orange grove that stood between the forge and the slaves' quarters, to pluck a fruit from the tree. To peel it hurriedly, bury the bright rind in the soil, and eat. Sometimes as Arin ate his meals of bread and stew he thought about it. When he walked under the trees, it was almost unbearable. The scent of citrus made his throat dry. But he didn't touch the fruit. He looked away and kept walking.

Arin wasn't sure which god he had offended. The god of laughter, maybe. One with an idle, cruel spirit who looked at Arin's unprecedented streak of good behavior, smiled, and said it couldn't last forever.

It was almost dusk and Arin was returning from the stables to the slaves' quarters when he heard it.

Music. He went still. His first thought was that the dreams he had almost every night were spooling out of his head. Then, as notes continued to pierce through wavering trees and dart over the whir of cicadas, he realized that this was real.

It was coming from the villa. Arin's feet moved after the music before his mind could tell them to stop, and by the time his mind understood what was happening, it was enchanted, too.

The notes were quick, limpid. They struggled with each other in gorgeous ways, like crosscurrents at sea. Then they stopped.

Arin looked up. He had reached a clearing in the trees. The sky grayed into purple.

Curfew was coming.

He had almost regained his senses, had almost turned back, when a few low notes stole into the air. The music now came in slow strokes, in a different key. A nocturne. Arin moved toward the garden. Past it, ground-floor glass doors burned with light.

Curfew had come and gone, and he didn't care.

He saw who was playing. The lines of her face were illuminated. She frowned slightly, leaned into a surging passage, and dappled a few high notes over the troubled sound.

Night had truly fallen. Arin wondered if she would lift her eyes, but wasn't worried he would be seen in the garden's shadows.

He knew the law of such things: people in brightly lit places cannot see into the dark.

YET AGAIN, THE STEWARD STOPPED KESTREL before she could leave the villa. "Going into the city?" he said, blocking the garden door. "Don't forget, my lady, that you need—"

"An escort."

"The general gave me orders."

Kestrel decided to irritate Harman as much as he did her. "Then send for the blacksmith."

"Why?"

"To serve as my escort."

He started to smile, then realized she was serious. "He is unsuitable."

She knew that.

"He's sullen," Harman said. "Unruly. I understand he broke curfew last night."

She did not care.

"He simply does not look the part."

"See to it that he does," she said.

"Lady Kestrel, he is trouble. You are too inexperienced to see it. You don't see what's right in front of you."

"Do I not? I see you. I see someone who has ordered our blacksmith to make hundreds of horseshoes over the two weeks he has been here, when his primary value to us is weapons making, and when only a fraction of the horseshoes made can be found in the stables. What I do not see is where those surplus shoes have gone. I imagine I might find them on the market, sold for a nice profit. I might find them transformed into what is no doubt a lovely watch."

Harman's hand went to the gold watch chain that trailed out of his pocket.

"Do as I say, Harman, or you will regret it."

Kestrel could have sent Arin to the kitchens upon their arrival at Jess's house. Once indoors, she had no official need of an escort. But she told him to remain in the parlor while she and Jess sat, drinking chilled osmanth tea and eating hibiscus cakes with peeled oranges. Arin stood stiffly against the far wall, the dark blue of his clothes blending with a curtain. Yet she found him hard to ignore.

He had been dressed to society's expectations. The collar of his shirt was high, the mark of Herrani aristocratic fashion before the war. All male house slaves wore them. But they did not, if they were wise, also wear expressions of obvious resentment.

At least his long sleeves hid the muscle and scars that showed a decade's worth of labor. This was a relief. Kestrel thought, however, that the slave was hiding more than that. She watched him out of the corner of her eye. She had a theory.

"The Trenex cousins are at it again," said Jess, and began describing their latest feud.

Arin looked bored. Of course he would, as someone with no understanding of the Valorian conversation. Yet Kestrel suspected he would look the same way even if he *were* following everything said.

And she thought that he was.

"I swear," Jess continued, fiddling with the earrings Kestrel had bought that day in the market. "It's only a matter of time before one of the cousins is dead and the other must pay the death-price."

Kestrel remembered Arin's one word of Valorian to her: *no*. How light his accent had been. He had also recognized Javelin's name. Perhaps this was not so unusual; Arin was a blacksmith and probably had made javelins for Valorians. Still, it struck her as an odd word for him to know.

Really, it was the *ease* with which he had recognized it that had given her pause.

"I can't believe Lady Faris's picnic is in only a few days!" Jess chattered on. "You'll stop here an hour before, won't you, and come in our carriage? Ronan told me to ask you."

Kestrel imagined sharing the close quarters of a carriage with Ronan. "I think it's best if I go separately."

"Only because you have no sense of fun!" Jess hesitated, then said, "Kestrel, could you try to be more . . . normal at the party?"

"Normal?"

"Well, you know, everyone thinks you're a bit eccentric."
Kestrel did know.

"Of course, people *love* you, they do. But when you freed
that nurse of yours, there was talk. It would have been forgotten, except that you always do something *else*. Your music is
an open secret—not that it's wrong, exactly."

They'd had this conversation before. The problem was
Kestrel's devotion. If she had played occasionally, like her
mother, it would have escaped notice. If the Herrani hadn't
prized music so highly before the war, that, too, might have
changed things. But in the eyes of Valorian society, music
was a pleasure to be taken, not made, and it didn't occur to
many that the making and the taking could be the same.

Jess was still speaking. ". . . then there was the auction—"
She glanced self-consciously at Arin.

Kestrel did, too. His face was impassive, yet somehow
more alert.

"Are you embarrassed to be my friend?" Kestrel asked
Jess.

"How can you say that?" Jess looked genuinely hurt, and
Kestrel regretted her question. It had been unfair, especially
when Jess had just invited her to attend the picnic with her
family.

"I'll try," Kestrel told her.

Jess was relieved. She did her best to dispel the tension
by predicting, in minute detail, which foods would be served
at the party and which sweethearts were most likely to behave
scandalously. "All the handsome young men will be there."

"Hmm," said Kestrel, turning her glass in a full circle
where it rested on the table.

"Did I tell you Faris will debut her baby at the picnic?"

"What?" Kestrel's hand stopped.

"The little boy is six months now, and we should have perfect weather. It's the ideal opportunity to introduce him to society. Why do you look so surprised?"

Kestrel shrugged. "It's a bold move."

"I don't see why."

"Because the baby's father is not Faris's husband."

"No," Jess whispered in mock horror. "How do you know?"

"I don't, not for certain. But I visited Faris at home recently and saw the baby. He is far too beautiful. He doesn't resemble Faris's older children one bit. Actually"—Kestrel tapped her glass—"if it *is* true, the best way to hide it is to do exactly as Faris plans. No one would believe a society lady would brazenly debut an illegitimate child at the season's biggest party."

Jess gaped, then laughed. "Kestrel, the god of lies must love you!"

Kestrel seemed to feel rather than hear the sharp intake of breath from across the room.

"What did you say?" Arin whispered in Valorian. He was staring at Jess.

She glanced between him and Kestrel, uncertain. "The god of lies. The Herrani one. Valorians don't have gods, you know."

"Of course you have no gods. You have no souls."

Kestrel rose to her feet. He had advanced on them. She thought of when the auctioneer had commanded him to sing and the slave's anger had practically trembled off his skin. "That's enough," she ordered.

"My god *loves* you?" Arin's gray eyes were narrow. His chest heaved once. Then he screwed his fury down, deep inside him. He held Kestrel's gaze, and she saw that he was aware he had betrayed exactly how well he knew her language. In a determinedly even voice, Arin asked Jess, "How do you know he loves her?"

Kestrel started to speak, but Arin lifted a hand to stop her. Shocked, Jess said, "Kestrel?"

"Tell me," Arin demanded.

"Well . . ." Jess tried to laugh. "He must, mustn't he? Kestrel sees the truth of things so clearly."

His mouth went cruel. "I doubt that."

"Kestrel, he is *your* property. Aren't you going to do something?"

These words, instead of making her act, were paralyzing.

"You think you see the truth," he said to Kestrel in Herrani, "because people *let* you believe it. If you accuse a Herrani of a lie, do you think he will dare deny it?"

A horrible thought struck her. She felt the blood trickle icily from her face. "Jess. Give me your earrings."

"What?" Jess was woefully confused.

"Loan them to me. Please. I'll bring them back."

Jess unhooked the earrings and set them in Kestrel's outstretched hand. The golden glass droplets glimmered up at her. Or *were* they glass? The Herrani jewelry seller in the market had said they were topaz before faltering under Kestrel's accusation that they were not.

Kestrel had paid more than glass was worth, but not nearly as much as jewels would cost. Maybe they *had* been topaz, and the seller too afraid to insist on the truth.

Shame shuddered through Kestrel. The room had fallen silent, Jess fidgeting with the lace cuffs on her sleeves, Arin looking maliciously glad that his words to Kestrel had shot home.

"We're leaving," she told him.

He gave no further sign of resistance. She knew it wasn't out of fear that she would punish him. It was because he was now secure in the certainty that she never would.

Kestrel burst out of the carriage and strode into the shop of the most reputed Valorian jeweler in the city. Arin followed.

"I want to know if these are real." Kestrel dropped the earrings with a rolling clatter onto the table in front of the jeweler.

"Topaz?" he asked.

She found it hard to speak. "That's what I'm here to find out."

The jeweler peered at the droplets through a lens, then said, "Hard to tell. I'd like to compare them with stones I know are true. It might take a while."

"Take your time."

"My lady." Arin spoke in his language, his voice all politeness, as if his outburst in the parlor had never happened. "May I walk around the market?"

She glanced at him. It was an unusual request, and he

couldn't have been very hopeful that it would be granted, especially not after his earlier behavior.

"You're indoors," he said, "and so don't need an escort at the moment. I'd like to see a friend."

"A friend?"

"I do have friends." He added, "I'll come back. Do you think I would get far if I tried to run away?"

The law was clear on captured runaways. Their ears and nose were cut off. Such disfigurement didn't impede a slave's ability to work.

Kestrel found that she couldn't bear the sight of Arin's face. She rather hoped he *would* run away, that he would succeed and she would never see him again.

"Take this." She pulled a ring off her finger, one stamped with a bird's talons. "You'll be questioned if you walk alone without a brand of freedom, or my seal."

She dismissed him.

Arin wanted to see her bright hair chopped and stuffed under a work scarf. He wanted her in prison. He wanted to hold the key. He could almost feel its cold weight. The fact that she hadn't claimed his god's favor somehow didn't temper his resentment.

A seller in the market cried his wares. The sound cut into Arin's thoughts, stilling the black spin of them. He had a purpose here. He needed to get to the auction house. And he needed to clear his head.

Nothing should dampen his mood now, not even that

bitter taste in the back of his throat. He let the sun bathe his face and inhaled the dust of the market air. It tasted fresher even than that of the general's citrus grove, because at least he could pretend to be free while he breathed it. He walked, thinking of the things he had learned in the parlor. His mind touched them, considering their shapes and sizes as if they were beads on a string.

He dwelled momentarily on one particular fact: his new mistress had freed a slave. Arin let this information slip along the string in his mind, click against the other beads, and be silent. It had no bearing on his situation.

There was much in the previous hour that he didn't understand. He had no idea why the girl had looked anxious, clutching those earrings. All he knew was that he had somehow gained the upper hand—if not without cost. She'd be careful, now, with what she said in Valorian within his hearing.

Arin was stopped only once on the way to his destination, and the soldier allowed him to pass. It didn't take him long to reach the auction house, where he asked to see Cheat, who relished his Valorian nickname to the point that no one knew what he had been called before the war. "Cheat is the perfect name for an auctioneer," he always said.

Cheat strode into the waiting room. When he saw Arin, he grinned. The wicked flash of teeth reminded Arin of what the auctioneer tried to hide from many people. Cheat was short, and while also thickset, he liked to cultivate an easygoing air, a lazy posture. Few would think that he was a fighter. Until he smiled.

"How did you pull *this* off?" Cheat sketched a hand in

the air to outline Arin standing before him, well dressed and unaccompanied.

"Guilt, I think."

"Good for you." The auctioneer beckoned him toward the holding cell. They slipped inside, then opened a narrow door within, one hidden from the view of any Valorian who might linger in the waiting room to collect a purchase. Arin and Cheat stood in the windowless room's darkness until the auctioneer lit a lamp.

"We can't count on you getting more opportunities like this," Cheat said, "so you'd better say everything, and say it fast."

Arin gave an account of the past two weeks. He described the layout of the general's villa, drawing a rough map with the scrap of paper and charcoal stub Cheat thrust at him. He sketched the grounds with their outbuildings, and indicated where the land was hilly and where flat. "I've only been inside the house once."

"Think you can change that?"

"Maybe."

"What have you learned about the general's movements?"

"Nothing unusual. Training sessions outside the city walls. He's rarely home, yet never far from it."

"And the girl?"

"She pays social calls. She gossips." Arin decided not to say that there had been something too shrewd in her comments about Lady Faris's baby. Nor did he mention the complete lack of surprise on her face when he had spoken in Valorian.

"Does she talk about her father?"

Did that conversation in the stables count? Not to Cheat, it wouldn't. Arin shook his head. "She never discusses the military."

"Doesn't mean she won't. If the general has a plan, he might include her. Everyone knows he wants her to enlist."

Arin hadn't meant to say it. Yet it slipped out and sounded like an accusation: "You should have told me she was a musician."

Cheat squinted at him. "It wasn't relevant."

"Relevant enough for you to try to sell me as a singer."

"Thank the god of chance I did. She wasn't biting at the opportunity for a blacksmith. Do you know how long I've tried to place someone at that house? You nearly wrecked everything with your childish defiance. I warned you what it would be like in the pit. All I did was tell you to sing for the crowd. All you had to do was obey."

"You're not my master."

Cheat ruffled Arin's short hair. "Course not. Look, lad, the next time I set you up as a spy in a high-ranking Valorian's household, I *promise* to tell you what the lady likes best."

Arin rolled his eyes. He moved to leave.

"Hey," said Cheat, "what about my weapons?"

"I'm working on it."

Out of the corner of her eye, Kestrel saw Arin walking into the jeweler's in time to hear the old man say, "I'm sorry, my lady, but these are false. Just pretty bits of glass."

Kestrel sagged in relief.

"No need to be too disappointed," the jeweler told her. "You can tell your friends they're topaz. None will be the wiser."

Later, in the carriage, she said to Arin, "I want you to tell me the truth."

His face seemed to pale. "The truth?"

She blinked. Then she understood the miscommunication. She couldn't help a twinge of offense: Arin believed her the sort of mistress who would pry into a slave's personal life, to want details about a meeting with a friend. She studied him, and his hand made an odd gesture, lifting toward his temple to brush away something invisible. "I'm not trying to invade your privacy," she said. "Your secrets are your own."

"So you want me to inform on other slaves," he said flatly. "To report their misdeeds to you. To say if someone steals bread from the larder, or an orange from the grove. I won't do it."

"That isn't what I am asking." Kestrel weighed her words before speaking again. "You were right. People tell me what they think I want to hear. What I hope is that you will feel free to be honest with me, as you were in Jess's parlor. I'd like to know how you truly see things."

Slowly, he said, "That would be valuable to you. My honesty."

"Yes."

There was a silence. Then he said, "I might feel more free to speak if I were more free to roam."

Kestrel heard the bargain in his words. "I can arrange that."

"I want the privileges of a house slave."

"They are yours."

"*And* the right to visit the city on my own. Just once in a while."

"To see your friend."

"My sweetheart, actually."

Kestrel paused. "Very well," she said.

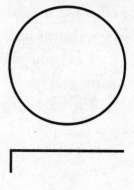

"OH, NO." KESTREL SMILED ACROSS THE GAMING table. She and the other three Bite and Sting players sat on the terrace, in full view of Lady Faris's guests, who wandered over the grass. "You don't want to do *that*," Kestrel told the young man sitting opposite her.

Lord Irex's finger paused on the blank-backed tile he had set down, ready to flip and show the engraving on its hidden side. His mouth tightened, then curled into a sneer.

Ronan glanced at Kestrel from his corner of the gaming table. He, too, knew Irex's ruthless nature, and they both knew that it served Irex well, at least in hand-to-hand combat. He had won the last spring tournament, an event organized every year to display the weapons skills of Valorians not yet enlisted in the military.

"I'd listen to her if I were you," Ronan said, idly mixing his ivory tiles. Benix, the fourth player, kept his thoughts to himself. Neither of them knew that Irex had approached Kestrel after taking the spring prize. At the celebratory party hosted by the governor, Irex had edged her into an alcove and made an advance. His eyes had looked almost black, oily with arrogance. Kestrel had laughed and slipped away.

"I am sure you're very pleased to have a pair of foxes," Kestrel told Irex now, "but you'll have to do better."

"I set down my tile," Irex said coldly. "I cannot take it back."

"I'll let you take it back. Just this once."

"You *want* me to take it back."

"Ah. So you agree that I know what tile you mean to play."

Benix shifted his weight on Lady Faris's delicate chair. It creaked. "Flip the damn tile, Irex. And you, Kestrel: Quit toying with him."

"I'm merely offering friendly advice."

Benix snorted.

Kestrel watched Irex watch her, his anger mounting as he couldn't decide whether Kestrel's words were a lie, the well-meant truth, or a truth she hoped he would judge a lie. He flipped the tile: a fox.

"Too bad," said Kestrel, and turned over one of hers, adding a third bee to her other two matching tiles. She swept the four gold coins of the ante to her side of the table. "See, Irex? I had only your best interests at heart."

Benix blew out a gusty sigh. He settled back in his protesting chair, shrugged, and seemed the perfect picture of amused resignation. He kept his head bowed while he mixed the Bite and Sting tiles, but Kestrel saw him shoot Irex a wary glance. Benix, too, had seen the rage that turned Irex's face into stone.

Irex shoved back from the table. He stalked over the

flagstone terrace to the grass, which bloomed with the highest members of Valorian society.

"That wasn't necessary," Benix told Kestrel.

"It was," she said. "He's tiresome. I don't mind taking his money, but I cannot take his company."

"You couldn't spare a thought for me before chasing him away? Maybe *I* would like a chance to win his gold."

"Lord Irex can spare it," Ronan added.

"Well, I don't like poor losers," said Kestrel. "That's why I play with you two."

Benix groaned.

"She's a fiend," Ronan agreed cheerfully.

"Then why do you play with her?"

"I enjoy losing to Kestrel. I will give anything she will take."

"While I live in hope to one day win," Benix said, and gave Kestrel's hand a friendly pat.

"Yes, yes," Kestrel said. "You are both fine flatterers. Now ante up."

"We lack a fourth player," Benix pointed out. Bite and Sting was played in pairs or fours.

Despite herself, Kestrel looked at Arin standing not too far away, considering the garden or the house beyond it. From his position he would have had a view of Irex's tiles, and Ronan's. He would not, however, have been able to see hers. She wondered what he had made of the game—if he had bothered to follow it.

Perhaps feeling her gaze on him, Arin glanced her way. His eyes were calm, uninterested. She could read nothing in them.

"I suppose our game is over then," she told the two lords in a bright voice. "Shall we join the others?"

Ronan poured the gold into her purse and slipped its velvet strap over her wrist, unnecessarily fiddling with the broad ribbon until it lay flat against Kestrel's skin without a wrinkle. He offered his arm and she took it, resting her palm on the cool silk of his sleeve. Benix fell in step, and the three walked toward the heart of the murmuring party. Kestrel knew, rather than saw, that Arin shifted position and followed, like the shadow line of a sundial.

This was precisely what he was supposed to do as her attendant at Lady Faris's picnic, yet she had the uncomfortable impression of being tracked.

She brushed aside this thought. It was due to the lingering unpleasantness of playing Bite and Sting with Irex. Well, that young lord's behavior was not her fault. He had pressed where he was not invited. And he seemed consoled, now, sitting at the feet of Senator Nicon's pretty daughters and Jess. Pinks, reds, and oranges were this season's fashion, and the women's skirts were filled with tulle. Lady Faris's lawn looked as if the grass had lured sunset clouds to earth and tethered them there.

Kestrel led Ronan to where their hostess sat, sipping lemon water while her baby crawled on the grass beside her under the watchful guard of a slave. Several young men lounged around Faris, and as Kestrel grew near she compared the chubby baby's face with each of the lady's favorites, trying to find a match.

". . . of course it is the most shocking scandal," Faris was saying.

Kestrel's curiosity sharpened. A scandal? If it was of a romantic nature, her estimation of Faris was about to rise. Only a steel-nerved woman would gossip about other people's follies while her own giggled and clutched at the grass with tiny fists.

"I love scandals," Ronan said as he, Kestrel, and Benix sat.

"You should," said Benix. "You're always causing them."

"Not the ones I most want." Ronan smiled at Kestrel.

Faris rapped his shoulder with her fan, a gesture that appeared to chastise him, but which everyone in the circle knew was an encouragement to continue the witty, flirty banter that would make a success of this party—provided that the compliments were turned toward its hostess.

Ronan immediately praised Faris's low-cut dress with its slashed sleeves. He admired the jewel-encrusted hilt of her dagger, strapped over her sash as all ladies wore their weapons.

Kestrel listened. She saw, yet again, that her friend's compliments were just bits of art and artifice. They were paper swans, cunningly folded so that they could float on the air for a few moments. Nothing more. Kestrel felt something within her lessen. She didn't know, however, whether that something was tension, easing into relief, or expectation, dwindling into disappointment.

She plucked a wildflower from the grass and offered it to the baby. He grabbed it, staring with dark-eyed awe at the petals as they crumpled in his grasp. He smiled, and one dimple sank into his left cheek.

Ronan's flattery had triggered the competition of the other young men present, so Kestrel had to wait some time before the conversation could be brought back to the meat of the matter: the scandal.

"But you gentlemen are distracting me!" Faris said. "Don't you want my news?"

"I do," said Kestrel, passing the baby another flower.

"As you should. Your father won't be pleased."

Kestrel glanced up from the child, and when she did, she saw Arin within earshot, his expression keen.

"What has my father to do with it?" She found it impossible to believe that he had romantically entangled himself. "He's not even in the city. He's leading a training session a day's ride from here."

"That may be. But when General Trajan returns, Senator Andrax will pay an even greater price."

"For what?"

"Why, for selling kegs of black powder to the eastern savages."

There was a stunned silence.

"Andrax has sold weapons to the empire's enemies?" Benix said.

"He claims the kegs were stolen. But I ask you, how could they be? They were under his guard. Now they're missing. Everyone knows Andrax likes to line his pockets with bribes. What's to stop him from trading illegally with the barbarians?"

"You're right," Kestrel said, "my father will be furious."

Lady Faris began listing in thrilled tones the possible punishments for the senator, who had been imprisoned until the capital could be reached for instructions. "My husband himself has gone to discuss the matter with the emperor.

Oh, what shall *happen* to Andrax? An execution, do you think? Banishment to the northern tundra at the very least!" Faris's circle of admirers joined in, concocting punishments so wildly cruel they became morbid jokes. Only Ronan was silent, watching Faris's baby clamber onto Kestrel's lap and drool on her sleeve.

Kestrel held the child, her eyes trained on but not really seeing his fine white hair, stirring in the faint wind like dandelion fluff. She dreaded her father's return. She knew what this news would bring. He would be appalled at the senator's betrayal and would use the news to urge Kestrel to see the necessity of adding loyal soldiers to the empire's ranks. His pressure on her would increase. She could not breathe.

"You're good at this," said Ronan.

"What?"

He leaned to touch the baby's head. "Being a mother."

"What is that supposed to mean?"

Ronan looked awkward. Then he said glibly, "Nothing, if you don't like it." He glanced at Benix, Faris, and the others, but they were discussing thumbscrews and nooses. "It didn't mean anything. I take it back."

Kestrel set the baby on the grass next to Faris. "You cannot take it back."

"Just this once," he said, echoing her earlier words during the game.

She stood and walked away.

He followed. "Come, Kestrel. I spoke only the truth."

They had entered the shade of thickly grown laran trees, whose leaves were a bloody color. They would soon fall.

"It's not that I wouldn't want to have a child someday," Kestrel told Ronan.

Visibly relieved, he said, "Good. The empire needs new life."

It did. She knew this. As the Valorian empire stretched across the continent, it faced the problem of keeping what it had won. The solutions were military prowess and boosting the Valorian population, so the emperor prohibited any activities that unnecessarily endangered Valorian lives—like dueling and the bull-jumping games that used to mark coming-of-age ceremonies. Marriage became mandatory by the age of twenty for anyone who was not a soldier.

"It's just—" Kestrel tried again: "Ronan, I feel trapped. Between what my father wants and—"

He held up his hands in flat-palmed defense. "*I* am not trying to trap you. I am your friend."

"I know. But when you are faced with only two choices— the military or marriage—don't you wonder if there is a third, or a fourth, or more, even, than that?"

"You have many choices. The law says that in three years you must marry, but not *whom*. Anyway, there is time." His shoulder grazed hers in the teasing push of children starting a mock fight. "Time enough for me to convince you of the right choice."

"Benix, of course." She laughed.

"Benix." Ronan made a fist and shook it at the sky. "Benix!" he shouted. "I challenge you to a duel! Where are you, you great oaf?" Ronan stormed from the laran trees with all the flair of a comic actor.

Kestrel smiled, watching him go. Maybe his silly

flirtations disguised something real. People's feelings were hard to know for certain. A conversation with Ronan resembled a Bite and Sting game where Kestrel couldn't tell if the truth looked like a lie, or a lie like the truth.

If it was true, what then?

She paused, nursing that glow of a laugh that remained inside her, the question she had posed to herself unanswered.

Someone—a man—came up behind her and snaked an arm around her waist.

Not flirtation. Aggression.

Kestrel sidestepped and spun, pulling her dagger from its sheath.

Irex. His dagger was drawn, too.

"A fight, dear Kestrel?" His stance was easy. He didn't know how to play Bite and Sting, but his skill at weapons outmatched hers.

"Not here," she said stiffly.

"No, not here." His voice was soft. "But anywhere, if you want it."

"Exactly what do you think you are doing, Irex?"

"You mean, a moment ago? Oh, I don't know. Maybe I was trying to pick your pocket." His tone hinted at a coarse double meaning.

Kestrel slid her dagger into its sheath. "Theft is the only way you will get my gold." She walked from the cover of trees and saw, with shaky gratitude, that the party was still there, that the sound of porcelain and spoons still tinkled over low talk, and that no one had noticed anything.

No one, except perhaps Arin. He was waiting for her. She felt a flash of something unpleasant—embarrassment, perhaps, as she wondered how much of this afternoon he had overheard. Dismay to think that he might have witnessed that last exchange with Irex, and misunderstood it. Or was she troubled by something else? Maybe it was the thought that Arin knew perfectly well what had been taking place behind the trees and had made no move to interfere, to help.

It was not his place to interfere, she reminded herself. She had not needed his help.

"We are leaving," she told him.

She let her bad mood seethe into the silence of the carriage. Finally, she couldn't bear the vicious cycle of her thoughts, the way they kept returning to Irex and her stupid decision to humiliate him at Bite and Sting. "Well?" she asked Arin.

He sat across from her in the carriage, but didn't lift his eyes to meet hers. He studied his hands. "Well, what?"

"What do you think?"

"About?"

"About the party. About anything. About the bargain we made that you could at least pretend to uphold."

"You want to gossip about the party." He seemed tired.

"I want you to *speak* to me."

He looked at her then. She found that she had clenched her silk skirts in a fist. She let go. "For example, I know you overheard about Senator Andrax. Do you think he merits torture? Death?"

"He deserves what he gets," he said, and went quiet again.

Kestrel gave up. She sank into her anger.

"That isn't what's bothering you." Arin sounded

reluctant, almost incredulous, as if he couldn't believe the words coming from his mouth.

Kestrel waited.

He said, "That man is an ass."

It was clear whom he meant. It was clear that no slave should ever say that of any Valorian. But it was magic to hear the words out loud. Kestrel breathed a laugh. "And I am a fool." She pressed chilly hands to her forehead. "I knew what he's like. I should have never played Bite and Sting with him. Or I should have let him win."

The corner of Arin's mouth twitched. "I enjoyed watching him lose."

There was a silence, and Kestrel, though she felt comforted, knew that Arin's understanding of the afternoon had been fairly complete. He *had* waited beyond the laran trees, listening to her and Irex. Would he have continued to do nothing, had something else happened?

"Do you know how to play Bite and Sting?" she asked.

"Maybe."

"Either you do or you don't."

"Whether I know or don't doesn't matter."

She made an impatient noise. "Because?"

His teeth flashed in the late, shifting light. "Because you would not want to play against *me*."

WHEN THE GENERAL RETURNED HOME AND heard the news about Senator Andrax, he didn't wait even to wash off the dirt of the previous days. He climbed back on his horse and spurred it in the direction of the prison.

It was afternoon when he strode back into the villa, and Kestrel, who had heard his horse coming from where she sat in one of her rooms, came down the stairs and saw him crouching by the pool in the entryway. He splashed water on his face and palmed it over his hair, which was spiky with sweat.

"What will happen to the senator?" asked Kestrel.

"The emperor doesn't like to punish by death, but in this case I think he will make an exception."

"Perhaps the kegs of black powder *were* stolen, as Andrax claims."

"He was the only one besides myself with a key to that particular armory, and there was no sign of forced entry. I had my key with me and have been away for three days."

"The kegs could still be in the city. I assume that some-one has ordered the ships to be kept at port and searched?"

Her father winced. "Trust you to think of what the governor should have done two days ago." He paused, then said, "Kestrel—"

"I know what you're going to say." This was why she had come to her father and broached the subject of the senator's betrayal: she hadn't wanted to wait for the general to turn it into a tool to use on her. "The empire needs people like me."

His brows rose. "So you'll do it? You'll enlist?"

"No. I have a suggestion. You claim that I have a mind for war."

Slowly, he said, "You have a way of getting what you want."

"Yet for years now my military training has focused on the physical, and all it has done is shape me into a barely competent fighter." Kestrel had an image of Irex standing before her, the dagger held so naturally that it seemed to have grown out of his hand. "It's not enough. You should be teaching me history. We should be inventing battle scenarios, discussing the benefits and drawbacks of battalion order. Meanwhile, I will keep an open mind about fighting for the empire."

His light brown eyes were crinkling at the corners, but he made his mouth stern. "Hmph."

"You don't like my suggestion?"

"I am wondering what it will cost me."

Kestrel readied herself. This was the hard part. "My sessions with Rax stop. He knows as well as I do that I have come as far as I can. We are wasting his time."

The general shook his head. "Kestrel—"

"*And* you will stop pressuring me to enlist. Whether I become a soldier is my choice."

The general rubbed his wet palms together, his hands still dirty. The water that dripped from them was brown. "Here is my counteroffer. You will study strategy with me as my schedule allows. Your sessions with Rax will continue, but only on a weekly basis. And you will make your decision by spring."

"I don't have to decide until I am twenty."

"It's better for us both, Kestrel, if we know soon on what ground we stand."

She was ready to agree, but he lifted one finger. "If you don't choose my life," he said, "you will marry in the spring."

"That's a trap."

"No, it's a bet. A bet that you like your independence too much not to fight alongside me."

"I hope you see the irony in what you have just said."

He smiled.

Kestrel said, "You will stop trying to persuade me? No more lectures?"

"None."

"I will play the piano whenever I like. You won't say a word about it."

His smile shrank. "Fine."

"And"—her voice faltered—"if I marry, it will be to whom I choose."

"Of course. Any Valorian of our society will do."

This was fair, she decided. "I agree."

The general patted her cheek with a damp hand. "Good girl."

Kestrel walked down the hall. The night before her father's return she had lain awake, seeing the three bee tiles behind her closed eyes, and Irex's knife, and her own. She had thought about how powerful she had felt in one situation, and how helpless in the other. She studied her life like a draw of Bite and Sting pieces. She believed she saw a clear line of play.

But she had forgotten that it was her father who had taught her that game.

Kestrel had the feeling that she had just made a very bad bargain.

She passed by the library, then stopped and returned to its open door. Two house slaves were inside, dusting. They paused at the sound of her feet on the threshold and looked at her—no, *peered*, as if they could see all her mistakes imprinted on her face.

Lirah, a lovely girl with greenish eyes, said, "My lady—"

"Do you know where Smith is?" Kestrel wasn't sure what had made her use Arin's other name. It wasn't until that moment that she realized she hadn't shared his true one with anybody.

"At the forge," Lirah said promptly. "But—"

Kestrel turned and walked toward the garden doors.

She thought that she had been seeking a light distraction. But when she heard the clang of metal on metal and saw Arin scraping a shaft of steel across the anvil with one set of tools and beating at it with another, Kestrel knew she had come to the wrong place.

"Yes?" he said, keeping his back to her. His workshirt was soaked through with sweat. His hands were sooty. He left the blade of the sword to cool on the anvil and moved to place another, shorter length of metal on the fire, which lined his profile with unsteady light.

She willed her voice to be her own. "I thought we could play a game."

His dark brows drew together.

"Of Bite and Sting," Kestrel said. More firmly, she added, "You implied you know how to play."

He used tongs to stoke the fire. "I did."

"You implied that you could beat me."

"I implied that there was no reason a Valorian would want to play with a Herrani."

"No, you worded things carefully so that what you said could be interpreted that way. But that isn't what you meant."

He faced her then, arms folded across his chest. "I have no time for games." The tips of his fingers had black rings of charcoal dust buried under the nail and into the cuticle. "I have work to do."

"Not if I say you don't."

He turned away. "I like to finish what I start."

She meant to leave. She meant to leave him to the noise and heat. She meant to say nothing more. Instead, Kestrel found herself issuing a challenge. "You are no match for me anyway."

He gave her the look she recognized well, the one of measured disdain. But this time, he also laughed. "Where do you propose we play?" He swept a hand around the forge. "Here?"

"My rooms."

"Your rooms." Arin shook his head disbelievingly.

"My sitting room," she said. "Or the parlor," she added, though it bothered her to think of playing Bite and Sting with him in a place so public to the household.

He leaned against the anvil, considering. "Your sitting room will do. I'll come when I've finished this sword. After all, I have house privileges now. Might as well use them." Arin started to say something else, then stopped, his gaze roving over her face. She grew uneasy.

He was staring, she realized. He was staring at her.

"You have dirt on your face," he said shortly.

He returned to his work.

Later, in her bathing room, Kestrel saw it. The moment she tilted the mirror to catch the low, amber light of late afternoon, she saw what he had seen, as had Lirah, who had tried to tell her. A faint smudge traced the slope of her high cheekbone, darkened her cheek, and skimmed the line of her jaw. It was a handprint. It was the shadow left from her father's gritty hand, from when he had touched her face to seal the bargain between them.

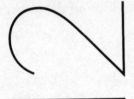

ARIN HAD BATHED. HE WAS WEARING HOUSE clothes, and when Kestrel saw him standing in the doorway his shoulders were relaxed. Without being invited, he strode into the room, pulled out the other chair at the small table where Kestrel waited, and sat. He arranged his arms in a position of negligent ease and leaned into the brocaded chair as if he owned it. He seemed, Kestrel thought, at home.

But then, he had also seemed so in the forge. Kestrel looked away from him, stacking the Bite and Sting tiles on the table. It occurred to her that it was a talent for Arin to be comfortable in such different environments. She wondered how she would fare in his world.

He said, "This is not a sitting room."

"Oh?" Kestrel mixed the tiles. "And here I thought we were sitting."

His mouth curved slightly. "This is a writing room. Or, rather"—he pulled his six tiles—"it was."

Kestrel drew her Bite and Sting hand. She decided to

show no sign of curiosity. She would not allow herself to be distracted. She arranged her tiles facedown.

"Wait," he said. "What are the stakes?"

She had given this careful consideration. She took a small wooden box from her skirt pocket and set it on the table. Arin picked up the box and shook it, listening to the thin, sliding rattle of its contents. "Matches." He tossed the box back onto the table. "Hardly high stakes."

But what were appropriate stakes for a slave who had nothing to gamble? This question had troubled Kestrel ever since she had proposed the game. She shrugged and said, "Perhaps I am afraid to lose." She split the matches between them.

"Hmm," he said, and they each put in their ante.

Arin positioned his tiles so that he could see their engravings without revealing them to Kestrel. His eyes flicked to them briefly, then lifted to examine the luxury of his surroundings. This annoyed her—both because she could glean nothing from his expression and because he was acting the gentleman by averting his gaze, offering her a moment to study her tiles without fear of giving away something to him. As if she needed such an advantage.

"How do you know?" she said.

"How do I know what?"

"That this was a writing room. I have never heard of such a thing." She began to position her own tiles. It was only when she saw their designs that she wondered whether Arin had really been polite in looking away, or if he had been deliberately provoking her.

She concentrated on her draw, relieved to see that she had a good set. A tiger (the highest tile); a wolf, a mouse, a fox (not a bad trio, except the mouse); and a pair of scorpions. She liked the Sting tiles. They were often underestimated.

Kestrel realized that Arin had been waiting to answer her question. He was watching her.

"I know," he said, "because of this room's position in your suite, the cream color of the walls, and the paintings of swans. This was where a Herrani lady would pen her letters or write journal entries. It's a private room. I shouldn't be allowed inside."

"Well," said Kestrel, uncomfortable, "it is no longer what it was."

He played his first tile: a wolf. That meant one less chance for her to add a wolf to her hand. She set down her fox.

"But how do you even know to recognize the room?" Kestrel pressed. "Were you a house slave before?"

His finger twitched against a tile's blind side. Kestrel hadn't meant to upset him, but saw that she had.

"All Herrani aristocratic houses had writing rooms," he said. "It's common knowledge. Any slave could tell you what I just did. Lirah could, if you asked her."

Kestrel hadn't quite realized that he knew Lirah—or at least, well enough to drop her name casually into the conversation. Though of course he did. She remembered how quick Lirah was to tell her of Arin's whereabouts earlier. The girl had spoken as if the answer had already been trembling on the surface of her mind, like a dragonfly on water, long before Kestrel had asked.

Kestrel and Arin played in silence, discarding tiles, drawing new ones, playing others, speaking only to bet.

Then Arin's hands paused. "You survived the plague."

"Oh." Kestrel hadn't noticed that her loose, slashed sleeves had slipped back to reveal the skin of her inner arms. She touched the short scar above her left elbow. "Yes. Many Valorians caught the plague during the colonization of Herran."

"Most Valorians weren't healed by a Herrani." He stared at the scar.

Kestrel drew the sleeves over her skin. She picked up a match and turned it around in her fingers. "I was seven at the time. I don't remember much."

"I'm sure you nevertheless know what happened."

She hesitated. "You won't like it."

"It doesn't matter what I like."

She set down the match. "My family had just arrived. My father didn't fall ill. I suppose he had a natural immunity. He has always seemed . . . invulnerable."

Arin's face tightened.

"But my mother and I were very sick. I remember sleeping next to her. Her skin was hot. The slaves were told to separate us, so that her fever wouldn't drive mine and mine hers, but I always woke up in her bed. My father noticed that no Herrani seemed very affected by the plague—and if they caught it, they didn't die. He found a Herrani physician." She should have left it at that. Yet Arin's gray gaze was unwavering, and she felt that to say no more would be a lie he would easily see. "My father told the doctor to heal us or be killed."

"So the doctor did." Arin sounded disgusted. "For fear of his life."

"That's not why." Kestrel looked down at her tiles. "I don't know why. Because I was a child?" Kestrel shook her head. "He cut my arm to bleed the disease. I suppose that's what all Herrani doctors did, if you recognize the scar. He stopped the blood. He stitched the wound. Then he turned the knife on himself."

Something flickered in Arin's eyes. Kestrel wondered if he was trying, as she often did when she looked in the mirror, to see her as a child, to see whatever it was in her that the doctor had decided to save. "And your mother?" he said.

"My father tried to cut her in the same way the doctor had cut me. I remember that. There was a lot of blood. She died."

In the silence, Kestrel heard a falling leaf scratch the glass of the window, opened out toward the dimming sky. It was warm, but summer was almost over.

"Play your tiles," Arin said roughly.

Kestrel turned them over, taking no joy in the fact that she had surely won. She had four scorpions.

Arin flipped his. The sound of ivory clacking against the wooden table was unnaturally loud.

Four vipers.

"I win," he said, and swept the matches into his hand.

Kestrel stared at the tiles, feeling a numbness creep along her limbs. "Well," she said. She cleared her throat. "Well played."

He gave her a humorless smile. "I did warn you."

"Yes. You did."

He stood. "I think I'll take my leave while I have the advantage."

"Until next time." Kestrel realized she had offered him her hand. He looked at it, then took it in his own. She felt the numbness ebb, only to be replaced by a different kind of surprise.

He dropped her hand. "I have things to do."

"Like what?" She tried for a lighthearted tone.

He answered in kind. "Like contemplate *what* I am going to do with my sudden windfall of matches." He widened his eyes in pretend glee, and Kestrel smiled.

"I'll walk you out," she said.

"Do you think I will lose my way? Or steal something as I go?"

She felt her expression turn haughty. "I am leaving the villa anyway," she said, though she had had no such plans until the words left her mouth.

They walked in silence through the house until they had reached the ground floor. Kestrel saw his stride pause, almost imperceptibly, as they passed the closed doors that hid her piano.

She stopped. "What is your interest in that room?"

The look he gave her was cutting. "I have no interest in the music room."

Her eyes narrowed as she watched him walk away.

KESTREL'S FIRST LESSON WITH HER FATHER
took place in their library, a dark room with inset shelves
jammed end-to-end with beautifully bound volumes. Only
some were in her language; the empire had little literary tra-
dition. The majority of the books were in Herrani, and if few
Valorians spoke that language well, fewer still could read it,
for the alphabet was in a different script. Yet all Valorian colo-
nizers had kept their conquered libraries intact. They
looked nicer that way.

Her father stood, looking out the window. He didn't
like to sit. Kestrel settled into a reading chair as a deliberate
gesture of difference.

He said, "The project of the Valorian empire began
twenty-four years ago when we took the northern tundra."

"An easy territory to conquer." Kestrel couldn't prove
herself to the general with a sword, but at least she could
show him that she knew her history. "Its people were few,
scattered into distant tribes who lived in tents. We invaded
in the summer, with little life lost on either side. It was a

trial, to see if Valoria's neighbors would object to our expansion. It was also a symbolic victory, meant to encourage our people. But the tundra offers no agriculture, little meat, and few slaves. It's mostly worthless."

"Worthless?" The general opened one of the drawers lining the walls below the bookshelves and pulled out a scrolled map, which he unfurled and pinned to a table with glass weights. Kestrel stood and came close to study the outline of the continent and the empire's reaches.

"Perhaps not *worthless*," she conceded. She pointed to the tundra, which maintained a thin strip of land over much of the empire's north—until the frozen territory stretched east and widened, dipping south to curve around the northeastern corner of the empire. "It provides Valoria with a natural barrier against a barbarian invasion. The tundra isn't a friendly land for war, particularly now that it's defended by us."

"Yes. But the tundra has another value to us, one that you can't see by looking at this map. It's a state secret, Kestrel. I'm trusting you to keep it."

"Of course." She couldn't help a thrill of intrigue as well as happiness to be brought into her father's confidence, though she knew that this was exactly what he wanted her to feel.

"Spies were sent into the tundra well before we attacked. We do this with every territory we want to acquire; the tundra wasn't special in this. But what the spies found there *was*: mineral deposits. Some silver, which has been mined and helps fund our wars. More important, there is a vast amount of sulfur, a key ingredient in making black powder."

He smiled when he saw her eyes widen. Then he described in great detail the preparations for invasion, the initial skirmishes, and how the tundra was won by General Daran, who had seen promise in Kestrel's father when he was a young officer and tutored him in the ways of war.

When her father finished, Kestrel touched the Herran peninsula. "Tell me about the Herran War."

"We wanted this territory long before I took it. Once I did, Valorian colonists were eager for a piece of the prize. For decades before the war, the Herrani flaunted their country's wealth, its goods, its beauty, its rich land—its near *perfection*, not least because it might as well have been an island." The general swept a finger around the peninsula, bordered on almost all sides by the southern sea except where a mountain range separated it from the rest of the continent. "The Herrani considered us nothing more than stupid, bloody savages. They liked us enough to send ships to our mainland with luxuries for sale. They didn't seem to think that every alabaster bowl or sack of spice was a temptation to the emperor."

Although Kestrel knew most of this, it was as if the story she had known was a rough sculpture, and her father's words sharp blows with a chisel, chipping details into marble until she could see the true shape hidden inside the stone.

"The Herrani believed they were untouchable," he said. "They were almost right. They had mastered the sea. Their navy was far more sophisticated than ours, both in ships and training. Even if our navy had been more of a match for theirs, the sea was against us."

"The green storms," said Kestrel. Storm season was

coming. It would last until spring, with squalls appearing out of nowhere along the sea routes and slamming into the shores, turning the sky an eerie green.

"Invasion by sea was suicide. By land it was impossible. There was no way to bring an army through the mountains. There was one pass, yet it was so narrow that an army would have had to squeeze through it almost in single file, and slowly, making it easy for Herrani forces to whittle away at ours until we were nothing."

Kestrel knew what her father had done, but she hadn't realized something until now. "You got all that black powder from the earlier conquest of the tundra."

"Yes. We used it to pack the mountains and explode our way through that pass, widening it until the army could sweep down to victory. The Herrani weren't prepared for a land invasion. Their strength was at sea.

"And their folly was in their early surrender. Of course, once I seized the city there was little they could do. Yet they still had their navy: a fleet of almost a hundred swift ships with cannon. I doubt they could have won the city back; the sailors would have had to come on land eventually and their numbers were smaller than ours, not very capable against cavalry. But their ships could have harassed us. Engaged in pirate attacks. They could have brought war to Valorian waters and used that damage to negotiate better terms of surrender. But I had the city and its people—and a reputation."

Kestrel turned. She tugged a book of Herrani poetry off the shelf and paged through it. Her father was no longer looking at her, but into the past.

"So the Herrani surrendered," he said. "They chose life as slaves over none at all. They gave us their ships, and with them our navy became the greatest in the known world. Every Valorian soldier can sail well now. I made sure you learned, too."

Kestrel found the passage she was searching for. It was the beginning of a canto about a journey to magical islands where time had no meaning. It was a call to sailors to steer the ship toward open water. *Set keel to the wave-breaks,* she read. *Set forth on the brine-hearted sea.*

"There are many reasons we won," her father said, "and I will teach them to you. But the most fundamental reason is simple. They were weak. We were not."

He took her book and closed it.

Her meetings with the general were not frequent. He was busy, and Kestrel was grateful. Their conversations tipped her too easily between fascination and revulsion.

More leaves drifted from the trees. Summer warmth drained from the air. Kestrel barely noticed, for she stayed indoors, finding that she was able to forget most of what she had learned from her father while she played the piano. She played almost every free hour, now that she could. Music made her feel as if she were holding a lamp that cast a halo of light around her, and while she knew there were people and responsibilities in the darkness beyond it, she couldn't see them. The flame of what she felt when she played made her deliciously blind.

Until the day she found something waiting for her in the music room. A small, ivory tile was balanced on the exact middle key of the piano. The Bite and Sting piece had been set facedown. The blank side looked up.

It searched her like a question . . . or an invitation.

someone you couldn't beat," said Arin.

Kestrel looked up from her piano to see him standing by the doors she had left open, then glanced at the Bite and Sting set lying on a table by the garden windows.

"Not at all," said Kestrel. "I have been busy."

His gaze flicked to the piano. "So I've heard."

Kestrel moved to sit at the table and said, "I'm intrigued by your choice of room."

He hesitated, and she thought he was ready to deny any responsibility of choice, to pretend that a ghost had left that tile on the piano. Then he shut the doors behind him. The room, though large, felt suddenly small. Arin crossed the room to join her at the table. He said, "I didn't like playing in your suite."

She decided not to take offense. She *had* asked him to be honest. Kestrel mixed the tiles, but when she set a box of matches on the table, he said, "Let's play for something else."

Kestrel didn't move her hand from the box's lid. Again

she wondered what he could offer her, what he could gamble, and she could think of nothing.

Arin said, "If I win, I will ask a question, and you will answer."

She felt a nervous flutter. "I could lie. People lie."

"I'm willing to risk it."

"If those are your stakes, then I assume my prize would be the same."

"*If* you win."

She still could not quite agree. "Questions and answers are highly irregular stakes in Bite and Sting," she said irritably.

"Whereas matches make the perfect ante, and are so exciting to win and lose."

"Fine." Kestrel tossed the box to the carpet, where it landed with a muffled sound.

Arin didn't look satisfied or amused or anything at all. He simply drew his hand. She did the same. They played in intent concentration, and Kestrel was determined to win.

She didn't.

"I want to know," Arin said, "why you are not already a soldier."

Kestrel couldn't have said what she had thought he would ask, but this was not it, and the question recalled years of arguments she would rather forget. She was curt. "I'm seventeen. I'm not yet required by law to enlist or marry."

He settled back in his chair, toying with one of his winning pieces. He tapped a thin side against the table, spun the tile in his fingers, and tapped another side. "That's not a full answer."

"I don't think we specified how short or long these answers should be. Let's play again."

"If you win, will you be satisfied with the kind of answer you have given me?"

Slowly, she said, "The military is my father's life. Not mine. I'm not even a skilled fighter."

"Really?" His surprise seemed genuine.

"Oh, I pass muster. I can defend myself as well as most Valorians, but I'm not good at combat. I know what it's like to be good at something."

Arin glanced again at the piano.

"There is also my music," Kestrel acknowledged. "A piano is not very portable. I could hardly take it with me if I were sent into battle."

"Playing music is for slaves," Arin said. "Like cooking or cleaning."

Kestrel heard anger in his words, buried like bedrock under the careless ripple of his voice. "It wasn't always like that."

Arin was silent, and even though Kestrel had initially tried to answer his question in the briefest of ways, she felt compelled to explain the final reason behind her resistance to the general. "Also . . . I don't want to kill." Arin frowned at this, so Kestrel laughed to make light of the conversation. "I drive my father mad. Yet don't all daughters? So we've made a truce. I have agreed that, in the spring, I will either enlist or marry."

He stopped spinning the tile in his fingers. "You'll marry, then."

"Yes. But at least I will have six months of peace first."

Arin dropped the tile to the table. "Let's play again."

This time Kestrel won, and wasn't prepared for how her blood buzzed with triumph.

Arin stared at the tiles. His mouth thinned to a line.

A thousand questions swam into Kestrel's mind, nudging, fighting to be first. But she was as taken aback as Arin seemed to be by the one that slipped out of her mouth. "Why were you trained as a blacksmith?"

For a moment, Kestrel thought he wouldn't answer. His jaw tightened. Then he said, "I was chosen because I was the last nine-year-old boy in the world suited to be a blacksmith. I was scrawny. I daydreamed. I cringed. Have you looked at the tools in the forge? At the hammer? You'd want to think carefully about what kind of slave you'd let pick that up. My first slaver looked at me and decided I wasn't the type to raise my hand in anger. He chose me." Arin's smile was cold. "Well, do you like your answer?"

Kestrel couldn't speak.

Arin pushed his tiles away. "I want to go into the city."

Even though Kestrel had said that he could, and knew that there was nothing wrong with a slave hoping to see his sweetheart, she wanted to say no. "So soon?" she managed.

"It's been a month."

"Oh." Kestrel told herself that a month must be a long time to go without seeing the person one loves. "Of course. Go."

"I've made about thirty weapons," Arin told the auctioneer. "Mostly daggers, good for close-range attack. A few swords. I've bundled them, and will drop them over the southwest wall of the general's estate tonight, four hours before dawn. Make sure someone's waiting on the other side."

"Done," said Cheat.

"You can expect more. What about the black powder kegs?"

"They're secure."

"I wonder if I should try to recruit any of the general's slaves. They could be useful."

Cheat shook his head. "It's not worth the risk."

"If we didn't have people in Senator Andrax's house, we never would have been able to steal the black powder. All our man had to do was take his master's key and return it to its proper place afterward. We might be missing a similar opportunity at the general's."

"I said no."

Arin's heart seemed to be punching its way out of his chest, he was so angry. But he knew that Cheat was right, and his mood wasn't the auctioneer's fault. It was his own. Or hers. He wasn't sure what bothered him more about that last Bite and Sting game: that he had played into her hands, or that she had played into his.

"What about the girl?" Cheat said, and Arin wished that he had asked him any other question.

Arin hesitated, then said, "Reports of Lady Kestrel's military skill are exaggerated. She won't be a problem."

"Here." Kestrel handed her old nurse a small ceramic pot. "Syrup for your cough."

Enai sighed, which triggered another bout of coughing. She leaned against the pillows Kestrel had tucked behind her shoulders, then raised her eyes to the cottage ceiling. "I hate autumn. And the god of good health."

Kestrel sat at the edge of the bed. "Poor Amma," she said, using the Herrani word for *mother*. "Shall I tell you a story, like you used to do for me when I was sick?"

"No. You Valorians are bad storytellers. I know what you'll say. 'We fought. We won. The end.'"

"I think I can do better than that."

Enai shook her head. "Best to recognize the things you can't change, child."

"Well, then when you're better, you'll come to the villa and I will play for you."

"Yes. I always like that."

Kestrel left her side and moved around the two-room cottage, unpacking a basket of food and tidying up.

"I met Smith," Enai called.

Kestrel's hands stilled. She returned to the bedroom. "Where?"

"Where do you think? In the slaves' quarters."

"I thought you didn't go there," Kestrel said. "You shouldn't go outside until you're better."

"Don't fuss. I went there a few days ago, before I fell ill."

"And?"

Enai shrugged. "We didn't speak much. But he seems to be well liked. He's made friends."

"Like who?"

"He and the groom—that new one, I forget his

name—get along. At meals, Smith usually sits with Lirah."

Kestrel focused on drawing Enai's blanket into a neat line across the woman's chest. She made it neater still, thinking of Lirah's oval face and sweet voice. "Lirah is kind. She is a good friend for him to have."

Enai reached for her hand. "I know you regret the purchase, but there are worse places for him to be."

Kestrel realized that she no longer did regret the purchase and frowned. What kind of person had she become, to feel that way?

"I gave him house privileges," she said, knowing that her tone was defensive. "He also often serves as my escort into the city."

Enai swallowed some syrup and made a face. "Yes, I heard from the others. Does society talk about it?"

"About what?"

"About Smith. Does society talk about him appearing as your escort?"

"Not to my knowledge. There was some gossip about the price I paid for him, but everyone's forgotten that."

"That may be, but I would think he'd still draw attention."

Kestrel searched the woman's face. "Enai, what are you trying to say? Why would people talk about him?"

Enai studied the very plain syrup pot. Finally, she said, "Because of how he looks."

"Oh." Kestrel was relieved. "Once he's dressed in house attire he doesn't appear so rough. He holds himself well." This thought seemed ready to give rise to other thoughts, but she shook her head. "No, I don't think he would give anyone cause to complain about his appearance."

Enai said, "I'm sure you're right."

Kestrel had the sense that the woman's words were less an agreement than a decision to let some unspoken matter drop.

ENAI'S WORDS TROUBLED KESTREL, BUT NOT so much that she changed her ways. She continued to bring Arin with her on visits into society. She enjoyed his sharp mind—even his sharp tongue. She had to admit, however, that their conversations in Herrani created a false sense of privacy. She thought this was due to the language itself; Herrani had always felt more intimate than Valorian, probably because after her mother's death her father had had little time for her, and it was Enai who had filled the void, distracting Kestrel from her tears by teaching her the Herrani word for them.

Kestrel frequently had to remind herself that Arin knew her language as well as she did his. Sometimes, when she caught a glimpse of him listening to an absurd dinner conversation, she wondered how he had mastered Valorian so completely. Few slaves did.

Not long after her second game of Bite and Sting with Arin, they went to Jess's home.

"Kestrel!" Jess embraced her. "You've neglected us."

Jess waited for an explanation, but when Kestrel mentally sifted through her reasons—the strategy lessons with her father, hours of practice at piano, and two Bite and Sting games that took up much more time in her mind than they had actual hours—she said only, "Well, I'm here now."

"And ready with an apology. If not, I shall take my revenge on you."

"Oh?" Kestrel followed Jess into the parlor, listening to Arin's footsteps behind them soften as he moved from the marble hallway to the carpeted floor. "Should I be afraid?"

"Yes. If you don't beg my forgiveness, I won't go with you to the dressmaker's to order gowns for the governor's Firstwinter ball."

Kestrel laughed. "The first day of winter is ages away."

"But your apology, I hope, isn't."

"I am very, very sorry, Jess."

"Good." Jess's brown eyes glittered with mirth. "I forgive you, on the condition that you let *me* choose your gown."

Kestrel gave her a helpless look. She glanced at Arin, who was standing against the wall. Though his expression was bland, she had the impression he was laughing at her.

"You dress too modestly, Kestrel." When Kestrel began to protest, Jess caught one of her hands with both of hers and shook it. "There. It is agreed. It is done. A Valorian honors her word."

Kestrel sank onto a sofa next to Jess, admitting defeat.

"Ronan will be sorry to have missed you," Jess said.

"He is out?"

"He is visiting Lady Faris's household."

Kestrel lifted one brow. "Then I am sure her charms will soothe any regret he might have in missing me."

"Don't tell me that you're jealous. You know what Ronan feels for you."

Kestrel became acutely conscious of Arin's presence in the room. She glanced at him, expecting the bored expression he usually wore in Jess's company. It wasn't there. He seemed oddly intent. "You may go," she told him.

It looked like he might disobey. Then he spun on his heel and strode from the room.

When the door had shut behind him, Kestrel told Jess, "Ronan and I are friends."

Jess huffed with impatience.

"And there is only one reason young men of his set visit Lady Faris," Kestrel continued, thinking of Faris's baby and his dimpled smile. She considered the possibility that the child was Ronan's. This didn't trouble her—which *did* trouble her. Shouldn't she care? Didn't she welcome Ronan's attention? Yet the idea that he had fathered a child skimmed the surface of her mind and slipped in quietly, without a splash or gulp or quiver.

Well, if the baby was his, he had been conceived more than a year ago. And if Ronan was with Faris now, what promise was there between him and Kestrel?

"Faris is notorious," she told Jess. "Plus, her husband is in the capital."

"Young men visit her because her husband is one of the most influential men in the city, and they hope Faris will help them become senators."

"What price do you think she makes them pay?"

Jess looked scandalized.

"Why would Ronan mind paying?" Kestrel said. "Faris is beautiful."

"He would never."

"Jess, if you think you can convince me that Ronan is an innocent who has never been with a woman, you are mistaken."

"If you think Ronan would prefer Faris over you, you are mad." Jess shook her head. "All he wants is a sign of your affection. He has given you plenty."

"Meaningless compliments."

"You don't want to see it. Don't you think he is handsome?"

Kestrel couldn't deny that Ronan was everything she might hope. He cut a fine figure. He was witty, good-natured. And he didn't mind her music.

Jess said, "Wouldn't you like for us to be sisters?"

Kestrel reached for one of Jess's many shining, pale braids. She slipped it out of the girl's upswept arrangement, then tucked it back in. "We already are."

"*Real* sisters."

"Yes," Kestrel said in a low voice. "I would like that." She had always wanted to be part of Jess's family, ever since she had been a child. Jess had the perfect older brother and indulgent parents.

Jess made a delighted sound. Kestrel looked at her sharply. "Don't you dare tell him."

"Me?" Jess said innocently.

Later that day, Kestrel sat with Arin in the music room. She played her tiles: a pair of wolves and three mice.

Arin turned his over with a resigned sigh. He didn't have a bad set, but it wasn't good enough, and beneath his usual level of skill. He stiffened in his chair as if physically bracing himself for her question.

Kestrel studied his tiles. She was certain he could have done better than a pair of wasps. She thought of the tiles he had shown earlier in the game, and the careless way in which he had discarded others. If she didn't know how little he liked to lose against her, she would have suspected him of throwing the game.

She said, "You seem distracted."

"Is that your question? Are you asking me why I am distracted?"

"So you admit that you are distracted."

"You *are* a fiend," he said, echoing Ronan's words during the match at Faris's garden party. Then, apparently annoyed at his own words, he said, "Ask your question."

She could have pressed the issue, but his distraction was a less interesting mystery compared to one growing in her mind. She didn't think Arin was who he appeared to be. He had the body of someone born into hard work, yet he knew how to play a Valorian game, and play it well. He spoke her language like someone who had studied it carefully. He knew—or pretended to know—the habits of a Herrani lady and the order of her rooms. He had been relaxed and adept around her stallion, and while that might not mean anything—he had not *ridden* Javelin—Kestrel knew that horsemanship among the Herrani before the war had been a mark of high class.

Kestrel thought that Arin was someone who had fallen far.

She couldn't ask if that was true. She remembered his angry response when she had asked why he had been trained as a blacksmith, and that question had seemed innocent enough. Yet it had hurt him.

She did not want to hurt him.

"How did you learn to play Bite and Sting?" she asked. "It's Valorian."

He looked relieved. "There was a time when Herrani enjoyed sailing to your country. We liked your people. And we have always admired the arts. Our sailors brought back Bite and Sting sets a long time ago."

"Bite and Sting is a game, not an art."

He folded his arms across his chest, amused. "If you say so."

"I'm surprised to hear that Herrani liked anything about Valorians. I thought you considered us stupid savages."

"Wild creatures," he muttered.

Kestrel was sure she had misheard him. "What?"

"Nothing. Yes, you were completely uncultured. You ate with your hands. Your idea of entertainment was seeing who could kill the other first. But"—his eyes met hers, then glanced away—"you were known for other things, too."

"What things? What do you mean?"

He shook his head. He made that strange gesture again, lifting his fingers to flick the air by his temple. Then he folded his hands, unfolded them, and began to mix the tiles. "You have asked too many questions. If you want more, you will have to win them."

He showed no sign of distraction now. As they played, he ignored her attempts to provoke him or make him laugh. "I've seen your tricks on others," he said. "They won't work with me."

He won. Kestrel waited, nervous, and wondered if the way she felt was how he felt when he lost.

His voice came haltingly. "Will you play for me?"

"Play for you?"

Arin winced. In a more determined tone, he said, "Yes. Something I choose."

"I don't mind. It's only . . . people rarely ask."

He stood from the table, searched the shelves along the wall, and returned with a sheaf of sheet music. She took it. "It's for the flute," he said. "It will probably take you time to transpose it for the piano. I can wait. Maybe after our next game—"

She fanned the paper impatiently to silence him. "It's not that hard."

He nodded, then sat in the chair farthest away from the piano, by the glass garden doors. Kestrel was glad for his distance. She settled on the piano's bench, flipping through the sheet music. The title and notations were in Herrani, the pages yellow with age. She propped the paper on the piano's rack, taking more time than necessary to neaten the sheets. Excitement coursed through her fingers as if she had already plunged her hands into the music, but that feeling was edged with a metallic lace of fear.

She wished that Arin hadn't chosen music for the flute, of all instruments. The beauty of the flute was in its simplicity, in its resemblance to the human voice. It always sounded clear. It sounded alone. The piano, on the other hand, was a network of parts—a ship, with its strings like rigging, its case a hull, its lifted lid a sail. Kestrel always thought that the piano didn't sound like a single instrument but a twinned one, with its low and high halves merging together or pulling apart.

Flute music, she thought with frustration, and would not look at Arin.

Her opening notes were awkward. She paused, then gave the melody over to her right hand and began inventing with her left, pulling dark, rich phrases out of her mind. Kestrel felt the counterpoint knit itself into being. Forgetting the difficulty of what she was doing, she simply played.

It was a gentle, haunting music. When it ended, Kestrel was sorry. Her eyes sought Arin across the room.

She didn't know if he had watched her play. He wasn't looking at her now. His gaze was unfocused, directed toward the garden without really seeing it. The lines of his face had softened. He looked different, Kestrel realized. She couldn't say why, but he looked different to her now.

Then he glanced at her, and she was startled enough to let one hand fall onto the keys with a very unmusical sound.

Arin smiled. It was a true smile, which let her know that all the others he had given her were not. "Thank you," he said.

Kestrel felt herself blush. She focused on the keys and played something, anything. A simple pattern to distract herself from the fact that she wasn't someone who easily blushed, particularly for no clear reason.

But she found that her fingers were sketching an outline of a tenor's range. "Do you truly not sing?"

"No."

She considered the timbre of his voice and let her hands drift lower. "Really?"

"No, Kestrel."

Her hands slid from the keys. "Too bad," she said.

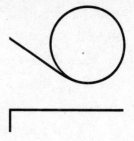

WHEN KESTREL RECEIVED A MESSAGE FROM Ronan inviting her to go riding with him and Jess at their estate, she remembered something her father had said recently about evaluating an enemy.

"Everything in war hinges on what you know of your adversary's skills and assets," he had said. "Yes, luck will play some part. The terrain will be crucial. Numbers are important. But how you negotiate the strengths of your opponent is more likely to decide the battle than anything else."

Arin wasn't Kestrel's enemy, but their Bite and Sting games had made her see him as a worthy opponent. So she considered her father's words. "Your adversary will want to keep his assets hidden until the final moment. Use spies if you can. If not, how might you trick him into revealing the knowledge you seek?" The general had answered his own question: "Nettle his pride."

Kestrel sent a house slave to the forge with a request for Arin to meet her in the stables. When he arrived, Javelin was already saddled and Kestrel was waiting, dressed for riding.

"What is this?" Arin said. "I thought you wanted an escort."

"I do. Pick a horse."

Warily, he said, "If I am to go with you, we need the carriage."

"Not if you know how to ride."

"I don't."

She mounted Javelin. "Then I suppose you must follow me in the carriage."

"You'll get in trouble if you ride alone."

She gathered the reins in her hands.

"Where are you going?" Arin demanded.

"Ronan invited me to ride on his grounds," she told him, and kicked Javelin into a canter. She rode out of the stables, then out of the estate, pausing only to tell the guards at the gate that a slave would be following her. "Probably," she added, spurring Javelin through the gate before the guards could question the irregularity of it all. She turned Javelin down one of the many horse paths Valorians had carved through the greener parts of the city, creating roads only for riders traveling at a good speed. Kestrel resisted the urge to slow her horse. She pressed him still further, listening to hooves hit the dirt with its blanket of fire-colored leaves.

It was some time before she heard galloping behind her, and then she did ease up, instinctively wheeling Javelin around to see the blur of horse and rider coming down the path.

Arin slowed, and sidled alongside Kestrel. The horses whickered. Arin looked at her, at the smile she couldn't hide, and his face seemed to hold equal parts frustration and amusement.

"You are a bad liar," she told him.

He laughed.

She found it hard to look at him then, and her gaze dropped to his stallion. Her eyes widened. "*That* is the horse you chose?"

"He is the best," Arin said seriously.

"He is my father's."

"I won't hold that against the horse."

It was Kestrel's turn to laugh.

"Come." Arin nudged the stallion forward. "Let's not be late," he said, and yet, without discussing it, they rode more slowly than was allowed on the path.

Kestrel no longer doubted that ten years ago Arin had been in a position much like hers: one of wealth, ease, education. Although she was aware she had not won the right to ask him a question, and didn't even want to voice her creeping worry, Kestrel couldn't bear remaining silent. "Arin," she said, searching his face. "Was it *my* house? I mean, the villa. Did you live there, before the war?"

He yanked on the reins. His stallion ground to a halt.

When he spoke, Arin's voice was like the music he had asked her to play. "No," he said. "That family is gone."

They rode on in silence until Arin said, "Kestrel."

She waited, then realized that he wasn't speaking to her, exactly. He was simply saying her name, considering it, exploring the syllables of the Valorian word.

She said, "I hope you're not going to pretend you don't know what it means."

He shot her a wry, sidelong look. "A kestrel is a hunting hawk."

"Yes. The perfect name for a warrior girl."

"Well." His smile was slight, but it was there. "I suppose neither of us is the person we were believed we would become."

Ronan was waiting in his family's stables. He played with the gloves in his hands as he stood watching Kestrel and Arin ride toward him.

"I thought you would take the carriage," Ronan said to Kestrel.

"To go riding? Really, Ronan."

"But your escort." His eyes cut to Arin sitting easily on the stallion. "I didn't think any of your slaves rode."

Kestrel watched Ronan tug at the gloves' fingers. "Is there a problem?"

"Now that you are here, certainly not." Yet his voice was strained.

"Because if you don't like the way in which I have come, you may ride to my house the next time you invite me, then escort me back to your estate, then see me safely home again, and go back the way you came."

He responded to her words as if they had been flirtatious. "It would be my pleasure. Speaking of pleasure, let's take some together." He mounted his horse.

"Where is Jess?"

"Sick with a headache."

Somehow Kestrel doubted that. She said nothing,

however, and let Ronan lead the way out of the stables. She turned to follow, and Arin did the same.

Ronan glanced back, blond hair brushing over his shoulder. "Surely you don't intend for him to join us."

Arin's horse, perfectly calm up until this point, began to shift and balk. It was sensing the tension Kestrel couldn't see in its rider, who looked impassively at her, waiting for her to translate Ronan's words into Herrani so that he could pretend it was necessary. "Wait here," she told him in his language. He wheeled the horse back toward the stables.

"You should vary your escorts," Ronan told Kestrel as Arin rode away. "That one stays too close to your heels."

Kestrel wondered who had orchestrated her ride alone with Ronan, the sister or the brother. She would have chosen Ronan—who, after all, had sent the invitation and would have encountered no resistance in asking Jess to stay indoors for the sake of a few private hours. But Ronan's uncharacteristically foul mood made her think otherwise. He was acting like one might if his matchmaking sister had tricked him into something he didn't wish to do.

The day, which had been beautiful to her, no longer looked as bright.

Yet when they stopped to sit under a tree, Ronan's smile returned. He opened his saddlebags to reveal lunch, then unfurled a picnic blanket with a flourish, settled onto it, and stretched out his long form. Kestrel joined him. He poured a glass of wine and offered it.

She lifted a brow. "That is a rather large amount of wine for this time of day."

"I hope to ply you with it, and make you say things you won't regret."

She sipped, watching him pour a second cup, and said, "Are you not afraid for yourself?"

He drank. "Why should I be?"

"Perhaps it is you who will reveal things he'd rather not. I understand you've been paying call to Lady Faris."

"Jealous, Kestrel?"

"No."

"Pity." He sighed. "The sad, dull truth is that Faris has the best gossip."

"Which you will share."

Ronan leaned back to rest on one elbow. "Well, Senator Andrax has been moved to the capital, where he awaits trial for selling black powder to our enemies. The black powder hasn't been found, despite the search—no surprise there, really. It probably vanished into the east long ago. Now, what else? Senator Linux's daughter stole quite a few hours with a certain sailor on board one of the ships in the harbor, and has been shut away in her rooms by her parents for the fall season—probably winter, too. My friend Hanan has gambled away his inheritance—don't worry, Kestrel, he'll get it back. Just please, please do not play Bite and Sting with him for a few months. Oh, and the captain of the city guard committed suicide. But you knew that."

She almost spilled her wine. "No. When did that happen?"

"The day before yesterday. You really didn't know? Well, your father's away *again*, I suppose. And you spend too much time sealed inside that villa. How you don't go mad with boredom is beyond me."

Kestrel knew the captain. Oskar had dined at her house. He was a friend of her father's, and unlike most of his friends he was jovial and well liked.

"It was an honor suicide," Ronan said, which meant that the captain had fallen on his sword.

"But why?"

Ronan shrugged. "The pressure of his position?"

"He was captain since the colonization. He was excellent at it, and respected."

"Personal troubles, perhaps." Ronan spread his hands. "Really, I don't know, and I wish I'd never brought up such a dreary topic. This day hasn't gone at all as I had hoped. Could we please talk about something other than suicide?"

On the way home, Arin said, "Was your ride not pleasant?"

Kestrel glanced up, startled by his biting tone. She realized she had been frowning, lost in thought. "Oh, it was very nice. I'm just troubled by some news."

"What news?"

"The captain of the city guard has killed himself."

"Does this . . . grieve you? Did you know him?"

"Yes. No. Yes, I knew him, as a friend of my father's, but not well enough to feel his death."

"Then I don't understand why it should concern you."

"It concerns the whole city. There's bound to be some disorder as the governor appoints a new captain, and the transition might not go smoothly. Oskar was very good at policing the city and his guards. That isn't what bothers me." Kestrel shook her head. "His suicide is the second thing to happen recently that doesn't make sense."

"What do you mean?"

"Senator Andrax. He loves gold, to be sure, but only because it buys him comfort. Good food, mistresses. He likes bribes: easy money. He won't sit down at a Bite and Sting table with me, he's so afraid of losing. How could *he* risk everything to sell black powder to the barbarians?"

"Maybe there is a side of him you have never seen. But he has nothing to do with the captain."

"*Except* that both events are strange. Oskar had no reason to commit suicide. Even the emperor had praised his performance as captain. His guards admired him. He seemed happy."

"So? You don't know everything. People are unhappy for many reasons." Arin's voice was impatient, and she thought that they were no longer talking about the captain. "What do you know of unhappiness?" he said. "What makes you think you can see into the hearts of men?"

He spurred his horse ahead, and the puzzle about the senator and the captain flew out of Kestrel's mind as she concentrated on keeping up.

KESTREL'S FATHER DIDN'T DISMISS THE CAPTAIN'S death as easily as Ronan and Arin had. During the next lesson in the library, he listened to Kestrel broach the topic, his brow furrowing into deep lines.

"Did Oskar have enemies?" she asked.

"Everyone has enemies."

"Perhaps someone made life difficult for him."

"Or someone *made* him fall on his sword." When the general saw her surprise he said, "It's not hard to make murder look like an honor suicide."

"I hadn't thought of that," she said quietly.

"And what do you think now?"

"If it was murder, he could have been killed by someone likely to inherit his position as captain."

Her father rested a hand on her shoulder. "The death may be only what it appears: a suicide. But I'll discuss our concerns with the governor. This matter bears further thought."

Kestrel, however, had little thought to spare. Enai wasn't getting better.

"Your cough is starting to worry me," she told her nurse as they sat near the fire in her cottage.

"I rather like it. It keeps me company. And it brings you to visit more frequently . . . when you are not playing Bite and Sting."

Kestrel didn't like the coy look on Enai's face, or the fact that it was almost impossible to keep anything that happened in the villa private. Those games were private.

In a sharp tone, Kestrel said, "Let me send for a doctor."

"He will only tell me that I am old."

"Enai."

"I don't want to see one. Don't try to order *me* around."

That silenced Kestrel. She decided not to press the issue. After all, the feverish glaze in Enai's eyes had vanished long ago. Kestrel, seeking to change the subject, asked about something that Arin had said. It had been like a needle in a dark part of her mind, stitching invisible patterns. "Did the Herrani enjoy trading with Valorians before the war?"

"Oh, yes. Your people always had gold for Herrani goods. Valoria was our biggest buyer of exports."

"But did we have a reputation for something else? Besides being rich and savage, with no manners."

Enai took a sip of tea, peering at Kestrel over the cup's rim. Kestrel grew uncomfortable, and hoped Enai wouldn't ask what inspired these questions. But the woman only said, "You were known for your beauty. Of course, that was before the war."

"Yes," said Kestrel softly. "Of course."

From the window of her dressing room, Kestrel could see the garden. One morning, her hair still loose, she noticed Arin and Lirah talking by the rows of autumn vegetables. Arin wore work clothes and his back was to the window, giving Kestrel no opportunity to read his expression. Lirah's, however, was as clear as the dawn.

Kestrel realized that she had drawn close to the window. The chill from the glass breathed onto her skin, and her nails were digging into the grain of the sill. She drew back. She wasn't eager to be caught spying. She pulled her velvet robe more tightly around her and let the view of the rosy sky fill her eyes, but still it seemed that all she saw was Lirah's frank adoration.

Kestrel sat in front of her dressing table's hinged mirror, then wondered why she had done such a foolish thing as to look at herself. The mirror's reflection only proved her displeasure. And why should she care about what she had seen in the garden? Why should she feel that some trust had been breached?

Her reflection frowned. Why should she *not* feel that way? She had a duty to the well-being of her slaves. There was something dishonorable in Arin accepting Lirah's attention when he had a sweetheart. Kestrel doubted Lirah knew about the woman in the market.

Kestrel's hand pushed the oval mirror, spinning it on its hinges until it faced the wall and she stared at its blank, mother-of-pearl back. She refused to consider this anymore. She would not become one of those mistresses who tracked her slaves' movements and gossiped about them for lack of anything interesting in her own life.

Later that day, Arin came to the music room with a request to visit the city. Kestrel was especially gracious. She gave him her seal ring and told him to take as much time as he liked, so long as he was back by curfew. When it seemed that he might linger, she sat at the piano, making her dismissal clear. Yet she didn't play until he had left and she felt that he had already walked out of the villa, and was some distance away.

When Cheat saw Arin, he greeted him in the way Herrani men used to do, with a palm pressed briefly to the side of his face. Arin smiled and did the same. He had known Cheat for years, since he was a boy and had just changed hands from his first slaver to his second. They had met in a quarry outside the city. Arin remembered how the gray rock dust had made everyone look old, powdering hair and drying out the skin. Cheat, however, had seemed almost viciously full of life, and there was no question in the slaves' quarters at night who led them.

"Things are going very well," Cheat said to him now. "Almost every household in the city has Herrani devoted to our cause—and now, thanks to you, they are armed."

"I'll drop the latest batch of weapons over the wall

tonight, but I'm not sure how many more I can make," Arin said. "No one's noticed what I do on the side because I fill the steward's orders on time, but if someone decides to check, it'll be clear that iron and steel have gone missing."

"Then stop. Your position is too important to risk. I'll arrange for someone to raid the city armory before the new captain is appointed to replace Oskar."

Cheat had been a city guard before the war. He had taken one look at the twelve-year-old Arin, called him a puppy with big paws, and said, "You'll grow into them." After curfew, he would teach Arin how to fight. Arin's misery eased, though some of it came back when Cheat flattered and connived his way out of the quarry after a stint of only two years. But the skills Cheat had given him remained.

"You should plan to raid the armory *after* the new captain is appointed," said Arin. "If it's noticed then that weapons are missing, it will make him look incompetent."

"Good idea. In the meantime, you and I will keep meeting. We need our moment at the general's estate. You'll give it to us."

This was when Arin should have told Cheat that Kestrel was beginning to see a pattern of events. He should have revealed that she found something strange in the death of the captain, though she couldn't know that two of the captain's slaves had held him while another knelt on the ground with the man's sword, waiting for the final push.

Arin should have said something to his leader. Yet he didn't.

He kept his distance from the villa. It was too easy to slip in Kestrel's presence.

One day, Lirah came to the forge. Arin was sure that he was being called to serve as Kestrel's escort somewhere. He felt an eager dread.

"Enai would like to see you," Lirah said.

Arin set the hammer on the anvil. "Why?" His interactions with Enai had been limited, and he liked to keep them that way. The woman's eyes were too keen.

"She's very sick."

Arin considered this, then nodded, following Lirah from the forge.

When they entered the cottage, they could hear the sounds of sleep from beyond the open bedroom door. Enai coughed, and Arin heard fluid in her lungs.

The coughing subsided, then gave way to ragged breath.

"Someone should fetch a doctor," Arin told Lirah.

"Lady Kestrel has gone for one. She was very upset. She'll return soon, I hope." Haltingly, Lirah said, "I'd like to stay with you, but I have to get back to the house." Arin barely noticed her touch his arm before leaving him.

Reluctant to wake Enai, Arin studied the cottage. It was snug and well maintained. The floor didn't creak. There were signs, everywhere, of comfort. Slippers. A stack of dry wood. Arin ran a hand along the smooth mantel of the fireplace until he touched a porcelain box. He opened it. Inside was a small braid of dark blond hair with a reddish tinge, looped in a circle and tied with golden wire.

Although he knew he shouldn't, Arin traced the braid with one fingertip.

"That's not yours," a voice said.

He snatched his hand away. He turned, his face hot. Through the open bedroom door, Arin saw Enai staring at him from where she lay. "I'm sorry." He set the lid on the box.

"I doubt it," she muttered, and told him to come near.

Arin did, slowly. He had the feeling he was not going to like this conversation.

"You spend a lot of time with Kestrel," Enai said.

He shrugged. "I do what she asks."

Enai held his gaze. Despite himself, he looked away first.

"Don't hurt her," the woman said.

It was a sin to break a deathbed promise.

Arin left without making one.

AFTER ENAI'S DEATH, KESTREL SAT IN HER rooms remembering how the woman had taught her to paint a tree by blowing through a hollow quill at a pool of ink on paper. Kestrel saw the white page. She felt the ache in her lungs, saw the black branches spreading, and thought this was what her grief felt like, digging roots and twigs into her body.

She had had a mother, and that mother was gone. Then she had had another mother, and that one was gone, too.

Daylight came and went and continued without Kestrel being truly aware that time was passing. She pushed away food that slaves brought her. She refused to read letters. She couldn't even think of playing the piano, for it was Enai who had encouraged her to keep practicing after her mother's death. She heard the memory of Enai saying what a pretty melody that was, and could Kestrel play it again? That memory became a refrain of its own: echoing, diminishing, returning. And then Kestrel saw again the skin and bone of Enai's face, the coughed-up blood, and knew that she was to blame, that she should have insisted on a doctor earlier, and now Enai was dead.

It was late afternoon and she was sitting alone in her breakfast room, blankly staring out a window at bad weather, when she heard rapid, fierce footfalls striding toward her.

"Stop crying." Arin's tone was brutal.

Kestrel lifted fingertips to her cheek. They came away wet. "You shouldn't be here," she said, her voice hoarse. The breakfast room was one into which men were not allowed.

"I don't care." He tugged Kestrel to her feet, and the shock of it forced her gaze to his. The blacks of his eyes were blown wide with feeling.

With anger. "Stop it," he said. "Stop pretending to mourn someone who wasn't your blood."

His hand was iron around her wrist. She pulled free, the cruelty of what he had said bringing fresh tears to her eyes. "I loved her," Kestrel whispered.

"You loved her because she did anything you wanted."

"That's not true."

"She didn't love *you*. She could never love you. Where is her *real* family, Kestrel?"

She didn't know. She had been afraid to ask.

"Where is her daughter? Her grandchildren? If she loved you, it was because she had no choice, and there was no one else left."

"Get out," she told him, but he was already gone.

The light dimmed. The sky through the windows turned emerald. It was the first green storm of the season, and as Kestrel heard the wind pummel the house, she knew that

Arin was wrong. He had wanted to punish her for months now. Hadn't she bought him? Didn't she own him? This was his revenge. That was all.

The rain drove nails against the windowpanes. The room grew almost black. Kestrel heard Arin's voice again in her mind and felt suddenly broken. Even if she didn't doubt her feelings for Enai, there had been truth in his words.

She didn't notice him return. This storm was loud, the room was dark. She sucked in her breath when she realized he stood next to her. For the first time, it occurred to her to be afraid of him.

But he merely struck a match and touched it to the wick of a lamp. He was soaked with rain. His skin glittered with it.

When she looked at him, he flinched. "Kestrel." He sighed. He rubbed a hand through his wet hair. "I shouldn't have said what I did."

"You meant it."

"Yes, but—" Arin looked weary and confused. "I would have been angry if you did *not* weep for her." He held out the hand that rested at his side in the shadows, and for an uncertain moment Kestrel thought he would touch her. But he was only offering something on his uplifted palm. "This was in her cottage," he said.

It was a braid of Kestrel's hair. She took it carefully; even so, her smallest finger brushed his wet palm. His hand instantly fell.

She considered the braid, turning the bright ring in her fingers. She knew that it didn't choose sides between her truth and Arin's. It wasn't proof of Enai's love. Yet it was a comfort.

"I should go," Arin said, though he didn't move.

Kestrel looked at his face glowing in the lamplight. She became aware that she was close enough to him that her bare foot rested on the damp edge of carpet where Arin stood, seeping rainwater. A shiver traveled up her skin.

Kestrel stepped back. "Yes," she said. "You should."

The next morning, her father strode into her visiting room and said, "This seclusion of yours has gone on long enough." He stood in front of her chair, feet planted. He often took this stance when he would rather pace. "I know your attachment to your nurse, and I suppose, all things considered, it's understandable. But you've missed a training session with Rax, a lesson with me, and I didn't raise you to fall apart at the slightest difficulty."

"I'm fine, Father." Kestrel poured a cup of tea.

It was only then that he truly looked at her. She was sure there were hollows under her eyes, but she was impeccably dressed for a late autumn day in society.

"Well," he said. "Good. Because I sent for Jess. She's waiting downstairs in the parlor."

Kestrel set the cup on its saucer and rose to greet her friend.

"Kestrel." The general touched her shoulder. When he spoke, his voice was uncharacteristically hesitant. "It's every child's duty to survive her parents. My profession isn't a safe one. I would like—Kestrel, when I die, do not mourn me."

She smiled. "You do not command me," she said, and kissed his cheek.

Jess was in her element. She whisked Kestrel away in her carriage and stopped in front of the city's finest dressmaker. "You promised," she warned Kestrel as they stepped from the carriage.

Kestrel eyed her. "I promised to let you choose the fabric for my gown."

"Liar. I get to choose *everything*."

"Oh, all right," Kestrel said, because Jess's enthusiasm made her own sadness ebb. How much damage, anyway, could Jess do?

When they entered the shop, Jess waved away the fabrics Kestrel would have chosen, and sketched designs for the dressmaker that made Kestrel's eyes widen. "Jess. This is for a *First-winter* ball. I am going to *freeze*. May I please have sleeves?"

"No."

"And the neckline—"

"Be quiet. Your opinion is not needed."

Kestrel gave up, and stood on the block while the dressmaker pinned cloth around her and Jess gave instructions. Then the two young women left Kestrel alone, ducking into the supply room where bolts of fabric shimmered on shelves. Jess whispered, the dressmaker whispered back, and as Kestrel strained to understand their excited confederacy, she began to suspect that Jess was arranging for not one but two dresses.

"Jess," called Kestrel, "did I hear you say that you wanted the evening dress to be embroidered, *and* the ball gown to be plain?"

"Of course. You need a new evening dress, too, for Lord Irex's dinner party."

A pin jabbed into Kestrel's waist. "He's having a party?"

"It is high time. He hopes to be a senator someday, so he must begin to show his friendly side to society. Plus, his parents have traveled to the capital for the winter season. He has the house to himself."

"I'm not going," Kestrel said flatly.

"You *have* to go."

"I wasn't invited."

"Obviously you were. You are General Trajan's daughter, and if now is the first time you have heard of the party, it's only because you haven't opened your letters in more than a week."

Kestrel remembered Irex's threatening leer. "No. Absolutely not."

"But why?"

"I don't like him."

"What does that matter? There will be scores of people, and his house is certainly large enough for you to avoid him. Everyone will be there. How will it look if you are not?"

Kestrel thought of a Bite and Sting game. She had to admit that if Irex's invitation were a tile and not a piece of paper folded and sealed, she would play it coolly.

Jess drew near and reached for Kestrel's hands. "I don't like to see you sad. Come with Ronan and me, and we will keep you away from Irex and make you laugh at him. Come, Kestrel. I won't give up until you say yes."

WHEN THE DRESS FOR IREX'S DINNER PARTY arrived wrapped in muslin and tied with twine, it was Arin who brought the package to Kestrel. She hadn't seen him since the first green storm. She didn't like to think about that day. It was her grief, she decided, that she didn't want to remember. She was learning to live around it. She had returned to her music, and let that and outings and lessons flow around the fact of Enai's death, smoothing its jagged edges.

She spent little time at the villa. She sent no invitations to Arin for Bite and Sting. If she went into society, she chose other escorts.

When Arin stepped into her sitting room that was really a writing room, Kestrel set her book next to her on the divan and turned its spine so that he wouldn't see the title.

"Hmm," Arin said, turning the packaged dress over in his hands. "What could this be?"

"I am sure you know."

He pressed it between his fingers. "A very soft kind of weapon, I think."

"Why are you delivering my dress?"

"I saw Lirah with it. I asked if I could bring it to you."

"And she let you, of course."

He lifted his brows at her tone. "She was busy. I thought she would be glad for one less thing to do."

"That was kind of you then," Kestrel said, though she heard her voice indicate otherwise and was annoyed with herself.

Slowly, he said, "What do you mean?"

"I mean nothing."

"You asked me to be honest with you. Do you think I have been?"

She remembered his harsh words during the storm. "Yes."

"Can I not ask the same thing of you?"

The answer was no, no slave could ask anything of her. The answer was no, if he wanted her secret thoughts he could try to win them at Bite and Sting. But Kestrel swallowed a sudden flare of nervousness and admitted to herself that she valued his honesty—and her own, when she was around him. There was nothing wrong with speaking the truth. "I think that you are not fair to Lirah."

His brows drew together. "I don't understand."

"It's not fair for you to encourage Lirah when your heart is elsewhere."

He inhaled sharply. Kestrel thought that he might tell her it was no business of hers, for it was not, but then she saw that he wasn't offended, only taken aback. He pulled up a chair in that possessive, natural way of his and sank into it, dropping the dress onto his knees. He studied her. She willed herself not to look away.

"I hadn't thought of Lirah like that." Arin shook his head. "I'm not thinking clearly at all. I need to be more careful."

Kestrel supposed that she should feel reassured.

Arin set the package on the divan where she sat. "A new dress means an event on the horizon."

"Yes, a dinner party. Lord Irex is hosting."

He frowned. "And you're going?"

She shrugged.

"Do you need an escort?"

Kestrel intended to say no, but became distracted by the determined set to Arin's mouth. He looked almost . . . protective. She was surprised that he should look that way. She was confused, and perhaps this made her say, "To be honest, I would be glad for your company."

His eyes held hers. Then his gaze fell to the book by Kestrel's side. Before she could stop him, he took it with a nimble hand and read the title. It was a Valorian history of its empire and wars.

Arin's face changed. He returned the book and left.

"Where are we going?" Arin stared out the carriage window at the trees of the Garden District, their bare branches slim and violet in the dusk.

Kestrel fidgeted with her skirts. "Arin. You know that we are going to Irex's party."

"Yes," he said shortly, but didn't tear his gaze away from the passing trees.

Better he look at them than at her. The velvet dress was a deep red, the skirts deliberately crushed in a pattern highlighted by golden embroidered leaves that twined up toward the bodice, where they interlaced and would catch the light. Conspicuous. The dress made her conspicuous. Kestrel sank into her corner of the carriage, feeling her dagger dig into her side. This evening at Irex's wouldn't be easy.

Arin seemed to think the same. He held himself so rigidly on the carriage seat across from her that he looked wooden. Tension seeped into the air between them.

When torches lit the darkness outside the windows and the driver lined up behind other carriages waiting to access the pathway to Irex's villa, Kestrel said, "Perhaps we should return home."

"No," said Arin. "I want to see the house." He opened the door.

They were silent as they walked up the path to the villa. Though not as large as Kestrel's, it was also a former Herrani home: elegant, prettily designed. Arin fell behind Kestrel, as was expected of slaves, but this made her uneasy. It was unsettling to feel him close and not see his face.

They entered the house with the other guests and made their way into the receiving room, which was lined with Valorian weapons.

"They don't belong there," she heard Arin say. She turned to see him staring in shock at the walls.

"Irex is an exceptional fighter," said Kestrel. "And not very modest."

Arin said nothing, so neither did Kestrel. She prepared

herself for the moment when the line of guests before her dwindled and she had to thank Irex for his hospitality.

"Kestrel." Irex took her hand. "I didn't think you would come."

"Why wouldn't I?"

He pulled her closer. Although his grip on her hand was painful, she let him. People milled around them, and she didn't think it would help matters to shame Irex in front of his guests. He said, "Let's have no bad blood between us." He smiled, and a dimple bit into his left cheek, making him look oddly childlike at the same time his voice was unpleasant. "Did you never wonder why I wanted to play with you at Bite and Sting?"

"Because you wanted to beat me. But you won't." She placed her free hand on top of his that gripped hers. The gesture would look friendly to anyone who watched, but Irex felt her pinch the nerve that forced his hand to release her captive one. "This is a lovely party. My thanks to you equals the grace you have shown me."

The smile slid from his face. But Lady Faris was behind Kestrel and Arin, eager for attention, so it was easy for Kestrel to step aside and let the woman push close to Irex, saying what a *shame* it was that her husband couldn't join her.

A slave in serving dress presented Kestrel with wine, then led the way to an open solarium with a low fountain and hothouse flowers. Musicians played discreetly behind an ebony screen as guests greeted each other, some chatting where they stood, others retreating for quiet conversations on the stone benches lining the fountain.

Kestrel turned to face Arin.

His eyes were dazed with anger, his hands clenched.

"Arin," she began, concerned, but his gaze flicked away and settled on some point across the room. "Your friends are here," he said.

She followed his line of sight to see Jess and Ronan laughing at something Benix had said.

"Dismiss me," Arin said.

"What?" she said, though in fact he was the only escort in the room. The slaves who threaded through the crowd were servers, and Irex's.

"Join your friends. I don't want to stay here anymore. Send me to the kitchens."

She took a breath, then nodded. He spun on his heel and was gone.

She felt instantly alone. She hadn't expected this. But when she asked herself what she had expected, she had a foolish image of her and Arin sitting on a bench together.

Kestrel looked up at the glass roof, a pyramid of purple sky. She saw the sharp cut of the moon, and remembered Enai saying that it was best to recognize the things one cannot change.

She crossed the room to greet her friends.

Kestrel ate little at dinner and drank less, though Ronan, who sat to her right, was attentive toward her plate and cup. She was glad when the last course was served and everyone moved into the adjoining ballroom, for she had begun to feel trapped at the table, and Ronan's talk had a pattern that was too easy to predict. She preferred listening to music. Even in a crowd, she would take a quiet pleasure in whatever the flutist played for the dance. She thought that Arin would, too, if he were here.

"Kestrel." Ronan touched her long earring to make it swing. "You are dreaming. What holds your mind so?"

"Nothing," she told him, and was relieved when Benix strode toward them to claim Ronan's assistance.

"The Raul twins," Benix said pleadingly, casting his eyes in the direction of the identical sisters. "One won't dance without the other, Ronan, so if you wouldn't mind . . ."

Ronan looked irritated.

"What?" said Benix. When he glanced between Ronan and Kestrel he waved a dismissive hand. "We are old friends, we three. Kestrel can spare you for one dance."

Kestrel certainly could. But she pretended to be cross in a way that indicated both that she didn't mind and that she did, a little, when the truth of the matter was that she didn't care at all. She told the boys she would find Jess and a corner in which they would gossip.

"Only *one* dance," Ronan told Benix, and they crossed the room to the twins. The dance began, but Kestrel didn't seek Jess. She found a chair in the shadows and sat listening, eyes closed, to the flute.

"Lady Kestrel?" said an anxious voice.

Kestrel opened her eyes to see a girl dressed in a Herrani serving uniform. "Yes?"

"Will you please follow me? There is a problem with your escort."

Kestrel stood. "What's wrong?"

"He has stolen something."

Kestrel rushed from the room, wishing the girl would move more quickly down the villa's halls. There must be some mistake. Arin was intelligent, far too canny to do something so dangerous. He must know what happened to Herrani thieves.

The girl led Kestrel into the library. Several men were gathered there: two senators, who held Arin by his arms, and Irex, whose expression when he saw Kestrel was gloating, as if he had just drawn a high tile in Bite and Sting. "Lady Kestrel," he said, "what exactly did you bring into my house?"

Kestrel looked at Arin, who refused to return her gaze. "He wouldn't steal." She heard something desperate in her voice.

Irex must have, too. He smiled.

"We saw him," said one of the senators. "He was slipping that inside his shirt." He nodded at a book that had fallen to the floor.

No. The accusation couldn't be true. No slave would risk a flogging for theft, not for a book. Kestrel steadied herself. "May I?" she asked Irex, nodding at the fallen book.

He swept a hand to indicate permission.

Kestrel stooped to retrieve the book, and Arin's eyes flashed to hers.

Her heart failed. His face was twisted with misery.

She considered the closed, leather-bound book in her hands. She recognized the title: it was a volume of Herrani poetry, a common one. There was a copy in her library as well. Kestrel held the book, not understanding, not seeing anything worth the risk of theft—at least not here, from Irex's library, when her own could easily serve Arin's purposes.

A suspicion whispered in her mind. She recalled Arin's odd question in the carriage. *Where are we going?* His tone had been incredulous. Yet he had known their destination. Now Kestrel wondered if he had recognized something in the passing landscape that she hadn't, and if his question had been less a question than the automatic words of someone sickened by a sudden understanding.

She opened the book.

"Don't," said Arin. "Please."

But she had already seen the inscription.

For Arin, it read, *from Amma and Etta, with love.*

This was Arin's home. This house had been his, this library his, this book his, dedicated to him by his parents, some ten years ago.

Kestrel breathed slowly. Her fingers rested on the page, just below the black line of writing. She lifted her gaze to meet Irex's smirk.

Her mind chilled. She assessed the situation as her father would a battle. She knew her objective. She knew her opponent's. She understood what she could afford to lose, and what she could not.

Kestrel closed the book, set it on a table, and turned her back to Arin. "Lord Irex," she said, her voice warm. "It is but a book."

"It is *my* book," Irex said.

There was a choked sound behind her. Without looking, Kestrel said in Herrani, "Do you wish to be removed from the room?"

Arin's answer was low. "No."

"Then be silent." She smiled at Irex. In their language, she said, "This is clearly not a case of theft. Who would dare steal from you? I'm certain he meant only to look at it. You can't blame him for being curious about the luxuries your house holds."

"He shouldn't have even been inside the library, let alone touching its contents. Besides, there were witnesses. A judge will rule in my favor. This is my property, so I will decide the number of lashes."

"Yes, your property. Let us not forget that we are also discussing *my* property."

"He will be returned to you."

"So the law says, but in what condition? I am not eager to see him damaged. He holds more value than a book in a language no one has any interest in reading."

Irex's dark eyes flicked to look behind Kestrel, then returned to her. They grew sly. "You take a decided interest in your slave's well-being. I wonder to what lengths you will go to prevent a punishment that is rightfully mine to give." He rested a hand on her arm. "Perhaps we can settle the matter between us."

Kestrel heard Arin inhale as he understood Irex's suggestion. She was angry, suddenly, at the way her mind snagged on the sound of that sharp breath. She was angry at herself, for feeling vulnerable because Arin was vulnerable, and at Irex for his knowing smile. "Yes." Kestrel decided to twist Irex's words into something else. "This is between us, and fate."

Having uttered the formal words of a challenge to a duel, Kestrel stepped back from Irex's touch, drew her dagger, and held it sideways at the level of her chest like a line drawn between him and her.

"Kestrel," Irex said. "That isn't what I had in mind when I said we might solve the matter."

"I think we'll enjoy this method more."

"A challenge." He tsked. "I'll let you take it back. Just this once."

"I cannot take it back."

At that, Irex drew his dagger and imitated Kestrel's gesture. They stood still, then sheathed their blades.

"I'll even let you choose the weapons," Irex said.

"Needles. Now it is to you to choose the time and place."

"My grounds. Tomorrow, two hours from sunset. That will give me time to gather the death-price."

This gave Kestrel pause. But she nodded, and finally turned to Arin.

He looked nauseated. He sagged in the senators' grip. It seemed they weren't restraining him, but holding him up.

"You can let go," Kestrel told the senators, and when they did, she ordered Arin to follow her. As they left the library, Arin said, "Kestrel—"

"Not a word. Don't speak until we are in the carriage."

They walked swiftly down the halls—Arin's halls—and when Kestrel stole sidelong looks at him he still seemed stunned and dizzy. Kestrel had been seasick before, at the beginning of her sailing lessons, and she wondered if this was how Arin felt, surrounded by his home—like when the eyes can pinpoint the horizon but the stomach cannot.

Their silence broke when the carriage door closed them in.

"You are mad." Arin's voice was furious, desperate. "It was my book. My doing. You had no right to interfere. Did you think I couldn't bear the punishment for being caught?"

"Arin." Fear trembled through her as she finally realized what she had done. She strove to sound calm. "A duel is simply a ritual."

"It's not yours to fight."

"You know *you* cannot. Irex would never accept, and if you drew a blade on him, every Valorian in the vicinity would cut you down. Irex won't kill me."

He gave her a cynical look. "Do you deny that he is the superior fighter?"

"So he will draw first blood. He will be satisfied, and we will both walk away with honor."

"He said something about a death-price."

That was the law's penalty for a duel to the death. The victor paid a high sum to the dead duelist's family. Kestrel dismissed this. "It will cost Irex more than gold to kill General Trajan's daughter."

Arin dropped his face into his hands. He began to swear, to recite every insult against the Valorians the Herrani had invented, to curse them by every god.

"Really, Arin."

His hands fell away. "You, too. What a stupid thing for you to do. Why did you do that? Why would you do such a stupid thing?"

She thought of his claim that Enai could never have loved her, or if she had, it was a forced love.

"You might not think of me as your friend," Kestrel told Arin, "but I think of you as mine."

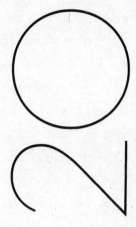

KESTREL SLEPT EASILY THAT NIGHT. SHE HADN'T known, before she claimed Arin's friendship, that this was what she felt. He had fallen silent in the carriage and looked strange, like someone who has drunk wine when he expected water. But he didn't deny her words, and she knew him well enough to believe that he would if he wished.

A friend. The thought calmed her. It explained many things.

When she closed her eyes, she remembered something her father had often told her as a child, and would say to soldiers the night before a battle: "Nothing in dreams can hurt you."

Sleep settled on her like velvet.

Then the dawn came, clear and cold. Kestrel's peace had vanished. She pulled on a dressing gown and hunted through a wardrobe for her ceremonial fighting garb. Her father ordered a new set every year, and this year's was buried behind dresses. But they were there: black leggings, tunic, and stiff jacket. A worm of misgiving ate through her as she looked at the clothes. She left them where they were for the moment.

It wasn't that she feared the duel, Kestrel thought as she shut the wardrobe door. She didn't balk at first blood, which could be no worse than she had received in training sessions. She didn't dread losing to Irex. Defeat at a duel brought no shame in the eyes of society.

But Kestrel's reasons for fighting might.

Does society talk about him? Enai had asked. Kestrel pressed a palm against the wardrobe door, then rested her forehead against her fingers. Society would talk about Arin now, if they hadn't before. She imagined news of the duel spreading among Irex's guests, who must have been shocked and enthralled by the details. A mistress to fight on behalf of her thieving slave? Had it ever been done?

Obviously not.

She could expect an audience at the duel. What would she tell them? That she sought to protect a friend?

Her easy sleep had been a lie. Nothing was easy about this.

Kestrel straightened. The challenge to duel had been issued, received, and witnessed. There was no dishonor in losing, but there was in cowering.

She pulled on a simple dress, intending to visit the barracks, where she hoped to confirm that her father wouldn't return from his training session before the next day. Kestrel knew she couldn't keep the duel a secret. Even her father couldn't fail to hear the gossip *this* would stir. Still, she would prefer for him to arrive after the fact.

When she opened the outermost door to her suite, she

found a slave in the hallway, her arms drooping under the weight of a small chest.

"Lady Kestrel," she said. "This just arrived from Lord Irex."

Kestrel accepted it, but her hands had gone limp with the realization of what the box must hold. Her fingers could not close.

The chest dropped to the hallway's marble floor, spilling its contents. Gold pieces spun and rolled, ringing like small bells.

Irex had sent the death-price. Kestrel didn't need to count the coins to know that they numbered five hundred. She didn't need to touch the gold to remember what she had won from Irex at Bite and Sting, and to think that he might become a better player someday, if he understood the psychology of intimidation enough to pay a death-price *before* a duel had begun.

She stood motionless, washed by acid fear. *Breathe,* she told herself. *Move.* But she could only stare as the slave chased the errant coins and another girl came down the hall to help refill the chest.

Kestrel's foot moved forward. Then another step, and another, and she was ready to run from the sight of spilled gold until a memory sliced through her mindless panic. She saw Irex's dimpled smile. She felt his hand gripping hers. She saw weapons on walls, him flipping a Bite and Sting tile, his boots crushing Lady Faris's lawn, heel digging a divot of grass and dirt. She saw his eyes, so dark they were almost black.

Kestrel knew what she had to do.

She went downstairs to the library and wrote two letters. One was to her father, the other to Jess and Ronan. She folded them, stamped the wax seals with her seal ring, and put the writing materials away. She was holding the letters in one hand, the wax firm yet still warm against the skin, when she heard footsteps beating down the marble hall, coming closer.

Arin stepped inside the library and shut the door. "You won't do it," he said. "You won't duel him."

The sight of Arin shook her. She wouldn't be able to think straight if he continued to speak like that, to look at her like that. "*You* do not give *me* orders," Kestrel said. She moved to leave.

He blocked her path. "I know about the delivery. He sent you a death-price."

"First my dress, and now this? Arin, one would think you are monitoring everything I send and receive. It is none of your business."

He seized her by the shoulders. "You are so *small*."

Kestrel knew what he was doing, and hated it, hated him for reminding her of her physical weakness, of the same failure that her father witnessed whenever he watched her fight with Rax. "Let go."

"*Make* me let you go."

She looked at Arin. Whatever he saw in her eyes loosened his hands. "Kestrel," he said more quietly, "I have been whipped before. Lashes and death are different things."

"I won't die."

"Let Irex set my punishment."

"You're not listening to me." She would have said more,

but realized that his hands still rested on her shoulders. A thumb was pressing gently against her collarbone.

Kestrel caught her breath. Arin startled, as if out of sleep, and pulled away.

He had no right, Kestrel thought. He had no right to confuse her. Not now, when she needed a clear mind.

Everything had seemed so simple last night in the close dark of the carriage.

"You are not allowed," Kestrel said, "to touch me."

Arin's smile was bitter. "I suppose that means we are no longer friends."

She said nothing.

"Good," he said, "then you can have no reason for fighting Irex."

"You don't understand."

"I don't understand your godsforsaken Valorian honor? I don't understand that your father would probably rather see you gutted than live with a daughter who turned away from a duel?"

"You have very little faith in me, to think that Irex would win."

He raked a hand through his short hair. "Where is *my* honor in all this, Kestrel?"

They locked eyes, and she recognized his expression. It was the same one she had seen across the Bite and Sting table. The same one she had seen in the pit, when the auctioneer had told Arin to sing.

Refusal. A determination so cold it could blister the skin like metal in winter.

She knew that he would stop her. Perhaps he would be

cunning about it. Maybe he would go to the steward behind her back, tell him of the theft and challenge, and ask
to be brought before the judge and Irex. If that plan didn't
suit Arin, he would find another.

He was going to be a problem.

"You're right," she told him.

Arin blinked, then narrowed his eyes.

"In fact," she continued, "if you had let me explain, I
would have told you that I had already decided to call off
the duel."

"You have."

She showed him the two letters. The one addressed to
her father was on top. She let the mere edge of the other letter show. "One is for my father, telling him what has happened. The other is for Irex, making my apologies and
inviting him to collect his five hundred gold pieces whenever he likes."

Arin still looked skeptical.

"He'll also collect *you*, of course. Knowing him, he'll
have you whipped until you're unconscious and even after
that. I'm sure that when you wake up, you'll be very glad
that I decided to do exactly as you wanted."

Arin snorted.

"If you doubt me, you're welcome to walk with me to
the barracks to watch as I give my father's letter to a soldier,
with orders for its swift delivery."

"I think I will." He opened the library door.

They left the house and crossed the hard ground. Kestrel shivered. She hadn't stopped to fetch a cloak. She
couldn't risk that Arin would change his mind.

When they entered the barracks, Kestrel looked among the six off-duty guards. She was relieved, since she had counted on finding only four, and not necessarily Rax, whom she trusted most. She approached him, Arin just a step behind her.

"Bring this to the general as swiftly as you can." She gave Rax the first letter. "Have a messenger deliver this other letter to Jess and Ronan."

"What?" Arin said. "Wait—"

"And lock this slave up."

Kestrel turned so that she wouldn't see what happened next. She heard the room descend into chaos. She heard the scuffle, a shout, the sound of fists thudding against flesh.

She let the door shut behind her and walked away.

Ronan was waiting for her beyond the estate's guarded gate. From the looks of things, he had been waiting for some time. His horse was nosing brown grass as Ronan sat on a nearby boulder, throwing pebbles at the general's stone wall. When he saw Kestrel ride through the gate on Javelin, he flung his handful of rocks to the path. He remained sitting, elbows propped on his bended knees as he stared at her, his face pinched and white. He said, "I have half a mind to tear you down from your horse."

"You got my message, then."

"And rode instantly here, where guards told me that the lady of the house gave strict orders not to let anyone—even me—inside." His eyes raked over her, taking in the black fighting clothes. "I didn't believe it. I *still* don't believe it.

After you vanished last night, everyone at the party was talking about the challenge, yet I was sure it was just a rumor started by Irex because of whatever has caused that ill will between you. Kestrel, how could you expose yourself like this?"

Her hands tightened around the reins. She thought about how, when she let go, her palms would smell like leather and sweat. She concentrated on imagining that scent. This was easier than paying heed to the sick feeling swimming inside her. She knew what Ronan was going to say.

She tried to deflect it. She tried to talk about the duel itself, which seemed straightforward next to her reasons for it. Lightly, she said, "No one seems to believe that I might win."

Ronan vaulted off the rock and strode toward her horse. He seized the saddle's pommel. "You'll get what you want. But what *do* you want? *Whom* do you want?"

"Ronan." Kestrel swallowed. "Think about what you are saying."

"Only what everyone has been saying. That Lady Kestrel has a lover."

"That's not true."

"He is her shadow, skulking behind her, listening, watching."

"He isn't," Kestrel tried to say, and was horrified to hear her voice falter. She felt a stinging in her eyes. "He has a girl."

"Why do you even *know* that? So what if he does? It doesn't matter. Not in the eyes of society."

Kestrel's feelings were like banners in a storm, snapping at their ties. They tangled and wound around her. She focused, and when she spoke, she made her words disdain-ful. "He is a slave."

"He is a *man*, as I am."

Kestrel slipped from her saddle, stood face-to-face with Ronan, and lied. "He is nothing to me."

Ronan's anger dimmed a little. He waited, listening.

"I never should have challenged Irex." Kestrel decided to weave some truth into her story, to toughen the fabric of it. "But he and I have an unfriendly history. He made me an offer last spring. I turned him down. Since then, he has been . . . aggressive."

She had Ronan's sympathy then, and she was grateful, for she didn't know what she would do if he and Jess turned their backs on her. She needed them—not only today, but always.

"Irex angered me. The slave was just an excuse." How much easier everything would be if that were so. But Kestrel wouldn't let herself consider the truth. She didn't want to know its shape or see its face. "I was thoughtless and rash, but I've drawn my tiles and must play them. Will you help me, Ronan? Will you do as I asked in my letter?"

"Yes." He still looked unhappy. "Though as far as I can see, there is little for me to do but stand and watch you fight."

"And Jess? Will she be at the duel?"

"Yes, as soon as she is done weeping her eyes out. What a fright you've given us, Kestrel."

Kestrel opened a saddlebag and passed Ronan the purse with the death-price. He took it, recognizing it by its weight and the fact that her letter had told him to expect it. Softly, he said, "You frightened *me*."

She embraced him, stepping into his arms. They relaxed around her. His chin rested on top of her head, and she felt his forgiveness. She tried to push away thoughts of Arin on the auction block, of the look in his eyes when he asked where his honor was, of him swearing at her guards in his tongue. She held Ronan more tightly, pressing her cheek against his chest.

Ronan sighed. "I'll ride with you to Irex's house," he said, "and see you safely home after you've won."

The path to Irex's house was clotted with carriages. Society had turned out in force for this duel: Kestrel saw hundreds of well-dressed men and women talking excitedly, their breath fogging the late autumn air. Ronan dismounted and so did she, letting their horses range to join the others.

Kestrel scanned the crowd ringed around the clearing in the trees. People smiled when they saw her, but they were not kind smiles. There were coy looks, and some faces held a morbid fascination, as if this were not a duel but a hanging, and the only question was whether the criminal's neck would break instantly. Kestrel wondered how many people gathered in the lowering sun knew that Irex had already paid the death-price.

Kestrel felt cold and hard. A walking skeleton.

Ronan slid an arm around her. She knew this was as much to prove a point to society as to soothe her. He was shielding her reputation with his own. She hadn't asked him for this, and the fact that he had seen something missing in her plan made her feel both relieved to have him at her side and more afraid than before.

"I don't see my father." Kestrel's fingers trembled. Ronan caught her hands in his, and even though his eyes were filled with doubt, he gave her a showy grin meant for the crowd. Loudly, he said, "How chilly your hands are. Let's get this dull thing over with, shall we, and then go somewhere warm?"

"Kestrel!" Benix detangled himself from the crowd, holding Jess's hand and waving boisterously at his friends. Benix had a jolly swagger as he walked toward them, but Jess couldn't play the game so well. She looked awful. Her eyes were red, her face splotched.

Benix swept Kestrel into a bear hug, then pretended to duel with Ronan—a move that amused some of those watching, but brought fresh tears to Jess's eyes. "This is not a joke," she said.

"Oh, sister," Ronan teased. "You take things too seriously."

The crowd shifted, disappointed that Kestrel's arrival hadn't triggered any emotional explosions among her closest friends. As people turned away, Kestrel saw a clear path to Irex, tall and black-clad in the center of the space marked for the duel. He smiled at her, and Kestrel was so thrown out of herself that she didn't know her father had arrived until she felt his hand on her shoulder.

He was dusty and smelled of horse. "Father," she said, and would have tucked herself into his arms.

He checked her. "This isn't the time."

She flushed.

"General Trajan," Ronan said cheerfully. "So glad you could come. Benix, do I see the Raul twins over there, in the front, closest to the dueling ground? No, you blind bat. *There*, right next to Lady Faris. Why don't we watch the match with them? You, too, Jess. We need your feminine presence so we can pretend that we're only interested in the twins because you'd like to chat about feathered hats."

Jess squeezed Kestrel's hand, and the three of them would have left immediately had the general not stopped them. "Thank you," he said.

Kestrel's friends dropped their merry act, which Jess wasn't performing well anyway. The general focused on Ronan, sizing him up like he would a new recruit. Then he did something rare. He gave a nod of approval. The corner of Ronan's mouth lifted in a small, worried smile as he led the others away.

Kestrel's father faced her squarely. When she bit her lip, he said, "Now is not the time to show any weakness."

"I know."

He checked the straps on her forearms, at her hips, and against her calves, tugging the leather that secured six small knives to her body. "Keep your distance from Irex," he said, his voice low, though the people nearest to them had withdrawn to give some privacy—a deference to the general. "Your best bet is to keep this to a contest of thrown knives. You can dodge his, throw your own, and might even get first blood. Make him empty his sheaths. If you both lose all six Needles, the duel is a draw." He straightened her jacket. "Don't let this turn into hand-to-hand combat."

The general had sat next to her at the spring tournament. He had seen Irex fight and directly afterward had tried to enlist him in the military.

"I want you to be at the front of the crowd," Kestrel said.

"I wouldn't be anywhere else." A small crease appeared between her father's brows. "Don't let him get close."

Kestrel nodded, though she had no intention of taking his advice.

She walked through the throngs of people to meet Irex.

PRIVATE CONVERSATION BETWEEN KESTREL and Irex was impossible, which probably pleased him. He liked to be heard as well as watched, and seemed to have no interest in stepping away from the crowd until he and she would move to their assigned places at opposite ends of the circular space, marked with black paint on the dead grass.

"Lady Kestrel." He spoke clearly for the listening audience. "Did you receive my gift?"

"And brought it back here."

"Does this mean that you forfeit? Come, agree to send me your slave and give me your hand. I'll prick your little finger. First blood will be mine, our friends will go home happy, and you will join me for dinner."

"No, I like the plans as they stand. With you in your place, and me fifty paces away from you."

Irex's dark eyes became slits. His mouth, which some might have called charming, dropped its grin. Irex turned his back to her and went to take his place. She took hers.

Irex, as the challenged, had appointed a friend to call

the start of the duel. When the young man shouted "Mark!" Irex snatched a dagger from his arm and threw.

Kestrel neatly dodged the blade, having expected he would take the offensive. The dagger sang through the air to bury itself in a tree.

Their audience shrank away from the dueling circle. Sideline casualties had happened before, and Needles was a particularly dangerous game to watch.

Irex appeared unworried that his first attempt had failed. He crouched, slipping a Needle from its sheath at his calf. He weighed it, watching Kestrel. He feinted, but if she was skilled at anything it was seeing through a bluff, particularly when Irex had no real desire to hide his feelings. He rushed forward, and threw.

His speed was terrifying. Kestrel hit the ground, her cheek scraping dirt, then shoved herself up before Irex could catch her in so vulnerable a position. As she stood, she saw something gleam on the ground: the very end of her braid, sheared off by the knife.

Kestrel's breath came quickly. Irex held his position at about thirty paces from her.

She balanced on her toes, waiting, and saw that Irex's anger at her insult was gone, or had mixed itself with pleasure to the point where he seemed to be in a good humor. His first throw had been wild, and not smart, since he had drawn a Needle from one of the two easiest points of access. When Needles became hand-to-hand, it was a disadvantage to have few knives, and to have lost those at the forearms, or even the hips. Kestrel knew he knew that, or he wouldn't have thrown his second Needle from his calf.

He was cocky, but he could be cautious. That would make Kestrel's task harder.

She could almost feel her father's frustration. People were shouting suggestions at her, but she didn't hear her father's voice. She briefly wondered if it was hard for him not to yell at her to throw a few Needles of her own. She knew that this was what he wanted. It was the sensible thing for a weaker fighter to do: hope to end the duel early with a strike anywhere.

But she wanted to get close to Irex, close enough to speak without anyone overhearing. She would need every knife she had once she was within arm's reach of him.

Irex cocked his head. He was either mystified that Kestrel wasn't taking the only sensible strategy or disappointed that she was doing little at all. He had probably expected more of a fight. Kestrel had taken great pains never to reveal her very ordinary skills at weapons, and society assumed that the general's daughter must be an excellent fighter.

He hung back, showing no interest in emptying more sheaths. He didn't advance, which was a problem—if Kestrel couldn't lure him to her, she would have to come to him.

The shouts were incoherent now. They swelled to something like a roaring silence.

Kestrel's father would say that she should stand her ground. Instead she pulled her two calf daggers and sped forward. A blade spun from her hand and went wide—a terrible throw, but one that distracted Irex from the second, which might have struck him had he not ducked and launched a Needle of his own.

She skidded on the dry grass to avoid the knife. Her

side hit the earth just as the Needle punched into the ground next to her leg. Her mind iced over, sealed itself shut.

He was quick, too quick. She hadn't even seen his hand move.

Then Irex's boot kicked her ribs. Kestrel gasped in pain. She forced herself to her feet and swept an arm knife out of its sheath. She sliced the air in front of her, but Irex danced back, knocked the blade out of her hand, and rolled to claim it as his own.

Her chest heaved. It hurt to breathe. It hurt to think. She fleetingly imagined her father closing his eyes in dismay. *Never arm your opponent,* he always said.

But she had what she wanted. She and Irex were in the circle's center now, too far from the shouting audience for their conversation to be overheard.

"Irex." Her voice was thin and weak. "We need to talk."

He kicked in her knee. She felt something grind and give just before she crumpled to the ground. The force of her fall drove the kneecap back in place. She cried out.

The shock was too great for pain. Then it came: a spasm that tunneled from her leg into her brain.

It wasn't fear that forced Kestrel to her feet. She was stupid with pain and didn't have room to feel anything else. She didn't know how she managed to get up, only that she did, and Irex let her.

"I never liked you," he hissed. "So superior."

Kestrel's vision was whitening. She had the odd impression that it was snowing, but as the whiteness ate its way toward Irex's face she realized there was no snow. She was about to faint.

Irex slapped her face.

That stung her to life. She heard a gasp, and wasn't sure if it came from the crowd or her own throat. Kestrel had to speak now, and quickly, or the duel was going to end with Irex crushing her well before he finished things off with a Needle. It was hard to find the air for words. She drew a dagger. It helped, a little, to feel its solidity against her palm. "You are the father of Faris's baby."

He faltered. "What?"

Kestrel prayed she wasn't wrong. "You slept with Senator Tiran's wife. You fathered her child."

Irex brought his guard back up, the dagger fire-bright in the setting sun. But he bit the inside of his cheek, making his face go lopsidedly lean, and that slight trace of worry made her think that maybe she would survive this duel. He said, "What makes you say that?"

"Strike a blow easy for me to block and I'll tell you."

He did, and the sound of her blade pushing his back made Kestrel stronger. "You have the same eyes," she said. "The baby has the trick of a dimple in his left cheek, as you do. Faris looked pale as we took our places to fight, and I notice that she is at the front of the crowd. I don't think she's worried about *me*."

Slowly, he said, "Your knowing a secret like that doesn't make me feel less inclined to kill you."

She took a shuddery breath, glad that she was right, glad that he hesitated even as the crowd continued to shout. "You won't kill me," she said, "because I have told Jess and Ronan. If I die, they will tell everyone else."

"No one would believe them. Society will think they mourn you and seek to damage me."

"Will society think that when they begin to compare the boy's face to yours? Will Senator Tiran?" Limping, she circled him, and he allowed it, though he drew a second Needle and held them both ready. He shifted his feet swiftly while she tried not to stumble. "If Ronan has any difficulty starting a scandal, he'll feed it with money. I have given him five hundred gold pieces, and he will bribe friends to swear that the rumor is true, that they witnessed you in bed with Faris, that you keep a lock of the boy's hair close to your heart. They will say anything, true or not. Few people are as rich as you. Ronan has many friends—like poor Hanan— who would gladly take gold to ruin the reputation of someone no one really likes."

Irex's arms slackened. He looked slightly ill.

Kestrel pressed her advantage. "You slept with Faris so that she would encourage her husband to help you gain a seat in the Senate. Maybe you did it for other reasons, too, but this is the one we care about. You *should* care, because if Tiran suspects you, he won't just withhold his help. He'll turn the Senate against you."

She saw the fight drain out of him.

"Even though this duel has broken no rules, it's not been clean," she said. "You began a brawl. Society will murmur its disapproval even before Ronan and Jess destroy your reputation."

"Society will disapprove of me?" Irex sneered. "*Your* reputation is not so lily white. Slave-lover."

Kestrel wobbled on her feet. It took her a moment to speak, and when she did, she wasn't sure that what she said was true. "Whatever people say about me, my father will be your enemy."

Irex's face was still sharp with hate, but he said, "Very well. You can live." His voice became hesitant. "Did you tell the general about Faris?"

Kestrel thought of her letter to her father. It had been simple. *I have challenged Lord Irex to a duel,* it had said. *It will take place on his grounds today, two hours before sunset. Please come.* "No. That would have defeated my purpose."

Irex gave Kestrel a look, one that she had seen before on the faces of her opponents in Bite and Sting. "Purpose?" he said warily.

Kestrel felt triumph surge through her, stronger even than the pain in her knee. "I want my father to believe that I've legitimately won this duel. You are about to lose. You'll throw the match, and give me a clear victory." She smiled. "I want first blood, Irex. My father is watching. Make this look good."

22

Kestrel onto her horse, which only went a few steps before
she swayed in the saddle. Her right knee throbbed. It felt as
if some knot inside had slipped and was unraveling, pressing
hot coils against the inner wall of her skin.

Her father halted Javelin. "We can borrow a carriage."

"No." What point was there in having defeated Irex if
she couldn't keep her seat on a horse? Kestrel hadn't realized
she had such pride. Maybe she didn't want her father's military life, but it seemed she wanted his approval as much as she
had as a girl.

The general looked as if he might argue, then said only,
"That was a decisive win." He mounted his horse and set the
pace.

It was slow, yet Kestrel grimaced with every jolt of the
stallion's hooves. She was glad when night dyed the sky. She
felt her face thinning with pain, but reminded herself that
not even her father could see through the dark. He couldn't
see her dread.

She kept expecting his question: why had she challenged Irex to a duel?

But he didn't ask, and soon it became impossible for her to think of anything other than staying on her horse. She bit her lip. By the time they reached home, her mouth tasted of blood.

She wasn't aware of passing through the gate. The house simply appeared, bright and sort of trembling at the edges. She vaguely heard her father say something to someone else, and then his hands were at her waist, lifting her off Javelin as if she were a child.

He set Kestrel on her feet. Her knee buckled. She felt a sound choke her throat, and blacked out.

When Kestrel opened her eyes, she was lying in her bed. Someone had built a fire, which sent ripples of orange light over the ceiling. An oil lamp burned on the night table, casting her father's face into extremes of shadow and bone. He had drawn a chair close and perhaps had been sleeping in it, but his eyes were alert.

"Your knee needs to be tapped," he said.

She looked at it. Someone—her father?—had cut away the right legging at her thigh, and below the sheared black cloth her knee was swollen to twice its normal size. It felt tight and hot.

"I don't know what that means," Kestrel said, "but it doesn't sound very nice."

"Irex dislocated your kneecap. It slipped back into place, but the blow must have torn your muscle. Your knee's filling with blood. That's what's causing you so much pain: the swelling." He hesitated. "I have some experience with this kind of wound, on the battlefield. I can drain it. You'll feel better. But I would have to use a knife."

Kestrel remembered him cutting her mother's arm, blood weaving through his fingers as he tried to close the wound. He looked at her now, and she thought that he was seeing the same thing, or seeing Kestrel remember it, and that they were mirroring each other's nightmare.

His gaze fell to his scarred hands. "I've sent for a doctor. You can wait until she comes, if you prefer." His voice was flat, yet there was a small, sad note that probably only she would have heard. "I wouldn't suggest this if I didn't feel myself capable and if I didn't think it would be better to do it now. But it's your choice."

His eyes met hers. Something in them made her think that he would never have let Irex kill her, that he would have pushed into the ring and planted a blade in Irex's back if he had thought his daughter might die, that he would have thrown away his honor with hers.

Of course, Kestrel couldn't be sure. Yet she nodded. He sent a slave for clean rags, which he eased under her knee. Then he went to the fire and held a small knife in the flames to sterilize it.

He returned to her side, the blackened knife in his hand. "I promise," he said, but Kestrel didn't know whether he meant to say that he promised this would help her, or that he knew what he was doing, or that he would have saved her from Irex if she had needed saving. He slid the knife in, and she fainted again.

He had been right. Kestrel felt better the moment she opened her eyes. Her knee was sore and wrapped in a bandage, but the fevered swelling was gone, and a great deal of pain with it.

Her father was standing, his back to her as he looked out the dark window.

"You'd better release me from our bargain," she said. "The military won't take me now, not with a bad knee."

He turned and echoed her faint smile. "Don't you wish that were so," he said. "Painful though it is, this isn't a serious wound. You'll be on your feet soon, and walking normally before a month's out. There's no permanent damage. If you doubt me and think I'm blinded by my hope to see you become an officer, the doctor will tell you the same thing. She's in the sitting room."

Kestrel looked at the closed door of her bedroom and wondered why the doctor wasn't in the room with them now.

"I want to ask you something," her father said. "I'd prefer she didn't hear."

Suddenly it seemed as if Kestrel's heart, not her knee, was sore. That it had been cut into, and bled.

"What kind of deal did you make with Irex?" her father asked.

"What?"

He gave her a level look. "The duel was going badly for you. Then Irex held back, and you two seemed to have quite an interesting conversation. When the fighting resumed, it was as if Irex was a different person. He shouldn't have lost to you—not like that, anyway—unless you said something to make him."

She didn't know how to respond. When her father had asked his question she was so horribly grateful he wasn't probing into her reasons for the duel that she missed some of his words.

"Kestrel, I just want to make sure that you haven't given Irex some kind of power over you."

"No." She sighed, disappointed that her father had seen through her victory. "If anything, he's in my power."

"Ah. Good. Will you tell me how?"

"I know a secret."

"*Very* good. No, don't tell me what it is. I don't want to know."

Kestrel looked at the fire. She let the flames hypnotize her eyes.

"Do you think I care how you won?" her father said softly. "You won. Your methods don't matter."

Kestrel thought about the Herran War. She thought about the suffering her father had brought to this country, and how his actions had led to her becoming a mistress, and Arin a slave. "Do you really believe that?"

"Yes," he said. "I do."

Arin heard the door to the barracks creak. The sound brought him immediately to his feet, for only one person would come to his cell this late at night. Then he heard the first heavy footfall, and his hands slackened around the metal bars. The footsteps coming were not hers. They belonged to someone big. Solid, slow. Probably a man.

Torchlight pulsed toward Arin's cell. When he saw who carried it, he pulled away from the bars. He saw a child's nightmare come to life.

The general set the torch in a sconce. He stared, taking in Arin's fresh bruises, his height, his features. The general's frown deepened.

This man didn't look like Kestrel. He was all mass and muscle. But Arin found her in the way her father lifted his chin, and his eyes held the same dangerous intelligence.

"Is she all right?" Arin said. When he received no response, he asked again in Valorian. And because he had already damned himself with a question he couldn't bear not to ask, Arin said something he had sworn he would never say. "Sir."

"She's fine."

A feeling flowed into Arin, something like sleep or the sudden absence of pain.

"If I had my choice, I would kill you," said the general, "but that would cause more talk. You'll be sold. Not right away, because I don't want to be seen reacting to a scandal. But soon.

"I'll be spending some time at home, and I will be watching you. If you come near my daughter, I will forget my better judgment. I will have you torn limb from limb. Do you understand?"

2

LETTERS CAME. DURING THE FIRST DAYS AFTER
the duel, Kestrel ripped into them, eager for anything to
distract her from being confined to her bed, desperate to
learn what society thought of her now. Surely she had gained
some respect by beating the city's finest fighter?

But the letters were mostly from Jess and Ronan and
filled with false cheer. And then came the note.

Small, folded into a thick square. Stamped with a blank
seal. Written in a woman's hand. Unsigned.

Do you think you are the first? it read. *The only Valorian
to take a slave to her bed? Poor fool!*

Let me tell you the rules.

*Do not be so obvious. Why do you think society allows a
senator to call a pretty housegirl to his rooms at a late hour? Or
for the general's daughter to take long carriage rides with such
an exquisite "escort"?*

*It is not because secret liaisons are impossible. It is because
pretending they are impossible lets everyone turn a blind eye to
the fact that we can use our slaves exactly as we please.*

Kestrel felt her face burn. Then it crumpled, just like the paper in her fist.

She would throw the letter in the fire. She would forget it, forget everything.

But when she shifted her right leg out from underneath the blankets, her knee screamed in protest. She sat at the edge of the bed, looking at the fire, then at her bare feet flat against the floor. She trembled, and told herself it was because of the ache in her bandaged knee. Because her legs couldn't bear her own weight. Because she couldn't do something so simple as get out of bed and walk across the room.

She tore the letter into a snowfall of paper.

That first night after the duel, Kestrel had woken to find her father gone. A slave was sleeping in the chair drawn close to the bed. Kestrel had seen the lines under the woman's eyes, the awkward crook of her neck, and how her head bobbed back and forth in the way of someone who needed sleep. But Kestrel shook her.

"You have to do something," Kestrel had said.

The woman blinked, bleary-eyed.

"Go tell the guards to let Smith out. He's imprisoned in the barracks. He—"

"I know," the woman had said. "He's been released."

"He has? By whom?"

The slave looked away. "It was Rax's decision. He said you could complain to him if you didn't like it."

Those last words sounded like a lie. They didn't even make sense. But the woman patted her hand and said, "I saw Smith myself, in the slaves' quarters. He's not too worse for wear. Don't worry, my lady." The face of the woman, whose name Kestrel had forgotten, filled with such sympathy that she had told her to leave.

Kestrel remembered the woman's expression. She looked at the shredded letter and saw again its written words—so snide, so understanding.

They didn't understand. No one did. They were wrong.

Kestrel slipped back under the blankets.

Some hours later, she called for a slave and asked her to open a window. Cold air poured in, and Kestrel shivered until she heard a distant ringing, the sound of hammer against anvil. Arin must know that she couldn't come to him. Why didn't he come to her?

She could make him. If she sent an order, he would obey.

But she didn't want his obedience. She wanted him to want to see her.

Kestrel flinched at this thought and the pain it brought with it.

She knew that even if everyone believed the wrong thing of her, they were also too close to being right.

"You should have let me visit earlier," Jess said, her cheeks radiant from the brisk air outside. "It's been a week since the duel."

Kestrel sank back against the pillows. She had known the sight of Jess would hurt, would remind her that there was a life outside this bedroom. "Ronan isn't allowed."

"I should say not! I'm not letting him see you until you're better. You look awful. No one wants to kiss an invalid."

"Thank you, Jess. I'm so happy you've come."

Jess rolled her eyes. She started to speak, then her gaze fell on the nightstand. "Kestrel. You haven't been opening your letters."

They had collected in a pile, like a nest of coiled snakes.

"What would the letters tell me?" Kestrel said. "That my reputation is as ruined as ever?"

"It's nothing we can't fix."

Kestrel guessed what Jess might say: that she should go with Ronan to the Firstwinter ball. Ronan would be willing. He would be glad. It would stop some of the gossip and start a different kind.

It was a solution of sorts.

Kestrel smiled a little. She shook her head. "You're so loyal."

"*And* clever. I have an idea. The ball is not long from now and—"

"I'm bored, sitting in bed all these hours. Why don't you distract me, Jess? Better yet, why don't *I* do something for *you*? I owe you."

Jess smoothed the hair off Kestrel's forehead. "No, you don't."

"You have stood by me. I'll make it up to you. Once I'm well, I'll wear whatever you like."

Jess jokingly pressed a palm to Kestrel's brow. "You must be feverish."

"I'll teach you to play Bite and Sting so that no one will beat you."

Jess laughed. "Don't bother. I don't like games."

"I know." Kestrel felt her smile leave. "It's one of the things I admire about you."

Jess's expression turned quizzical.

"You never hide who you are," Kestrel said.

"Do you think that you do? Do you think I don't realize that even though you have asked me to distract you, you are trying to distract *me*?"

Kestrel winced.

"You'd be better at it," Jess said, "if you weren't bedridden. And miserable."

Kestrel reached for her hand and gripped it. "I meant what I said."

"Then stop playing games. There is an obvious answer to your problems."

She realized that Jess had more on her mind than the ball. Kestrel's hand slipped away.

Jess sighed. "Fine. We won't talk about Ronan. We won't talk about marriage. We won't talk about the fact that as much as you like to win, you're acting as if you're determined to lose."

Arin stoked the forge's fire. Not for warmth but for color. He craved it in the cold months. He had been a sickly child, and this time of year reminded him most of his home, of feeling cooped up inside, not knowing that one day he would dream of those painted walls, the curtains in a sweep of indigo, the blue of his mother's dress.

Cold without, color within. This was how it had been.

Arin watched the fire flare crimson. Then he went outside and surveyed the grounds, saw through leafless trees that no one was near. He could steal a few minutes.

When he stepped back inside the forge, he leaned against the anvil. With one hand he pulled a book from its hiding place behind the kindling box, and in the other he held a hammer so that, if in danger of being caught, he could more quickly pretend to have been working.

He began to read. It was a book he had seen in Kestrel's possession, one on the history of the Valorian empire. He had taken it from the library after she had returned it, weeks ago.

What would she say, if she saw him reading a book about his enemy, in his enemy's tongue? What would she do?

Arin knew this: her gaze would measure him, and he would sense a shift of perception within her. Her opinion of him would change as daylight changed, growing or losing shadow. Subtle. Almost indiscernible. She would see him differently, though he wouldn't know in what way. He wouldn't know what it meant. This had happened, again and again, since he had come here.

Sometimes he wished he had never come here.

Well. Kestrel couldn't see him in the forge, or know what he read, because she couldn't leave her rooms. She couldn't even walk.

Arin shut the book, gripped it between rigid fingers. He nearly threw it into the fire.

I will have you torn limb from limb, the general had said.

That wasn't why Arin stayed away from her. Not really.

He forced his thoughts from his head. He hid the book where it had been. He busied himself with quiet work, heating iron and charcoal in a crucible to produce steel.

It took some time before Arin realized he was humming

a dark tune. For once, he didn't stop himself. The pressure of song was too strong, the need for distraction too great. Then he found that the music caged behind his closed teeth was the melody Kestrel had played for him months ago. He felt the sensation of it, low and alive, on his mouth.

For a moment, he imagined it wasn't the melody that touched his lips, but Kestrel.

The thought stopped his breath, and the music, too.

WHEN NO ONE WAS LOOKING, KESTREL practiced walking around her suite. She often had to rest a hand against a wall, but she could make it to the windows.

She never saw what she wanted, which made her wonder whether this was mere chance or if Arin was avoiding her so completely that he took other paths across the grounds than those that passed through her view.

She couldn't handle the stairs, which meant that a visit to the music room on the ground floor was impossible unless she consented to be carried, and she didn't. Yet Kestrel caught her fingers playing phantom melodies on the furniture, on her thighs. The absence of music became an ache inside her. She wondered how Arin could bear not to sing, if he was indeed a singer.

Kestrel thought of the long flights of stairs, and forced her weak muscles to work.

She was standing in her visiting room, hands holding the carved back of a chair, when her father entered.

"There's my girl," he said. "On her feet already. You'll be a military officer in no time with an attitude like that."

Kestrel sat. She gave him a slight, ironic smile.

He returned it. "What I meant to say is that I'm glad you're better, and that I'm sorry I can't go to the Firstwinter ball."

It was good that she was already sitting. "Why would *you* want to go to a *ball*?"

"I thought I would take you."

She stared.

"It occurred to me that I have never danced with my daughter," he said. "And it would have been a wise move."

A wise move.

A show of force, then. A reminder of the respect due to the general's family. Quietly, Kestrel said, "You've heard the rumors."

He raised a hand, palm flat and facing her.

"Father—"

"Stop."

"It's not true. I—"

"We will not have this discussion." His hand lifted to block his eyes, then fell. "Kestrel, I'm not here for that. I'm here to tell you that I'm leaving. The emperor is sending me east to fight the barbarians."

It wasn't the first time in Kestrel's memory that her father had been sent to war, but the fear she felt was always the same, always keen. "For how long?"

"As long as it takes. I leave the morning of the ball with my regiment."

"The entire regiment?"

He caught the tone in her voice. He sighed. "Yes."

"That means there will be no soldiers in the city or its surroundings. If there's a problem—"

"The city guard will be here. The emperor feels they can deal with any problem, at least until a force arrives from the capital."

"Then the emperor is a fool. The captain of the city guard isn't up to the task. You yourself said that the new captain is nothing but a bungler, someone who got the position because he's the governor's toady—"

"Kestrel." His voice was quelling. "I've already expressed my reservations to the emperor. But he gave me orders. It's my duty to follow them."

Kestrel studied her fingers, the way they wove together. She didn't say *Come back safely,* and he didn't say *I always have.* She said what a Valorian should. "Fight well."

"I will."

He was halfway to the door when he glanced back and said, "I'm trusting you to do what's right while I'm gone."

Which meant that he didn't trust her—not quite.

Later that day, Lirah brought Kestrel's lunch. The slave wouldn't look at her. She set the tray down on a low table near the divan where Kestrel rested, and her movements were hurried, shaky. She spilled some tea.

"There's no need to rush," Kestrel said.

The girl's hands quieted, but her breath became uneven and harsh. A tear slipped down her cheek.

Kestrel suddenly understood why Lirah was rushing: because it was unbearable to stay any longer than necessary in the same room as her mistress.

Her mistress, who everyone thought had taken the lover Lirah wished were hers.

Kestrel should have felt pity. An urge to explain that what Lirah believed—what the whole city must believe—wasn't true. Instead, Kestrel couldn't help gazing at the girl's beauty, at the way tears made her green eyes greener. She wondered what Arin's sweetheart must be like, if Lirah couldn't change his choice.

As Kestrel tried to imagine the girl in the market—Arin's girl—a slow thought came to her.

Was this why Arin avoided her? Because the scandal had reached his sweetheart's ears?

A surge of anger pushed up Kestrel's throat.

She hated her. She hated that faceless, nameless woman.

"Fetch me a parasol," Kestrel told Lirah. "And get out."

The parasol wasn't a very good cane. Its tip dug into the hard, grassless earth, and the folded frame creaked as Kestrel limped across the grounds. But it brought her where she needed to go.

She found Arin walking through the bare orange grove, horse tack draped over his shoulder. It jangled when he stopped and stared at her. He stood, shoulders stiff. As Kestrel came close she saw that his jaw was clenched, and that there was no trace of what her guards had done to him. No bruises. Nor would there be, not for something that had happened nearly a month ago.

"Did I shame you?" Kestrel said.

Something strange crossed his face. "Shame me," Arin repeated. He looked up into the empty branches as if he expected to see fruit there, as if it weren't almost winter.

"The book. The inscription I read. The duel. The way I tricked you. The order I gave to have you imprisoned. Did I shame you?"

He crossed his arms over his chest. He shook his head, his gaze never wavering from the trees. "No. The god of debts knows what I owe."

"Then what is it?" Kestrel was trying so hard not to ask about the rumors or the woman in the market that she said something worse. "Why won't you look at me?"

"I shouldn't even be speaking with you," he muttered.

It dawned on her why it had never made sense that Rax had been the one to release Arin. "My father," she said. "Arin, you don't have to worry about him. He'll be leaving the morning of the Firstwinter ball. The entire regiment has been ordered east to fight the barbarians."

"What?" He glanced at her, eyes sharp.

"Things can be as they were."

"I don't think so."

"But . . . you are my friend." His expression changed, though not in a way Kestrel could read. "Just tell me what's wrong, Arin. Tell me the truth."

When he spoke, his voice was raw. "You own me. How can you believe I'll tell you the truth? Why would I?"

The parasol trembled in Kestrel's grip. She opened her mouth to speak, yet realized that if she did, she wouldn't be able to control what she said.

"I will tell you something you can trust is true." Arin's eyes held hers. "We are not friends."

Kestrel swallowed. "You're right," she whispered. "We're not."

Arin nearly got his throat cut.

"The god of life preserve you," Cheat gasped. He staggered back, his knife glinting in the shadows of his small bedroom. "What the hell are you doing here? Breaking into my home like a thief in the night. Climbing through the window. You're lucky I saw your face in time."

"There's something I have to tell you."

"Start with why you couldn't come by the auction house at a decent hour. I thought you had a free pass. What about the girl's seal ring?"

"Unavailable."

Cheat squinted up at Arin, tapping the flat of the short blade against his thigh. In the dim light of a streetlamp, a slow grin spread across his face. "Had a falling-out with your lady, did you? A lovers' quarrel?"

Arin felt his face go dark and tight.

"Easy, lad. Just tell me: are the rumors true?"

"*No.*"

"All right." Cheat held up his hands as if in surrender, the knife held loosely. "If you say they're not, they're not."

"Cheat. I broke curfew, scaled the general's wall, and stole through a guarded city to speak with you. Don't you think we have more important things to discuss than Valorian gossip?"

Cheat cocked one brow.

"The general is leaving to fight in the east. He's taking the entire regiment. The morning of the Firstwinter ball. It's the opportunity we've been waiting for."

Cheat dropped the knife to a table. He let out a breath that swelled into laughter. "This is beautiful," he said. "Perfect."

Arin saw, in his mind's eye, Kestrel's delicate face. He saw her bandaged knee. How her knuckles had whitened. He heard her voice crack.

"The revolution will happen the night of the ball," Cheat said. "Black powder kegs will be in place. I'll lead the assault on the general's estates. He'll leave his personal guard behind, so we can expect resistance. But it's nothing we can't handle, with your weapons, and seizing that property will be an important victory. Meanwhile, those high society Valorians at the ball will find a poisoned surprise in their wine. Arin." Cheat frowned at him. "Don't look like that. Even you can't find a flaw in this plan. It'll come off nicely. The city will be ours." Cheat rested a hand on Arin's shoulder and gripped it. "Freedom will be ours."

Those words sliced through the knots tangled within Arin. He slowly nodded. He turned toward the window.

"What're you doing?" Cheat said. "You risked enough coming here, and you'll risk the same returning to the estate. Stay. I can hide you until the assault."

Why won't you look at me? Kestrel had said. The hurt in her voice had hurt him. It hurt him still. It made him remember how his father had given him a blown-glass horse for his eighth nameday. Arin remembered its tapered legs, the arched neck: a thing of starlike clarity. He had fumbled, and it had smashed on the tiles below.

"No," Arin told Cheat. "I'm going back. I need to be there when it happens."

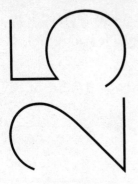

THE WALK TO THE ORANGE GROVE HAD
helped Kestrel's knee, if nothing else. The stiffness had eased,
and she forced herself to walk more every day. Soon she had
only the barest of limps, then none at all. She returned to
her music, let her fingers fly, let wild notes riddle her mind
until she couldn't think. It was bliss not to think, not to
remember the cold orange grove, and what she had said and
done and asked and wanted.

Kestrel played. She forgot everything but the music un-
furling around her.

The day before Firstwinter, the Valorian housekeeper delivered a muslin-wrapped package to Kestrel. "From the dressmaker's," she said.

Kestrel held the package and almost seemed to see a
gleam through the muslin.

She set it aside.

That evening, a slave brought a note from her father. *There is someone here who wishes to see you.*

Ronan, perhaps. The thought didn't make her glad. It came and went and didn't touch her, except when she realized that it hadn't touched her and that it should have.

There was something wrong with her. She should be glad to see her friend. She should hope Ronan was more than that.

We are not friends, Arin had said.

But she would not think of Arin.

She dressed for dinner with care.

Kestrel recognized the man's voice drifting down the hall from the dining room, but couldn't place it at first. "Thank you for not requisitioning my ship," he was saying. "I would have lost a great deal of profit—maybe even the ship itself—if the empire had borrowed it for the war effort."

"Don't thank me," said Kestrel's father. "If I had needed it, I would have taken it."

"Not big enough for you, Trajan?" the voice teased. Kestrel, hovering outside the door, suddenly knew who it was. She remembered being a little girl, a gray-haired man's easy smiles, sheaves of sheet music brought to her from far-off territories.

"On the contrary, Captain Wensan," she said, entering the room. The men rose from their seats. "I believe my father has not taken your ship for the military because it is one of the best, loaded with cannon, and he doesn't like to leave the harbor unprotected when he leaves tomorrow."

"Kestrel." The captain didn't take her hand in greeting, but rested his briefly on her head, as one did with a beloved child. She felt no disappointment that he, and not Ronan, was their guest. "You overestimate me," Wensan said. "I'm a simple merchant."

"Maybe," Kestrel said as the three sat at the table in their expected places, her father at the head, she at his right, the captain at his left. "But I doubt the two decks' worth of ten-pound cannon are there for decoration."

"I carry valuable goods. The cannon keep pirates away."

"As do your crew. They have quite the reputation."

"Fine fighters," her father agreed, "though they don't have the best memory."

The captain gave him a keen glance. "You can't possibly have heard about that."

"That your crew can't remember the code of the call to save their lives?"

The code of the call was the password sailors on deck demanded from shipmates in launches far below on the water when it was too dark to see who had rowed up from shore.

"I inspected each ship and crew before deciding which to take for battle," said Kestrel's father. "I like to be thorough." He studied his plate. It was empty, waiting for the first course. He touched its white rim, shifting it to center its design of a bird. There was something deliberate in his gesture.

Wensan looked at the plate, then at his own, Kestrel's, and the three others on the table in honor of the family dead. "You certainly are." He added unnecessarily, "I agree."

A message was being passed between the two men. Kestrel considered the porcelain her father must have chosen tonight for a reason. Her household had countless sets of dishes with various patterns. This particular set was of Valorian design, each showing a bird of prey: falcon, kite, lanceling, harrow owl, osprey, and kestrel. They referred to a marching song Valorian children learned.

"Are you using the birds from 'The Song of Death's Feathers' as passwords for your ship?" Kestrel asked the captain.

Wensan showed only a moment's surprise, and her father none. Kestrel had always been quick to guess secrets.

Mournfully, Wensan said, "It's the only thing the crew can seem to keep straight. The password must change every night, you know. The order of bird names in the song is an easy pattern to remember."

The general rang for slaves to bring the first course. Wensan began spinning stories of his travels, and Kestrel thought that perhaps this was why her father had invited him: to lift her spirits. Then she looked more closely at the captain's plate and realized that this was not the reason.

His plate showed the kestrel.

Clearly, it wasn't because the captain was an old friend that her father hadn't requisitioned his ship, or because its cannon might protect the harbor. It was a trade. A favor that demanded repayment. "I agree," Captain Wensan had said, looking at his plate.

He had agreed to watch over Kestrel in her father's absence.

Kestrel became aware that she had gone still. Her eyes lifted to her father, who said, "Captain Wensan will be attending the Firstwinter ball."

Slaves came bearing food, and served. Kestrel looked at the three empty plates, two for her father's brother and sister, who had died in battle, and the harrow owl for her mother. Kestrel wondered if things would have been different if her mother had lived. Maybe Kestrel and her father wouldn't communicate in code, or strategize against each other, and for each other. Maybe Kestrel could speak her heart.

What would she say? That she knew her father wanted the captain to watch over her, yes, but also to make certain that she didn't err, didn't sin against society and him?

She could say that she didn't blame his lack of faith when she no longer trusted herself.

She could say that she saw her father's love as well as his worry.

"How nice for Captain Wensan," she said with a smile, reaching for her knife and fork. "I'm sure he will enjoy the ball. I, however, am not going."

At dawn, Kestrel took the carriage into the city and down to the harbor. Her father had said that he didn't want her to see him off, so she hadn't been there during the gray hours as the ships made ready to set sail. But she stood in the cold sunrise on the almost empty docks. The wind rose, and salty air knifed through her cloak.

She saw the ships, two hundred strong, sailing toward open water. Only six merchant ships remained, including Captain Wensan's, rocking against their anchors. A handful of fishing boats clung to the shore, too small to do the military any good. She idly counted them.

Kestrel wondered if the general was on the deck of one of the warships, and if he could see her.

The fleet glided away, almost like dancers in a dance where one doesn't touch.

Happiness depends on being free, Kestrel's father often said, *and freedom depends on being courageous.*

She thought of the muslin-wrapped ball gown.

Why shouldn't she go to the ball? What had she to fear? The stares?

Let them stare. She was not defenseless, nor did she need her father's protection, or the captain's.

Kestrel had been injured, but she wasn't anymore.

The cloth was almost liquid. The dress lay cool against her skin, falling in simple, golden lines, pale as a winter sun. It left her arms bare, and was low enough to show the wings of her collarbone.

The dress was easy to slip on—a slave had only to fasten a few tiny pearl buttons that ran up the low back—and Kestrel was accustomed to belting the jeweled dagger around her waist herself. But once she was alone she knew her hair would be trouble, and she wasn't going to call for Lirah, the person most able to help.

She sat at her dressing table, eyeing her reflection warily. Her hair was loose, spilling over her shoulders, a few shades darker than the dress. She gathered a handful and began to braid.

"I hear you're going to the ball tonight."

Kestrel glanced in the mirror to see Arin standing

behind her. Then she focused on her own shadowed eyes. "You're not allowed in here," Kestrel said. She didn't look again at him, but sensed him waiting. She realized that she was waiting, too—waiting for the will to send him away.

She sighed and continued to braid.

He said, "It's not a good idea for you to attend the ball."

"I hardly think you're in a position to advise me on what I should or shouldn't do." She glanced back at his reflection. His face frayed her already sheer nerves. The braid slipped from her fingers and unraveled. "What?" she snapped. "Does this amuse you?"

The corner of his mouth lifted, and Arin looked like himself, like the person she had grown to know since summer's end. "'Amuse' isn't the right word."

Heavy locks fell forward to curtain her face. "Lirah usually does my hair," she muttered. She heard Arin inhale as if to speak, but he didn't.

Then, quietly, he said, "I could do it."

"What?"

"I could braid your hair."

"You?"

"Yes."

Kestrel's pulse bit at her throat. She opened her mouth, but before she could say anything he had crossed the room and swept her hair into his hands. His fingers began to move.

It was strange that the room was so silent. It seemed that there should have been some kind of sound when a fingertip grazed her neck. Or when he drew a lock taut and pinned it in place. When he let a ribbon-thin braid fall forward so that it tapped her cheek. Every gesture of his was as resonant as music, and Kestrel didn't quite believe that she couldn't hear any notes, high or low. She let out a slow breath.

His hands stilled. "Did I hurt you?"

"No."

Pins disappeared from the dressing table at a rapid rate. Kestrel watched small braids lose themselves inside larger ones, dip in and under and out of an increasingly intricate design. She felt a gentle tug. A twist. A shiver of air.

Although Arin wasn't touching her, he was touching no living part of her, it felt as if a fine net had been cast over Kestrel, one that hazed her vision and shimmered against her skin.

"There," he said.

Kestrel watched her reflection lift a hand to her head. She couldn't think of what to say. Arin had drawn back, hands in his pockets. But his eyes held hers in the mirror, and his face had softened, like when she had played the piano for him. She said, "How . . . ?"

He smiled. "How did a blacksmith pick up such an unexpected skill?"

"Well, yes."

"My older sister used to make me do this when I was little."

Kestrel almost asked where Arin's sister was now, then imagined the worst. She saw Arin watch her imagine it, and saw from his expression that the worst was true. Yet his smile didn't fade. "I hated it, of course," he said. "The way she ordered me around. The way I let her. But now . . . it's a nice memory."

She rose and faced Arin. The chair stood between them,

and she wasn't sure whether she was grateful for that barrier or not.

"Kestrel, if you must go to the ball, take me with you."

"I don't understand you," she said, frustrated. "I don't understand what you say, how you *change*, how you act one way and then come here and act another."

"I don't always understand myself either. But I know I want to go with you tonight."

Kestrel let the words echo in her mind. There had been a supple strength to his voice. An unconscious melody. Kestrel wondered if Arin knew how he exposed himself as a singer with every simple, ordinary word. She wondered if he meant to hold her in thrall.

"If you think it's stupid for me to go to the Firstwinter ball," she said, "you can be certain that it is far worse for me to take *you* along."

He lifted one shoulder. "Or it could send a bold message of what we both know to be true: that you have nothing to hide."

The governor's wife, Neril, faltered for only the briefest of moments when she saw Kestrel in the receiving line for the ball. But the governor thought highly of General Trajan and, more important, relied upon him. This made the men allies—which, in turn, meant that Neril had to be careful around the general's daughter, as Kestrel knew very well.

"My dear!" said Neril. "You look stunning." Her eyes, however, didn't rest on Kestrel. They darted behind her to where Arin stood.

"Thank you," said Kestrel.

Neril's smile was stiff. Her gaze didn't leave Arin's face. "Lady Kestrel, could I beg a favor? You see, half of my slaves fell ill tonight."

"So many?"

"They're faking, of course. But beating the lies out of them won't make me any less shorthanded tonight. A whipped slave could hardly serve my guests, at least not with the necessary poise and posture."

Kestrel didn't like where this was going. "Lady Neril—"

"May I borrow your slave tonight?"

Kestrel sensed the tension in Arin as clearly as if he stood next to her, shoulder brushing hers, instead of behind her, barely out of sight. "I might need him."

"*Need* him?" Neril dropped her voice: "Kestrel, I am doing *you* a favor. Send him to the kitchens now, before the ball has truly begun and more people notice. I doubt he'll mind."

Kestrel watched Arin as she went through the charade of translating Neril's Valorian for him. She thought that, yes, he *would* mind. Yet when he spoke, his voice was humble. His words were in Valorian, as if he no longer cared who knew how well he spoke the empire's language. "My lady," he said to Neril. "I don't know the way to your kitchens, and it would be easy to get lost in such a grand house. One of your slaves could guide me, but I see they are all busy . . ."

"Yes, fine." Neril waved an impatient hand. "I'll send a slave to find you. *Soon,*" she added, that last word directed at Kestrel. Then she turned her attention to the guests next in line.

The governor's home was Valorian-built, after the

conquest, so the reception hall led to a shield chamber, where embossed shields studded the walls and flared in the torchlight as guests chatted and drank.

A house slave placed a glass of wine in Kestrel's hand. She lifted it to her lips.

It was knocked away. It smashed at her feet, wine splashing near her shoes. People broke off their conversations and stared.

"I'm sorry," Arin muttered. "I tripped."

Kestrel felt the heat in the way everyone looked at her. At him. At her, standing next to him. She saw Neril, still visible at the threshold between the reception hall and the shield chamber, turn and take in the scene. The woman rolled her eyes. She grabbed a slave by the elbow and pushed him toward Kestrel and Arin.

"Kestrel, don't drink any wine tonight," Arin said.

"What? Why not?"

Neril's slave came closer.

"You should keep your head clear," Arin told her.

"My head is perfectly clear," she hissed at him, out of earshot of the murmuring crowd. "What is *wrong* with you, Arin? You ask to accompany me to an event you don't think I should attend. You're silent in the carriage the entire way here, and *now*—"

"Just promise me that you won't drink."

"Very well, I won't, if it's important to you." Did this moment, like others at Irex's dinner party, hide some past trauma of Arin's that she couldn't see? "But what—"

"Arin." It was Neril's slave. The man seemed surprised to see Arin, yet also pleased. "You're supposed to follow me."

When Arin entered the kitchens, the Herrani fell silent. He saw their expressions change, and it made him feel as if something sticky had been wiped on his skin, the way they looked at him.

As if he were a hero.

He ignored them, pushing past footmen and serving girls until he reached the cook, roasting a pig on a spit over the fire. Arin grabbed him. "Which wine?" he demanded. Once the poison was served, destruction would fall on every Valorian in this house.

"Arin." The cook grinned. "I thought you were supposed to be at the general's estate tonight."

"Which wine?"

The cook blinked, finally absorbing the urgency in Arin's voice. "It's in an iced apple wine, very sweet, sweet enough to mask the poison."

"When?"

"When's it going to be served? Why, right after the third round of dancing."

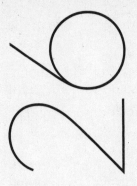

BEYOND ITS ENTRYWAY, THE BALLROOM RANG
with laughter and loud talk. Heat seethed over the threshold and into the hall where Kestrel stood.

She wove her fingers into a tight lattice. She was nervous.
She *looked* nervous.

No one must know how she felt.

Kestrel pulled her hands apart and stepped inside the
ballroom.

There was a sudden valley of silence. If the windows had
been open and air had rushed through them, Kestrel would
have heard the chandeliers tinkle, it was so quiet.

Faces chilled. One by one, they turned away.

She sought the crowd for a friend and hadn't realized
she'd been holding her breath until she noticed Benix. She
smiled. She moved toward him.

He saw her. She knew that he saw her. But his eyes refused to see her. It was as if she were transparent. Like ice, or
glass, or something equally breakable.

She stopped.

Benix turned his back. He went to the other side of the room.

Whispers began. Irex, far away but not far enough, laughed and said something in Lady Faris's ear. Kestrel's cheeks prickled with shame, yet she couldn't retreat. She couldn't move.

She saw the smile first. Then the face: Captain Wensan, coming to her rescue, weaving past people. He would ask Kestrel for the first dance, and her appearance would be salvaged, at least for now, even if her reputation was ruined. And she would say yes, for she had no choice but to accept the captain's pity.

Pity. The thought of it chased the blush from her face.

She scanned the crowd. Before the captain could reach her, she approached a senator standing alone. Senator Caran was twice Kestrel's age. Thin-haired, thin-faced. His reputation was spotless, if only because he was too timid to break ranks with society.

"Ask me to dance," she said quietly.

"Pardon me?"

At least he was speaking with her. "Ask me to dance," she said, "or I'll tell everyone what I know about you."

His gaping mouth clamped shut.

Kestrel didn't know any of Caran's secrets. Perhaps he had none. She was counting, however, on his being too afraid to risk whatever she might say.

He asked her to dance.

He wasn't, obviously, the ideal choice. But Ronan hadn't arrived, and Benix still wouldn't meet her gaze. Either he had changed his mind about her since the duel or his courage failed him in the absence of Ronan and Jess. Or maybe he was simply no longer willing to sink his reputation along with Kestrel's.

The dance began. Caran remained silent the entire time.

When the instruments slowed to an end, a lute picking a light tune downward until there was no more music, Kestrel broke away. Caran gave her an awkward bow and left.

"Well, *that* didn't look very fun," said a voice behind her. Kestrel turned. Gladness washed over her.

It was Ronan. "I'm ashamed of myself," he said. "Heartily ashamed, to be so late that you had to dance with such a boring partner as Caran. How did that happen?"

"I blackmailed him."

"Ah." Ronan's eyes grew worried. "So things aren't going well."

"Kestrel!" Jess threaded through milling people and came close. "We didn't think you'd come. You should have told us. If we'd known, we'd have been here from the first." Jess took Kestrel's hand and drew her to the edge of the dance floor. Ronan followed. Behind them, dancers began the second round. "As it was," Jess continued, "we barely made it into the carriage. Ronan was so *listless*, saying he saw no point in coming if he couldn't be with you."

"Sweet sister," said Ronan, "is it now my turn to share private things about you?"

"Silly. I have no secrets. Neither do you, where Kestrel is concerned. Well?" Jess looked triumphantly between them. "Do you, Ronan?"

He pinched the bridge of his nose between his fingers

and thumb, brows rumpling into a pained expression. "Not anymore."

"You look lovely, Kestrel," Jess said. "Wasn't I right about the dress? And the color will go perfectly with the iced apple wine."

Kestrel felt giddy, whether from the relief of seeing her friends or because of Ronan's forced confession, she wasn't sure. She smiled. "You chose the fabric of my dress to coordinate with wine?"

"A *special* wine. Lady Neril is very proud of it. She told me months ago that she planned to import several casks from the capital for the ball, and it occurred to me that it is simply too easy to match a dress only to jewels, dagger, and shoes. A glass of wine in one's hand *is* rather like a jewel, isn't it, a large, liquid one?"

"I'd better have a glass then. To complete my ensemble." Kestrel didn't quite forget her promise to Arin not to drink, but rather willed it away along with everything else about him.

"Oh, yes," said Jess. "You must. Don't you think so, Ronan?"

"I don't think. I am thinking of nothing other than what Kestrel could be thinking, and whether she will dance with me. If I'm not mistaken, there is one final dance before this legendary wine is served."

Kestrel's happiness faltered. "I'd love to, but . . . won't your parents mind?"

Ronan and Jess exchanged a glance. "They're not here," Ronan said. "They've left to spend the winter season in the capital."

Which meant that, were they here, they *would* object—as would any parents, given the scandal.

Ronan read Kestrel's face. "It doesn't matter what they think. Dance with me."

He took her hand, and for the first time in a long while, she felt safe. He pulled her to the center of the floor and into the motions of the dance.

Ronan didn't speak for a few moments, then touched a slim braid that curved in a tendril along Kestrel's cheek. "This is pretty."

The memory of Arin's hands in her hair made her stiffen.

"Gorgeous?" Ronan tried again. "Transcendent? Kestrel, the right adjective hasn't been invented to describe you."

She attempted a light tone. "What will ladies do, when this kind of exaggerated flirtation is no longer the fashion? We shall be spoiled."

"You know it's not mere flirtation," Ronan said. "You've always known."

And Kestrel had, it was true that she had, even if she hadn't wanted to shake the knowledge out of her mind and look at it, truly see it. She felt a dull spark of dread.

"Marry me, Kestrel."

She held her breath.

"I know things have been hard lately," Ronan continued, "and that you don't deserve it. You've had to be so strong, so proud, so cunning. But all of this unpleasantness will go away the instant we announce our engagement. You can be yourself again."

But she *was* strong. Proud. Cunning. Who did he think she was, if not the person who mercilessly beat him at every

Bite and Sting game, who gave him Irex's death-price and told him exactly what to do with it? Yet Kestrel bit back her words. She leaned into the curve of his arm. It was easy to dance with him. It would be easy to say yes.

"Your father will be happy. My wedding gift to you will be the finest piano the capital can offer."

Kestrel glanced into his eyes.

"Or keep yours," he said hastily. "I know you're attached to it."

"It's just . . . you are very kind."

He gave a short, nervous laugh. "Kindness has little to do with it."

The dance slowed. It would end soon.

"So?" Ronan had stopped, even though the music continued and dancers swirled around them. "What . . . well, what do you think?"

Kestrel didn't know what to think. Ronan was offering everything she could want. Why, then, did his words sadden her? Why did she feel like something had been lost? Carefully, she said, "The reasons you've given aren't reasons to marry."

"I love you. Is that reason enough?"

Maybe. Maybe it would have been. But as the music drained from the air, Kestrel saw Arin on the fringes of the crowd. He watched her, his expression oddly desperate. As if he, too, were losing something, or it was already lost.

She saw him and didn't understand how she had ever missed his beauty. How it didn't always strike her as it did now, like a blow.

"No," Kestrel whispered.

"What?" Ronan's voice cut into the quiet.

"I'm sorry."

Ronan swiveled to find the target of Kestrel's gaze. He swore.

Kestrel walked away, pushing past slaves bearing trays laden with glasses of pale gold wine. The lights and people blurred in her stinging eyes. She walked through the doors, down a hall, out of the palace, and into the cold night, knowing without seeing or hearing or touching him that Arin was at her side.

Kestrel didn't see why carriage seats had to face each other. Why couldn't they have been designed for moments like these, when all she wanted to do was hide? She took one look at Arin. She had given no order for the carriage lamps to be lit, but the moonlight was strong. Arin was silvered by it. He was staring out the window at the governor's palace dwindling as the carriage trundled toward home. Then he tore his gaze from the window with a sharp turn of the head and sagged against his seat, face filled with something that looked like shocked relief.

Kestrel felt a flicker of instinctive curiosity. Then she reminded herself bitterly that this was what curiosity had bought her: fifty keystones for a singer who refused to sing, a friend who wasn't her friend, someone who was hers and yet would never be hers. Kestrel looked away from Arin. She swore to herself that she would never look back.

Softly, he said, "Why are you crying?"

His words made the tears flow faster.

"Kestrel."

She drew a shaky breath. "Because when my father comes home, I will tell him that he has won. I will join the military."

There was a silence. "I don't understand."

Kestrel shrugged. She shouldn't care whether he understood or not.

"You would give up your music?"

Yes. She would.

"But your bargain with the general was for spring." Arin still sounded confused. "You have until spring to marry or enlist. Ronan . . . Ronan would ask the god of souls for you. He would ask you to marry him."

"He has."

Arin didn't speak.

"But I can't," she said.

"Kestrel."

"I can't."

"Kestrel, please don't cry." Tentative fingers touched her face. A thumb ran along the wet skin of her cheekbone. She suffered for it, suffered for the misery of knowing that whatever possessed him to do this could be no more than compassion. He valued her that much. But not enough.

"Why can't you marry him?" he whispered.

She broke her word to herself and looked at him. "Because of you."

Arin's hand flinched against her cheek. His dark head bowed, became lost in its own shadow. Then he slipped from his seat and knelt before hers. His hands fell to the fists on her lap and gently opened them. He held them as if cupping water. He took a breath to speak.

She would have stopped him. She would have wished herself deaf, blind, made of unfeeling smoke. She would have stopped his words out of terror, longing. The way terror and longing had become indistinguishable.

Yet his hands held hers, and she could do nothing.

He said, "I want the same thing you want."

Kestrel pulled back. It wasn't possible his words could mean what they seemed.

"It hasn't been easy for me to want it." Arin lifted his face so that she could see his expression. A rich emotion played across his features, offered itself, and asked to be called by its name.

Hope.

"But you've already given your heart," she said.

His brow furrowed, then smoothed. "Oh. No, not the way you think." He laughed a little, the sound soft yet somehow wild. "Ask me why I went to the market."

This was cruel. "We both know why."

He shook his head. "Pretend that you've won a game of Bite and Sting. Why did I go? Ask me. It wasn't to see a girl who doesn't exist."

"She . . . doesn't?"

"I lied."

Kestrel blinked. "Then why did you go to the market?"

"Because I wanted to feel free." Arin raised a hand to brush the air by his temple, then awkwardly let it fall.

Kestrel suddenly understood this gesture she'd seen many times. It was an old habit. He was brushing away a ghost, hair that was no longer there because she had ordered it cut.

She leaned forward, and kissed his temple.

Arin's hand held her lightly to him. His cheek slid against hers. Then his lips touched her brow, her closed eyes, the line where her jaw met her throat.

Kestrel's mouth found his. His lips were salted with her tears, and the taste of that, of him, of their deepening kiss, filled her with the feeling of his quiet laugh moments ago. Of a wild softness, a soft wildness. In his hands, running up her thin dress. In his heat, burning through to her skin . . . and into her, sinking into him.

He broke away, barely. "I haven't told you everything," he said. The carriage jostled, swaying the weight of his body against hers, then away again.

Kestrel smiled. "Do you have more imaginary friends?"

"I—"

A distant explosion rumbled through the night. One of the horses screamed. The carriage shook, knocking Kestrel's head against the window frame. She heard the driver's shout, the crack of a whip. The carriage ground to a halt. The hilt of Kestrel's dagger jabbed her side.

"Kestrel? Are you all right?"

Dazed, she touched the side of her head. Her fingers came away wet.

There was a second explosion. The carriage jerked again as the horses shied, but Arin's hand held Kestrel steady. She looked out the window, toward the city, and saw a faint glow in the sky. "What was that?"

Arin was silent. Then: "Black powder. The first explosion was at the city guards' barracks. The second was at the armory."

That might have been a guess, but it didn't sound like one. Half of Kestrel's mind knew exactly what it meant if Arin knew this, but the other half slammed a door on this knowledge, letting her understand only what it meant if he was correct.

The city was under attack.

Sleeping city guards had been killed.

Enemies were ransacking weapons from the armory.

Kestrel scrambled out the carriage door.

Arin was right behind her. "Kestrel, you should get back in the carriage."

She ignored him.

"You're bleeding," he said.

Kestrel looked at the Herrani driver hauling on the reins and swearing at the shifting horses. She saw the growing light over the city's center, a sure sign of fire. She stared up the road. They were only minutes away from her estate.

Kestrel took a step toward home.

"No." Arin seized her arm. "We need to go back together."

The horses quieted. The uneven rhythm of their snorts and stamped hooves floated into the night as Kestrel thought about Arin's word: *need*.

The door she had slammed shut in her mind sailed open.

Why had Arin told her not to drink the wine?

What had been wrong with the wine?

She thought of Jess and Ronan, and all the dancers at the ball.

"Kestrel." Arin's voice was low but insistent, the beginning of an explanation she did not want to hear.

"Let me go."

His hand fell, and Kestrel saw that he saw that she knew. She knew that, whatever was happening tonight, it was no surprise to him. That whatever awaited her at home was as dangerous as black powder or poisoned wine.

Both Arin and Kestrel were aware that her options here—on this road, isolated, at night—were few.

"What is going on?" The Herrani driver climbed down from his seat. He came close, then stared out over the dark crest of a hill at the city's faint glow. He met Arin's eyes. "The god of vengeance has come," he breathed.

Kestrel drew her dagger and pressed it to the driver's throat. "Curse your gods," she said. "Unhitch a horse."

"Don't," Arin told the driver, who swallowed nervously against Kestrel's blade. "She won't kill you."

"I'm Valorian. I will."

"Kestrel, there will be . . . changes, after tonight. But give me a chance to explain."

"I don't think so."

"Then think about this." In the moonlight, Arin's jaw hardened into a black line. "What would your next move be, after killing your driver? Will you attack me? Would you succeed?"

"I'll kill myself."

Arin took a step back. "You wouldn't." Yet there was fear in his eyes.

"An honor suicide? All Valorian children are taught how, when we come of age. My father showed me where to stab."

"No. You wouldn't. You play a game to its end."

"The Herrani were enslaved because they were too poor

at killing and too cowardly to die. I told you I didn't want to kill, not that I wouldn't. And I never said I was afraid of death."

Arin looked at the driver. "Unhitch both horses."

Kestrel held the knife steady as the driver stripped the first horse of its gear.

When she mounted its bare back, Arin lunged for her. She had expected this, and had the advantage of height and a wooden-heeled shoe. She kicked his brow, saw him reel. Then she dug one hand into the horse's mane and forced it to gallop.

Kestrel could see well enough by the moon to avoid deep ruts in the road. She concentrated on that, not on the betrayal seared into her skin. Branded on her mouth. The shoes fell from her feet and braids whipped her back.

It wasn't long before she heard the beating of hooves behind her.

The gate to the estate was open and the path strewn with the bodies of the general's guard. Kestrel saw Rax, his dead eyes staring. A short sword was buried in his gut.

Her horse was hurtling across the grounds to the house when the quarrel of a crossbow whined through the air and punched into the beast's side.

The horse screamed. Kestrel was thrown to the ground. She lay there, stunned. Then the fingers of her right hand realized what they no longer held and began scrabbling for the knife.

Her hand closed around its hilt just as a boot material-
ized in her line of sight. The heel drove into the winter dirt,
the sole hovering over her knuckles.

"It's the lady of the house," said the auctioneer. Kestrel
stared up at him, at the crossbow he held so easily, at the way
he appraised her, moving from bare feet to torn dress to
bleeding forehead. "The piano player." His boot lowered and
rocked a slight pressure over the bones of her fingers. "Drop
the knife or I'll crush your hand."

Kestrel dropped it.

He grabbed the back of her neck and hauled her up.
Her breath came quickly, in short bursts of fear. He smiled,
and she saw him again as he had been in the pit, pitching
the sale of Arin. *This slave has been trained as a blacksmith,*
the auctioneer had said. *He would be perfect for any soldier,
especially for an officer with a guard of his own and weapons
to maintain.*

No Valorian in the city had a guard of his own save
General Trajan.

Kestrel saw again how the auctioneer had met her eyes
that day. His delight when she had bid, his expression when
others had joined. He hadn't been excited to see the price
drive higher, Kestrel realized. He had been anxious.

As if the sale of Arin had been meant for *her*, her alone.

The ground trembled with approaching hooves.

The auctioneer's smile grew wider as Arin dragged his
horse to a halt. The auctioneer motioned toward the shadows of trees. Armed Herrani appeared. They trained their
weapons on Kestrel.

The auctioneer walked toward Arin, who dismounted. He placed one palm against Arin's cheek. Arin did the same to him. They stood, creating an image Kestrel had seen only in dust-covered Herrani art. It was a gesture of friendship as deep as family.

Arin's eyes met hers.

"*You* are the god of lies," she hissed.

THEY MARCHED HER TO THE HOUSE. KESTREL said nothing as rocks and twigs cut into her bare feet. When the auctioneer pushed her into the entryway, she left bloody footprints on the tile.

But she was distracted from this by another sight. Harman, her steward, floated facedown in the fountain, blond hair rippling like sea grass.

The general's slaves crowded the hallway beyond the fountain, shouting questions at the armed men, whose answers were a jumble of phrases like *We've seized the city*, *The governor's dead*, and, over and over, *You're free*.

"Where's the housekeeper?" said the auctioneer.

There was a shuffling among the slaves. It wasn't so much that the Valorian housekeeper was thrust forward as that the slaves stepped away to reveal her.

The auctioneer seized the woman's shoulders, backed her up against the wall, pressed a broad arm across her chest, and drew a knife.

She began to sob.

"Stop," Kestrel said. She turned toward the slaves. "Stop this. She was good to you."

They didn't move.

"Good to you?" the auctioneer said to them. "Was she good to you when she made you clean the privies? When she beat you for breaking a plate?"

"She wouldn't have hurt anyone." Kestrel's voice rode high with the fear she could no longer contain. It made her say the wrong thing. "I wouldn't have allowed it."

"You don't give orders anymore," the auctioneer said, and cut the woman's throat.

She sagged against the wall's painted flowers, choking on her blood, pressing hands to her throat as if she could hold everything inside. The auctioneer didn't step away. He let her blood splash him until she slid to the floor.

"But she didn't do anything." Kestrel couldn't stop herself, even though she knew that it was stupid, utterly stupid, for her to speak. "She only did what I paid her to do."

"Kestrel." Arin's voice was sharp.

The auctioneer turned to face her. He raised his knife again. Kestrel had just enough time to remember the sound of a hammer against anvil, to think of all the weapons Arin had forged, and to realize that if he had wanted to make more on the side it wouldn't have been hard.

The auctioneer advanced on her.

Not hard at all.

"No," said Arin. "She's mine."

The man paused. "What?"

Arin strolled toward them, stepping in the housekeeper's blood. He stood next to the auctioneer, his stance loose and careless. "She's mine. My prize. Payment for services rendered. A spoil of war." Arin shrugged. "Call her what you like. Call her my slave."

Shame poured into Kestrel, as poisonous as anything her friends must have drunk at the ball.

Slowly, the auctioneer said, "I'm a little worried about you, Arin. I think you've lost clarity on the situation."

"Is there something wrong with treating her the way she treated me?"

"No, but—"

"The Valorian army will return. She's the general's daughter. She's too valuable to waste."

The auctioneer sheathed his knife, but Kestrel couldn't sheathe her dread. This sudden alternative to death didn't seem like a better one.

"Just remember what happened to your parents," the auctioneer told Arin. "Remember what Valorian soldiers did to your sister."

Arin's gaze cut to Kestrel. "I do."

"Really? Where were you during the assault on the estate? I expected to find my second-in-command here. Instead, you were at a party."

"Because I learned that a slave to the harbormaster would be there. He gave me valuable information. We still have to deal with the merchant ships, Cheat. Send me. Let me do this for you." The need to please this man was clear on Arin's face.

Cheat saw it, too. He sighed. "Take some fighters. You'll find more at the docks. Seize all the ships or burn them. If even one leaves to alert the empire that we've taken the city, this is going to be a very short-lived revolution."

"I'll take care of it. They won't leave the harbor."

"Some might already have. The sailors on board will have heard the explosions."

"All the more reason for them to wait until their ship-mates on shore return."

Cheat acknowledged this with a grimace of guarded optimism. "Go. I'll mop up what's left at the governor's house."

Kestrel thought of her friends. She stared at the blood on the floor. She wasn't watching or listening as Arin strode toward her. Then the auctioneer said, "Her hands."

She glanced up. Arin's gaze flicked toward her fists. "Of course," he said to the auctioneer, and Kestrel understood that they had just discussed the best way to threaten her.

Her arm went limp when Arin gripped it. She remembered the auctioneer in the pit, in the full heat of summer. *This lad can sing,* he had said. She remembered the man's boot on her hand. The fact that the whole city knew her weakness for music. As Arin pulled her from the room, Kestrel thought about how this might be what hurt the most.

That they had used something she loved against her.

She had sworn to herself not to speak to Arin, but then he said, "You're coming with me to the harbor."

This surprised her into saying, "To do what? Why not lock me up in the barracks? It would be a perfect prison for your prize."

He continued to walk her down the halls of her home. "Unless Cheat changes his mind about you."

Kestrel imagined the auctioneer unlocking her cell door. "I suppose I'm no good to you dead."

"I would never let that happen."

"What a touching concern for Valorian life. As if you hadn't let your leader kill that woman. As if you're not responsible for the death of my friends."

They stopped before the door to Kestrel's suite. Arin faced her. "I will let every single Valorian in this city die if it means that you don't."

"Like Jess?" Her eyes swam with sudden, unshed tears. "Ronan?"

Arin looked away. The skin above his eye was beginning to blacken from where she had kicked him. "I spent ten years as a slave. I couldn't be one anymore. What did you imagine, tonight, in the carriage? That it would be fine for me to always be afraid to touch you?"

"*That* has nothing to do with anything. I am not a fool. You sold yourself to me with the *intention* of betrayal."

"But I didn't know you. I didn't know how you—"

"You're right. You don't know me. You're a stranger."

He flattened a palm against the door.

"What about the Valorian children?" she demanded. "What have you done with them? Have they been poisoned, too?"

"*No.* Kestrel, no, of course not. They will be cared for. In comfort. By their nurses. This was always part of the plan. Do you think we're monsters?"

"I think *you* are."

Arin's fingers curled against the door. He shoved it open.

He led her to the dressing room, opened the wardrobe,

and riffled through her clothes. He pulled out a black tunic, leggings, and jacket and thrust them at Kestrel.

Coolly she said, "This is a ceremonial fighting uniform. Do you expect me to fight a duel on the docks?"

"You're too noticeable." There was something strange about his voice. "In the dark. You . . . you look like an open flame." He found another black tunic and tore it between his hands. "Here. Wrap this around your hair."

Kestrel stood still, the black cloth limp in her arms as she remembered the last time she had worn such clothes.

"Get dressed," said Arin.

"Get out."

He shook his head. "I won't look."

"That's right. You won't, because you are going to *get out*."

"I can't leave you alone."

"Don't be absurd. What am I going to do, take back the city single-handedly from the comfort of my dressing room?"

Arin dragged a hand through his hair. "You might kill yourself."

Bitterly, she said, "I should think it was clear from the way I let you and your friend push me around that I want to stay alive."

"You might change your mind."

"And do what, exactly?"

"You could hang yourself with your dagger belt."

"So take it away."

"You'll use clothes. The leggings."

"Hanging is an undignified way to die."

"You'll break the mirror to your dressing table and cut

yourself." Again Arin's voice seemed foreign. "Kestrel, I won't look."

She realized why his words sounded rough. She had switched, at some point, to speaking in Valorian, and he had followed her. It was his accent that she heard.

"I promise," he said.

"Your promises are worth nothing." Kestrel turned and began to undress.

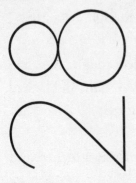

HE TOOK HER HORSE.

Kestrel saw the logic. Her carriage had been abandoned on the road and the stables were largely empty, since many horses had gone with her father. Javelin was the best of those that remained. In war, property goes to those who can seize and keep it, so the stallion was Arin's. But it hurt.

He studied her warily as he saddled Javelin. The stables rang with noise: the sounds of other Herrani readying horses to ride, the beasts whickering as they smelled human tension, the thumps of wood under hooves and feet. Yet Arin was silent, and watched Kestrel. The first thing he had done after entering the stables was grab a set of reins, slice the leather with a knife, bind Kestrel's hands, and place her under guard. It didn't matter that she was powerless. He watched her as if she weren't.

Or maybe he was just contemplating how hard it would be to bring a captive on horseback into the city and down to the harbor. This would have given Kestrel some satisfaction if she hadn't been very aware of what he should do.

Knock her unconscious, if he wanted to keep his prize. Kill her, if he had changed his mind. Imprison her, if she was too much trouble either way.

She saw his solutions as well as he must.

Someone called Arin's name. He and Kestrel turned to see a Herrani woman leaning against the stable door, sides heaving. Her face was damp with sweat. She looked familiar, and Kestrel realized why at the same time she understood why the woman was here.

She was one of the governor's slaves. She had come as a messenger, with news of what had happened at the ball after Kestrel and Arin had left.

Arin strode toward the woman. Kestrel tried to do the same, but was hauled back by her guard. Arin glanced at Kestrel, and she didn't like that look. It was the expression of someone who had just gained leverage.

As if he needed any more.

"In private," he said to the woman. "Then tell Cheat, if you haven't already."

Arin and the governor's slave stepped out of the stables. The doors slammed shut behind them.

When he returned, he was alone.

"Are my friends dead?" Kestrel demanded. "Tell me."

"I will tell you after I have set you on that horse and you haven't fought me, and after I am seated behind you and you don't have any clever ideas to shove me off or throw us both. I'll tell you when we've made it to the harbor." He came close. She didn't say anything, and he must have decided that she agreed, or maybe he didn't want to hear her voice any more than she wanted to speak, because he didn't wait for an answer. He lifted Kestrel onto Javelin, then settled behind her in a swift, fluid movement. Kestrel felt the lines of his body fit along hers.

His closeness was a shock. Kestrel decided, however, to agree to the bargain. She didn't signal Javelin to rear. She didn't drive her head back into Arin's jaw. She decided to behave. She focused on what mattered.

That kiss had meant nothing. Nothing. What remained was the hand she had drawn, and how she would play it.

The horses burst from the stables.

Kestrel felt Arin breathe as soon as they sighted the harbor, and knew it was from relief, since all of the boats she had seen that morning were still there. Kestrel was disappointed, though not surprised, since she knew from her time learning how to sail that crews considered their ships to be islands. Sailors on board wouldn't consider a threat on land to be a threat to them, and loyalty to their mates on shore would keep them anchored as long as they could safely wait. As for the fishermen who owned the smaller boats, most had homes on shore and would be there, in the thick of black powder smoke and fire and the bodies Javelin had sidestepped as they had ridden through the city. Any fishermen who had been sleeping on their boats weren't likely to risk sailing to the capital during the height of green storm season, and Kestrel had seen clouds gathering in the night as they'd ridden to the harbor. Small ships were particularly vulnerable.

As Kestrel considered them a tiny idea flickered.

The ships could not be burned. Especially not the fishing boats. She might need one of them later.

Arin dismounted and lifted Kestrel off Javelin. She winced. She pretended it wasn't because of the touch of his hands but the sting when her cut feet, stuffed into fighting boots, reached the ground.

"Tell me," she said to Arin. "Tell me what happened at the ball."

His face was lit with firelight. The burning barracks of the city guard, though not close to the docks, had collapsed into an inferno. The sky around it had an ashy orange halo. "Ronan is fine," Arin said.

Kestrel's breath hitched—his phrasing of words could mean only one thing. "Jess."

"She's alive." Arin reached for Kestrel's bound hands.

She jerked away.

Arin paused, then glanced at the Herrani circling them, well within hearing. They regarded her with open hatred and him with suspicion. He grabbed her wrists and tightened the knots. "She's sick," he said curtly. "She drank some of the poisoned wine."

The words trembled through Kestrel, and as much as she told herself not to show anything to anyone, especially not to Arin, never him, she couldn't help that her voice sounded stricken. "Will she live?"

"I don't know."

Jess is not dead, Kestrel told herself. She will not die. "And Benix?"

Arin shook his head.

Kestrel remembered Benix turning away from her at the ball. The way he had lowered his eyes. But she also remembered his belly laugh, and knew she could have teased him into admitting his wrong. She could have told him that she understood how fragile one felt when stepping out of line and into society's glare. She could have, if death hadn't robbed the chance to mend their friendship.

She would not cry. Not again. "What of Captain Wensan?"

Arin frowned. "No more questions. You're strategizing now. You're no longer asking after friends, but stalling me or seeking an advantage I can't see. He was no one to you."

Kestrel opened her mouth, then closed it. She had her answer—and no desire to correct him or show anything more of herself.

"I don't have time to give you a list of the living and the dead, even if I had one," said Arin. He cast a quick glance at the armed Herrani, then flicked his hand in an order for them to follow. Those who hadn't already dismounted their horses did so now and moved toward the small building near the centermost docks, the one that housed the harbormaster. As they drew closer, Kestrel saw a new group of Herrani dressed in the clothes of dock slaves. They encircled the building. The only Valorians in sight lay dead on the ground.

"The harbormaster?" Arin asked a man who seemed to be this new group's leader.

"Inside," the Herrani said, "under guard." His gaze fell on Kestrel. "Tell me that's not who I think it is."

"She doesn't matter. She's under my authority, just as you

are." Arin shoved open the door, but not before Kestrel caught the defensive set to his mouth and the distaste on the other man's face. And while Kestrel had already known that the rumors about her and Arin must have been as disturbing to his people as to hers, only now did that knowledge take a shape that felt like a weapon.

Let the Herrani think she was Arin's lover. It would only make them doubt the intentions and loyalty of the man Cheat had called his second-in-command.

Kestrel followed Arin into the harbormaster's house on the pier.

It smelled of pitch and hemp, since the harbormaster sold goods as well as working as a kind of clerk, noting in his ledger which ships came and went, and were docked at each pier. The house was stocked with barrels of tar and coils of rope, and the shipyard smell was stronger than even that of the urine that stained the harbormaster's pants.

The Valorian was afraid. Although the last several hours had already shaken Kestrel's sense of what she had believed, this man's fear shook her yet again, for he was in his prime, he had trained as a soldier, his role on the docks was similar to that of a city guard. If he was afraid, what could that mean to the rule that a true Valorian never was?

How could the Valorians have been so easily surprised, so easily taken?

As she had been.

It was Arin. Arin, who had been a spy in the general's household. Arin, whose sharp mind had been whittling away at a secret plan, carving it with weapons made on the sly, with information she had let slip. Who had dismissed her concerns about the captain of the city guard's suicide, which could not have been a suicide but a murderous step toward revolution. Arin had waved away the oddity of Senator Andrax selling black powder to the eastern barbarians, and of course Arin had, for he had known that it had not been sold, but stolen by Herrani slaves.

Arin, who had set hooks into her heart and drawn her to him so that she wouldn't see anything but his eyes.

Arin was her enemy.

Any enemy should be watched. *Always identify your opponent's assets and weaknesses,* her father had said. Kestrel decided to be grateful for this moment, crammed into the harbormaster's house with twenty-some Herrani, and fifty more waiting outside. This was a chance to see whether Arin was as good a leader as a spy and a player at Bite and Sting.

And perhaps Kestrel could seize an opportunity to tip the odds in her favor.

"I want names," Arin told the harbormaster, "of all sailors ashore at the moment, and their ships."

The harbormaster gave them, voice trembling. Kestrel saw Arin rub his cheek, considering the man, surely thinking, as she thought, that any plan of Arin's to take or burn the ships would require as many people as possible. No one should be left on shore to guard the harbormaster, who was now useless.

Killing him was the obvious and quickest next step.

Arin hit the man's head with the side of his fist. It was a precise strike, aimed at the temple. The man slumped over his desk. His breath stirred the pages of his ledger.

"We have two choices," Arin told his people. "We've

done well up to this point. We've taken the city. Its leadership has been removed or is under our power. Now we need time, as much as possible before the empire learns what's happened. We have people guarding the mountain pass. The only other way to bring news to the empire is by sea. We take the ships, or we burn them. We must decide now.

"Either way, our approach is the same. Storm clouds are blowing in from the south. When they cover the moon, we'll row small launches in the darkness, hugging the bay's curve until we can come around the boats and approach their sterns. Each prow is pointed toward the city and its light. We'll be on the dark side of the open sea while the sailors gather at the bow, watching the city's fire. If we hope to seize all the ships, we split into two teams. One will start with the biggest and deadliest: Captain Wensan's. The other waits at the nearest largest ship. We take Wensan's ship, then turn its cannons on the second one, which will be overrun by the second group. With those two ships, we can force the surrender of the next nearest and largest and continue to shrink the possibility for the merchants to fight back. The fishermen have no cannons, so they'll be ours after the sea battle. We'll sink any ship that tries to flee the bay. Then we will not only buy the time we need, we will also have the ships as *our* weapons against the empire, as well as any goods they have on board."

Apparently Arin wasn't half as clever as Kestrel had thought, to discuss such a plan in front of *her*. Or he thought she could do no harm with the information. Maybe he didn't care what she heard. Still, it was a decent plan . . . except for one thing.

"*How* will we seize Wensan's ship?" a Herrani asked.

"We'll climb its hull ladder."

Kestrel laughed. "You'll be picked off one at a time by Wensan's crew as soon as they realize what's happening."

The room went still. Spines stiffened. Arin, who had been facing the Herrani, turned to stare at Kestrel. The look he gave her prickled the air between them like static.

"Then we'll pretend we're their Valorian sailors who have been on shore," he said, "and ask for our launches to be winched up to the deck from the water."

"Pretend to be Valorian? *That* will be believable."

"It will be dark. They won't see our faces, and we have the names of sailors on shore."

"And your accent?"

Arin didn't answer.

"I suppose you hope that the wind will blow your accent away," Kestrel said. "But maybe the sailors will still ask you for the code of the call. Maybe your little plan will be dead in the water, just like all of you."

There was silence.

"The code of the call," she repeated. "The password that any sane crew uses and shares with no one but themselves, in order to prevent people from attacking them as you so very foolishly hope to do."

"Kestrel, what are you doing?"

"Giving you some advice."

He made an impatient noise. "You want me to burn the ships."

"Do I? Is that what I want?"

"We'll be weaker against the empire without them."

She shrugged. "Even with them, you won't stand a chance."

Arin must have felt the mood in the room shift as Kestrel's words exposed what everyone should have known: that the Herrani revolution was a hopeless endeavor, one that would be crushed once imperial forces marched, as planned, through the mountain pass to replace the regiments sent east. They would lay siege to the city and send messengers for more troops. This time, when the Herrani lost, they would not be enslaved. They would be put to death.

"Start loading the launches with those barrels of pitch," Arin told the Herrani. "We'll use them to burn the ships."

"That won't be necessary," Kestrel said. "Not when I know Wensan's code of the call."

"You," Arin said. "*You* know it."

"I do."

She didn't. She had, however, a good guess. She had a limited range of possibilities—all the birds in "The Song of Death's Feathers"—and the memory of the way Captain Wensan had looked at the kestrel plate. She would have bet gold on which code he would have chosen for the evening of the ball. Kestrel could read an expression as if looking through shifting water to see the grainy bottom, the silt rising or settling, the dart of a fish. She had seen Wensan making his decision like she could see the suspicion in Arin's eyes now.

Her certainty wavered.

Arin. Didn't Arin disprove her ability to read others? For she had thought him truthful in the carriage. She had thought that his lips had moved against hers as if in prayer. But she had been wrong.

Arin tugged Kestrel out of the harbormaster's house. The door slamming shut behind them, Arin marched her to the far end of an empty pier. "I don't believe you," he said.

"I think you have had quite an intimate knowledge of my household. What's delivered, what letters leave. Who comes, who goes. I think you know that Captain Wensan dined at our house the night before this one."

"He was your father's friend," Arin said slowly.

"Whose ship brought my mother's piano from the capital when I was a child. He was always kind to me. And now he's dead. Isn't he?"

Arin didn't deny it.

The moonlight was dimming, but Kestrel knew that Arin could see the sorrow seep into her face.

Let him see it. It served her purposes. "I know the password," she said.

"You would never reveal it." Clouds blotted the moon, casting Arin's features into shadow. "You're taunting me. You want me to hate myself for what I've done. You will never forgive me, and you certainly won't *help* me."

"You have something I want."

The cold dark seemed to pour around them.

"I doubt it," Arin said.

"I want Jess. I will help you seize the ships, and you will give her to me."

The truth can deceive as well as a lie. Kestrel *did* want to barter for the chance to help Jess, or at least be by her side if death came. Yet Kestrel also counted on this truth to be so believable that Arin wouldn't see that it disguised something else: that she needed at least one fishing boat to remain in the harbor.

"I can't just *give* her to you," Arin said. "Cheat will decide what happens to the survivors."

"Ah, but you seem to be entitled to special privileges. If you can claim one girl, why not two?"

His mouth twisted in what looked like disgust. "I'll arrange for you to see her as soon as I can. Will you trust my word?"

"I have little choice. Now, to the purpose. You told Cheat that you went to the ball to collect information from the harbormaster's slave. You will share that information with me."

"That's not why I went to the ball."

"What?"

"There is no information. I lied."

Kestrel raised one brow. "How very surprising. Didn't you just make a promise and ask me to trust your word? Really, Arin. You must sort out your lies and your truths or even you won't know which is which."

Silence. Had she wounded him? She hoped so.

"Your plan to seize the ships is solid enough," she said, "but you'll need to finesse a few important details." She told him what she had in mind. She wondered if Arin knew that accepting her help would increase his people's suspicion that they were lovers, that he was collaborating with a Valorian who didn't necessarily have their best interests at heart. She wondered if he knew that if he achieved his objective tonight, the winning would be undermined by the way he had won it.

Arin probably did. He must know that there was no such thing as a clear win.

But Kestrel doubted that he would guess that Captain Wensan had taught her how to sail. Even if Arin somehow knew that she could, she thought his mind was too occupied to notice that a fishing boat was her best chance of escape to the capital.

When she saw the opportunity to flee, she would take it. She would bring the hounds of the empire howling down on this city.

ARIN HAD WORKED ON THE HARBOR BEFORE.
He'd been sold out of the quarry into another forge, and
when his second blacksmith master had died, Arin was part
of the goods divided by the heirs. His name was still listed
as Smith, but he had hidden the skills of that trade from his
new owners and was sold at a loss to the shipyards. He had
never sailed, yet he knew a Herrani ship when he saw it. He
had dry-docked them along with other slaves, had hauled
on ropes to tip the massive things onto their sides at low
tide. Then he had waded in the mud to scrape the hardened
sea life off the hull, shards of barnacles flaking around him,
cutting skin, hatching thin red lines. He remembered the
taste of sweat in his mouth, water oozing up his calves, and
everything quick, so quick, so that the slaves could drag on
the pulleys and flip the boat again and clean its other side
before the tide rose.

Then the Valorians would take their stolen ship and sail
away.

As he rowed the launch toward Wensan's ship, which

was Herrani-made and studded with Valorian cannon, Arin remembered the exhaustion of that work, but also how it had corded his muscles until the ache in his arms became stone. He was grateful to the Valorians for having made him strong. If he was strong enough, he might live through this night. If he lived, he could reclaim the shreds of who he had been, and explain himself to Kestrel in a way she would understand.

She sat silent next to him in the launch. The other Herrani at the oars watched as she lifted her bound hands to tug at the black cloth covering her hair. It was an awkward business. It was also necessary, since a new twist in the plan called for Kestrel to be seen and recognized.

The Herrani watched her struggle. They watched Arin drop an oar in its lock to offer a hand. She flinched hard enough that her shifted weight shook the boat. It was only a slight tremor along wood, but they all felt it.

Shame ate into his gut.

Kestrel pulled the cloth from her head. Even though clouds swelled in the sky, swallowing the moon and deepening the dark around them, Kestrel's hair and pale skin seemed to glow. It looked like she was lit from within.

It wasn't something Arin could bear to see. He returned to the oars and rowed.

Arin knew, far better than any of the ten Herrani in the launch, that Kestrel could be devious. That he shouldn't trust her plan any more than he should have fallen for her ploys at Bite and Sting, or followed her blindly into the trap she had set and sprung for him the morning of the duel.

Her plan to seize the ship was sound. Their best option. Still, he kept examining it like he might a horse's hoof, tapping the surface for a flaw, a dangerous split.

He couldn't see it. He thought that there must be one, then realized that the flaw he sensed lay inside him. Tonight had cracked Arin open. It had brought the battle inside him to a boiling war.

Of course he was certain that something was wrong.

Impossible. It was impossible to love a Valorian and also love his people.

Arin was the flaw.

Kestrel watched the other four launches slip along the inky water. Two drew alongside Wensan's ship and paused by the hull ladder, hidden by the dark and the angle of the hull as it sloped inward from the broad main deck to the ship's narrow section at the waterline. To see those launches, sailors on the main deck would have to hang over the sides.

The sailors raised no cry of alarm.

Two more launches approached the next largest ship, a two-master with one row of cannons, a clear second player to Wensan's three-masted ship with double gun decks.

The Herrani glanced at Arin. He nodded, and they began to row with no interest in stealth, only speed. Oars rattled in their locks, dunked and splashed and swept in the water. When the launch reached Wensan's ship, sailors were already ringing the rail, looking far below at them. Their faces were blurs in the dark.

Kestrel stood. "Riot in the city!" she called to sailors, stating what they could no doubt see for themselves beyond the harbor and the city walls. "Bring us aboard!"

"You're none of ours," a voice floated down from the main deck.

"I'm a friend of Captain Wensan's: Kestrel, General Trajan's daughter. The captain sent me along with your crew for my protection."

"Where's the captain?"

"I don't know. We were separated in the city."

"Who's there with you?"

"Terex," called Arin, careful to roll the *r*. One by one, the Herrani in the launch shouted names given by the harbormaster of the ship's missing sailors. They said them quickly, some swallowing syllables, but each gave a passable version of the pronunciations Kestrel had drilled into them when they had first left shore.

The sailor spoke again: "What's the code of the call?"

"I am," Kestrel said with all the confidence she didn't feel. "My name: Kestrel."

A pause. A few sharp seconds during which Kestrel hoped she was right, hoped she was wrong, and hated herself for what she was doing.

A clank. A metallic unwinding.

Hooked pulleys were being lowered from the main deck. There was an eager clatter as Herrani attached them to the launch.

Arin, however, did not move. He stared at Kestrel. Perhaps he hadn't been convinced that she had known the password. Or perhaps he couldn't believe she would betray her own kind.

Kestrel looked at him as if looking through a window. What he thought didn't matter. Not anymore.

The roped pulleys creaked. The launch was lifted dripping out of the water. It jerked and swayed as sailors on board hauled on the ropes. Then it began to climb.

Kestrel couldn't see the hull ladder along the stern or the Herrani in the other launches on the water below. They were vague, night-colored shadows. But she noticed a ripple of movement up the hull. Herrani were scaling the ladder.

It wasn't too late for her to cry warning to the sailors on board.

She could choose not to betray them. She didn't understand how her father could do this again and again: make decisions that fed lives into the jaws of a higher purpose.

Yet would it be worth it, if Kestrel secured an escape route to alert the capital?

That, she supposed, might depend on how many Valorians died on Wensan's ship.

Kestrel's cool calculation appalled her. This was part of what had made her resist the military: the fact that she *could* make decisions like this, that she *did* have a mind for strategy, that people could so easily become pieces in a game she was determined to win.

The launch swayed higher.

Kestrel pressed her lips shut.

Arin glanced at the black cloth that had covered her hair, then at her. He must have considered gagging Kestrel with it, now that she had completed her role in the plan. That's what she would have done in his place. But he didn't, which made her feel worse than if he had. It was pure hypocrisy for him not to live up to a ruthlessness she now knew him to be capable of.

As was she.

The launch drew level with the main deck. Kestrel had just enough time to register the shock on the sailors' faces before the Herrani in the launch leaped onto the deck, weapons raised. The small boat rocked wildly, empty save for Kestrel.

Arin ducked the slice of a sailor's knife, beat it away with his own, and punched the man's throat. The sailor staggered back. Arin hooked the legs out from under him at the same moment he delivered another blow. The sailor was down.

It was like that all over the deck. Herrani hammered at Valorians, many of whom had had no time to draw weapons. As the sailors dealt with the sudden threat they had brought aboard, they didn't see the second one: more Herrani climbing onto the deck from the hull ladder. As Kestrel had planned, this second wave attacked the Valorians from the back. Trapped, the sailors quickly surrendered. Even though more sailors were pouring up from the decks below, they did so through narrow hatches, like mice emerging from tunnels. The Herrani attacked them one by one.

Blood stained the planks. Many of the fallen sailors didn't move. From the swaying launch, Kestrel could hear the man Arin had attacked first. He was clutching his throat. The noises he made were horrible, something between gasping and choking. And there was Arin, shouldering through the fray and landing blows that might not kill, but would still hurt and bruise and bleed.

Kestrel had seen this in him on the day that she had bought him. A brutality. She had let herself forget it because his mind had been so finely tuned. Because his touch had been gentle. Yet this was what he had become.

This was what he *was*.

And what of her, orchestrating the fall of a Valorian ship into enemy hands? Kestrel couldn't quite believe it. She couldn't believe it had been so relatively *easy*. Valorians were never ambushed. They never surrendered. They were brave, they were fierce, they would rather die than be taken.

Her launch swayed to a stop. She stood and faced the water far below. Earlier that night, when she had threatened to kill herself, she had said it without considering whether she could. Making the threat had been the right move. So she had made it.

Then Cheat had set his boot on Kestrel's fingers.

There was no music after death.

She had chosen to live.

Now she stood in the launch, knowing that if she hit the water's surface from this height, something was likely to break and she would sink quickly without the use of her bound hands.

What would Kestrel's father choose for her? An honorable death, or life as Arin's prize? She closed her eyes, imagining the general's face if he had seen her surrender to Cheat, if he could see her now.

Could she really find a way to sail to the capital? Was

it worth it to stay alive to see Jess, if only to watch her friend die?

Kestrel listened to the slap of waves against the ship, the cries of struggle and death. She remembered how her heart, so tight, like a scroll, had opened when Arin kissed her. It had unfurled.

If her heart were truly a scroll, she could burn it. It would become a tunnel of flame, a handful of ash. The secrets she had written inside herself would be gone. No one would know.

Her father would choose the water for Kestrel if he knew.

Yet she couldn't. In the end, it wasn't cunning that kept her from jumping, or determination. It was a glassy fear.

She didn't want to die. Arin was right. She played a game until its end.

Suddenly, Kestrel heard his voice. She opened her eyes. He was shouting. He was shouting her name. He was barreling past people, driving a path between the mainmast and the railing alongside the launch. Kestrel saw the horror in him mirror what she had felt when facing the water.

Kestrel gathered the strength in her legs and jumped onto the deck.

Her feet hit the planks, the force of movement toppling her. But she had learned from fighting Rax how to protect her hands. She tucked them to her, pressed the hard knots of her bonds against her chest, fell shoulder first, and rolled.

Arin hauled her to her feet. And even though he had seen her choice, must have seen it still blazing on her face, he shook her. He kept saying the words he had been shouting as he had neared the railing. "Don't, Kestrel. Don't."

His hands cradled her face.

"Don't touch me," she said.

Arin's hands fell. "Gods," he said hoarsely.

"Yes, it would be rather unfortunate for you, wouldn't it, if you lost your little bargaining chip against the general? Never fear." She smiled a brittle smile. "It turns out that I am a coward."

Arin shook his head. "It's harder to live."

Yes. It was. Kestrel had known there would be no escape tonight, and probably not for some time to come.

Her plan had worked brilliantly. Even now, the seized ship was turning its cannons on the two-master where more Herrani waited, ready to pounce on the sailors once they were distracted by the surprise of cannon fire. After that vessel fell into Arin's hands, the others in the harbor would fall, too.

It began to rain. A fine, icy spray. Kestrel didn't shiver, though she knew she should, from apprehension if not from cold. She had chosen to live, and so should be afraid of what living in this new world would mean.

KESTREL WAS TAKEN DOWN THE RECEPTION
hall of Irex's home—no, Arin's. Valorian weapons winked
at her from their mounts on the walls, asking why she didn't
knock her nearest guard off balance and seize the hilt of a
blade. Even with hands bound, she could do damage.

Arin had been the first into the house. He strode ahead
of her, back turned. He moved so eagerly that his emotion
was obvious. He would be easy to surprise. A dagger between
the shoulder blades.

Yet Kestrel made no move.

She had a plan, she told herself, one that didn't include
her death, which was the logical course of events should she
kill Arin.

The Herrani pushed her down the hall.

A dark-haired young woman was waiting in the atrium
by the fountain. When she saw Arin, her face filled with
light and tears. He almost ran across the short space between
them to gather her in his arms.

"Sister or lover?" Kestrel said.

The woman looked up from their embrace. Her expression hardened. She stepped away from Arin. "What?"

"Are you his sister or lover?"

She walked up to Kestrel and slapped her across the face.

"Sarsine!" Arin hauled her back.

"His sister is dead," Sarsine said, "and I hope you suffer as much as she did."

Kestrel's fingers went to her cheek to press against the sting—and cover a smile with the heels of her tied hands. She remembered the bruises on Arin when she had bought him. His surly defiance. She had always wondered why slaves brought punishment upon themselves. But it had been sweet to feel a tipping of power, however slight, when that hand had cracked across her face. To know, despite the pain, that for a moment Kestrel had been the one in control.

"Sarsine is my cousin," Arin said. "I haven't seen her in years. After the war, she was sold as a house slave. I was a laborer, so—"

"I don't care," Kestrel said.

His shadowed eyes met hers. They were the color of the winter sea—the water far below Kestrel's feet when she had looked down and imagined what it would be like to drown.

He broke the gaze between them. To his cousin he said, "I need you to be her keeper. Escort her to the east wing, let her have the run of the suite—"

"Arin! Have you lost your mind?"

"Remove anything that could be a weapon. Keep the outermost door locked at all times. See that she wants for nothing, but remember that she is a prisoner."

"In the *east wing*." Sarsine's voice was thick with disgust.

"She's the general's daughter."

"Oh, I know."

"A political prisoner," Arin said. "We must be better than the Valorians. We are more than savages."

"Do you truly think that keeping your clipped bird in a luxurious cage will change how the Valorians see us?"

"It will change how we see ourselves."

"No, Arin. It will change how everyone sees *you*."

He shook his head. "She's mine to do with as I see fit."

There was an uneasy rustle among the Herrani. Kestrel's heart sickened. She kept trying to forget this: the question of what it meant to belong to Arin. He reached for her, pulling her firmly toward him as her boots dragged and squeaked against the tiles. With the flick of a knife, he cut the bonds at her wrists, and the sound of leather hitting the floor was loud in the atrium's acoustics—almost as loud as Sarsine's choked protest.

Arin let Kestrel go. "Please, Sarsine. Take her."

His cousin stared at him. Eventually, she nodded, but her expression made clear that she thought he was indulging in something disastrous. "Follow me," she told Kestrel, and led the way from the atrium.

They had not gone far before Kestrel realized that Arin must have returned to the reception hall. She heard the sound of weapons ripped off walls and flung to the floor.

The harsh noise echoed throughout the house.

Rooms radiated from the suite's center: the bedroom, an utterly quiet space lit with gray as the coming dawn filtered through the windows. The suite was elegant the way a pearl is: smooth and pure. Its colors were muted, though Kestrel knew, from what Arin had once said long ago, that they had meaning. Despite its ornate Valorian furniture, this had been the suite of an aristocratic Herrani woman.

Sarsine said nothing, only lifted the apron of her house uniform so that it made a cradle. She began filling it with mirrors, a candle snuffer, a heavy marble inkpot . . . objects bulged the cloth and threatened to rip through.

"Fetch a basket," Kestrel said, "or a trunk."

Sarsine glared, because they both knew she would have to do just that. There were too many things in the suite that could become weapons in the right hands. Kestrel hated to see them leave, but was glad that when they did, at least it would feel as if she had given an order and Sarsine had obeyed.

But Sarsine went to the outermost door and called for assistance. Soon, Herrani were trooping in and out of the rooms, carrying fireplace pokers. A copper pitcher. A clock with pointed hour and minute hands.

Kestrel watched it all go. Apparently, Sarsine could see almost as many threats in everyday objects as Kestrel did. No matter. Kestrel could always unscrew a leg from one of the tables.

But she would need more than a weapon to escape. The suite was too high to jump from a window to the ground. Only one room, and one door, led to the rest of the house—and it seemed to have a very solid-looking lock.

When the Herrani had filed out, leaving Sarsine alone with her, Kestrel said, "Wait."

Sarsine didn't lower the thick key in her hand.

"I'm supposed to see my friend," Kestrel said.

"Your days of social calls are over."

"Arin promised." A lump rose in Kestrel's throat. "My friend is ill. Arin said that I could see her."

"He didn't mention that to me."

Sarsine pulled the outermost door shut behind her, and Kestrel didn't beg. She didn't want to give her the satisfaction of knowing how much it hurt to hear the key grate in the lock, and to hear the bolt thud home.

"Just what do you think you're doing, Arin?"

He looked up at Sarsine, blearily rubbing his eyes. He had fallen asleep in a chair. It was full morning. "I couldn't sleep in my old rooms. At least here, in Etta's suite—"

"I'm not talking about your choice of bedchamber, though I can't help but notice how *conveniently* close it is to the east wing."

Arin winced. There was usually only one reason why a man kept a conquered woman prisoner after a battle. "This isn't what it seems."

"Oh, no? Too many people heard you call her a spoil of war."

"It's not true."

Sarsine threw her hands up in the air. "Then why did you say it?"

"Because I couldn't think of any other way to save her!"

Sarsine stood still. Then she leaned over him and shook his shoulder as if waking him from a nightmare. "You? Save a *Valorian*?"

Arin captured her hand. "Please listen to me."

"I will when you say something I can understand."

"I did your lessons for you, when we were children."

"So?"

"I told Anireh to shut up when she made fun of your nose. Do you remember? She pushed me down."

"Your sister was too beautiful for her own good. But all this was long ago. What's your point?"

Arin held both her hands now. "We share something, and probably not for very long. The Valorians will come. There will be a siege." He groped for what to say. "By the gods, just listen."

"Oh, Arin. Haven't you learned? The gods won't hear you." She sighed. "But I will."

He told her about the day he had been sold to Kestrel, and every day since. He held nothing back.

When he finished, Sarsine's expression had changed. "You're still a fool," she said, but gently.

"I am," he whispered.

"What do you plan to do with her?"

Arin tilted his head helplessly against the carved back of his father's chair. "I don't know."

"She demanded to see a sick friend. Said you made her a promise."

"Yes, but I can't do it."

"Why not?"

"Kestrel hates me, but she still speaks to me. Once she sees Jess . . . she'll never do that again."

Kestrel sat in the sunroom. It was warm, filled with potted plants and their mineral, almost milky fragrance. The sun was already high above the skylight. It had burned through the ripples of rain left on the glass from the night's storm, which had drummed out the fire in the city. From the southernmost window, Kestrel had watched the flames fade.

It had been a long night, a long morning. But Kestrel didn't want to sleep.

Her eyes fell on a plant. The Herrani word for it was damselthorn. It was large and thick-stemmed, at least as old as the war. It had leaves that looked like flowers, because their green became a brilliant red in the sun.

Despite herself, Kestrel thought of Arin's kiss. How it had flared a light inside her, and transformed her from plain leaf into fire.

Kestrel opened the sunroom door and stepped into a high-walled rooftop garden. She breathed the chilled air. Everything was dead here. Fans of brown leaves. Stems that would snap as soon as touched. Stones lay strewn in artful patterns on the ground, in gray, blue, and white, the shape of birds' eggs.

She passed her hands over the cold walls. There were no rough edges, nothing that might give her fingers or toes purchase. She couldn't climb. There was a door set into the far wall, but where it led Kestrel would probably never know. It was locked.

Kestrel stood, considering. She bit her lips hard. Then she walked back into the sunroom and brought out the damselthorn.

She smashed the pot on the stones.

The day aged. Kestrel watched the light outside yellow. Sarsine came and saw the wreckage of plants in the garden. She gathered the ceramic shards, then had a group of Herrani search the suite for more.

Kestrel had made certain to hide some wicked-looking shards in places where they would be found. But the best— one that could cut a throat as easily as a knife—she had hung outside from the window. She had tied it with a strip of cloth, dangled it into the thick evergreen ivy that climbed the walls outside the bathing room, and closed the window on the strip's edge, securing it between the frame and the sill.

It wasn't discovered, and Kestrel was left alone again.

Her eyes itched and her bones turned to lead, yet she refused to sleep.

Finally she did something she had been dreading. She tried to unbraid her hair. She yanked at the plaits, swore as they snarled into knots. The pain kept her awake.

So did the shame. She remembered Arin's hands sinking into her hair, the brush of a fingertip against the hollow behind her ear.

Sarsine returned.

"Bring me scissors," Kestrel said.

"You know I won't do that."

"Because you're afraid I'll kill you with them?"

The woman didn't answer. Kestrel glanced at her, surprised at the silence and the way Sarsine's face had become thoughtful, curious.

"Cut it off then," Kestrel said. She would have done it

herself with the makeshift dagger hiding in the ivy if it wouldn't have raised questions.

"You might regret cutting your hair, a society lady like you."

Kestrel felt another wave of tiredness. "Please," she said. "I can't bear it."

Arin's sleep was fitful, and when he woke he was disoriented to be in his father's rooms. But happy, in spite of everything, to be there. Maybe it was the happiness, and not the place, that was disorienting. It was an unfamiliar feeling. Old and somewhat stiff, as if its joints ached when it moved.

He passed a hand across his face and got to his feet. He had to leave. Cheat wouldn't begrudge Arin his homecoming, but plans had to be made.

He was walking down the stairs of the west wing when he saw Sarsine on the floor below. She was coming from the east wing, a basket in her arms. He stopped.

It looked like she held a basketful of woven gold.

Arin leaped down the stairs. He strode up to his cousin and seized her arm.

"Arin!"

"What did you *do*?"

Sarsine jerked away. "What she wanted. Pull yourself together."

But Arin saw Kestrel as she had been last night before the ball. How her hair had been a spill of low light over his palms. He had threaded desire into the braids, had wanted her to sense it even as he dreaded that she would. He had met her eyes in the mirror and didn't know, couldn't tell, her feelings. He only knew the fire of his own.

"It's just hair," Sarsine said. "It will grow back."

"Yes," said Arin, "but not everything does."

Afternoon tipped toward evening. It was almost one full day since the Firstwinter ball, and more since Kestrel had slept. She stayed awake, staring at the outermost door to her rooms.

Arin opened it. Then he stepped back, inhaling as if she had frightened him. His hand tightened on the doorjamb, and he stared. Yet he said nothing of the fact that she still wore her black dueling uniform. He didn't mention the jagged ends of hair brushing her shoulders.

"You need to come with me," he said.

"To see Jess?"

His mouth thinned. "No."

"You said you would take me. Apparently there *is* no such thing as Herrani honor."

"I will as soon as I can. Right now, I can't."

"When?"

"Kestrel, Cheat is here. He wants to see you."

Her hands curled shut.

Arin said, "I can't say no."

"Because you're a coward."

"Because if I do, things will go worse for you."

Kestrel lifted her chin. "I will come," she said, "if

you never again pretend that anything you do is on my behalf."

Arin didn't comment on the obvious: that she had no choice in the matter. He simply nodded. "Be careful," he said.

Cheat wore a Valorian jacket Kestrel was sure she had seen on the governor the night before. He sat at the right hand of the empty head of the dining table, but stood when Kestrel and Arin entered. He approached.

His eyes dragged over her. "Arin, your slave looks positively wild."

Lack of sleep made her thoughts broken and shiny, like pieces of mirrors on strings. Cheat's words spun in her head. Arin tensed beside her.

"No offense," Cheat told him. "It was a compliment to your taste."

"What do you want, Cheat?" Arin said.

The man stroked a thumb over his lower lip. "Wine." He looked straight at Kestrel. "Get some."

The order itself wasn't important. It was how Cheat had meant it: as the first of many, and how, in the end, they translated into one word: obey.

The only thing that kept Kestrel's face clean of her thoughts was the knowledge that Cheat would take pleasure in any resistance. Yet she couldn't make herself move.

"I'll get the wine," Arin said.

"No," Kestrel said. She didn't want to be left alone with Cheat. "I'll go."

For an uncertain moment, Arin stood awkwardly. Then

he walked to the door and motioned a Herrani girl into the room. "Please escort Kestrel to the wine cellar, then bring her back here."

"Choose a good vintage," Cheat said to Kestrel. "You'll know the best."

As she left the room, his eyes followed her, glittering.

She returned with a clearly labeled bottle of Valorian wine dated to the year of the Herran War. She placed it on the table in front of the two seated men. Arin's jaw set, and he shook his head slightly. Cheat lost his grin.

"This was the best," Kestrel said.

"Pour." Cheat shoved his glass toward her. She uncorked the bottle and poured—and kept pouring, even as the red wine flowed over the glass's rim, across the table, and onto Cheat's lap.

He jumped to his feet, swatting wine from his fine stolen clothes. "Damn you!"

"You said I should pour. You didn't say I should stop."

Kestrel wasn't sure what would have happened next if Arin hadn't intervened. "Cheat," he said, "I'm going to have to ask you to stop playing games with what is mine."

It was almost alarming how quickly Cheat's rage vanished. Revealing a simple tunic beneath, he stripped off the spattered jacket and used it to mop up wine. "Plenty more clothes where this came from." He tossed the jacket aside. "Especially with so many dead. Why don't we get down to business?"

"I would be grateful if you did," said Arin.

"Listen to him," Cheat said to Kestrel in a friendly tone. "So quick to slip back into his high-class ways. Arin was never a commoner, even when breaking rock. Not like me." When Kestrel was silent, Cheat said, "I have a small task for you, my girl. I want you to write a letter to your father."

"I assume that I'm to tell him that all is well, so that you can keep the secret of your revolution as long as possible."

"You should be glad. Such letters of misinformation are keeping Valorians like you alive. If you want to live, you must be good for something. Though I get the sense that you're not interested in being good. Remember, you don't need all of your fingers to write a letter. Probably three on one hand will do."

Arin's breath was a hiss.

"And stain the pages with my blood?" Kestrel said coolly. "I doubt that will convince the general that I'm in good health." When Cheat started to reply, Kestrel cut him off. "Yes, I'm sure you have a long list of inventive threats you'd enjoy making. Don't bother. I'll write the letter."

"No," said Arin. "You'll *transcribe* it. I'll dictate. Otherwise, you'll find a way to warn him through code."

Kestrel's heart sank. That had, in fact, been her plan.

Paper and ink were set before her.

Arin said, "Dear Father."

Her pen wavered. She held her breath against a sudden pain in her throat. But it was for the best if the inked letters sloped and wobbled, she decided. Her father might see the distress in her handwriting.

"The ball went better than expected," Arin continued. "Ronan has asked me to marry him, and I have accepted." He paused. "This news must disappoint you, but you will have to bring glory to the empire's army for both of us. I know you will. I also know that you cannot be surprised. I made clear to you my wishes regarding a military life. And Ronan's affection has been clear for some time."

Kestrel lifted her pen, wondering when Arin had become aware of something she had refused to see for so long. Where was Ronan now? Did he despise her as much as she did herself?

"Be happy for me," Arin said. It took her a moment to realize that these words were meant for the page. "Now sign."

It was exactly the kind of letter Kestrel would have written in normal circumstances. She felt how deeply she had failed her father. Arin understood her heart, her thoughts, the very way she would speak to someone she loved. And she didn't know him at all.

Arin took the letter and studied it. "Again. Neatly this time."

She wrote several copies before he was satisfied. The final letter was in a firm hand.

"Good," Cheat said. "One last thing."

Kestrel rubbed tiredly at the ink on her skin. She could have slept then. She wanted to. Sleep was blind, it was deaf, and it would take her away from this room and these men.

Cheat said, "Tell us how long we have before the reinforcements come."

"No."

"Now might be the time when I start making my inventive threats."

"Kestrel will tell us," Arin said. "She'll see the wisdom of it."

Cheat raised his brows.

"She'll tell us once she sees what we can do to her people." Arin's expression was trying to tell her something his words didn't. Kestrel focused, and realized she had seen this look in his eyes before. It was the careful gleam of Arin striking a bargain. "I'm going to take her to the governor's palace, where she'll see the dead and the dying. She will see her friends."

Jess.

"DON'T PROVOKE CHEAT," ARIN SAID AS THEY stepped out of the carriage and onto the dusky path that led to the governor's palace, which looked eerie to Kestrel because its impressive façade was the same as the night before, but the lights burning in the windows were now few.

"Kestrel, do you hear me? You can't toy with him."

"He started it."

"That's not the point." Gravel crunched under Arin's heavy boots as he stalked up the path. "Don't you understand that he wants you dead? He'd leap at the chance," Arin said, hands in pockets, head down, almost talking to himself. He strode ahead, his long legs quicker than hers. "I can't—Kestrel, you must understand that I would never claim you. Calling you a prize—my prize—it was only words. But it worked. Cheat won't harm you, I swear that he won't, but you must . . . hide yourself a little. Help a little. Just tell us how much time we have before the battle. Give him a reason to decide you're not better off dead. Swallow your pride."

"Maybe that's not as easy for me as it is for you."

He wheeled on her. "It's not easy for me," he said through his teeth. "You know that it's not. What do you think *I* have had to swallow, these past ten years? What do you think *I* have had to do to survive?"

They stood before the palace door. "Truly," she said, "I haven't the faintest interest. You may tell your sad story to someone else."

He flinched as if slapped. His voice came low: "You can make people feel so small."

Kestrel went hot with shame—then was ashamed of her own shame. Who was he, that *she* should apologize? He had used her. He had lied. Nothing he said meant anything. If she was to feel shame, it should be for having been so easily fooled.

He ran fingers through his cropped hair, but slowly, anger gone, replaced by something heavier. He didn't look at her. His breath smoked the chill air. "Do what you want to me. Say anything. But it frightens me how you refuse to see the danger you risk with others. Maybe now you'll see." He opened the door to the governor's home.

The smell struck her first. Blood and decaying flesh. It pushed at Kestrel's gut. She fought not to gag.

Bodies were piled in the reception hall. Lady Neril was lying facedown, almost in the same place where she had stood the night of the ball, greeting guests. Kestrel recognized her by the scarf in her fist, fabric bright in the guttering torchlight. There were hundreds of dead. She saw Captain Wensan, Lady Faris, Senator Nicon's whole family, Benix . . .

Kestrel knelt next to him. His large hand felt like cold

clay. She could hear her tears drip to his clothes. They beaded on his skin.

Quietly, Arin said, "He'll be buried today, with the others."

"He should be burned. We burn our dead." She couldn't look at Benix anymore, but neither could she get to her feet.

Arin helped her, his touch gentle. "I'll make certain it's done right."

Kestrel forced her legs to move, to walk past bodies heaped like rubble. She thought that she must have fallen asleep after all, and that this was an evil dream.

She paused at the sight of Irex. His mouth was the stained purple of the poisoned, but he had sticky gashes in his side, and one final cut to the neck. Even poisoned, he had fought.

Tears came again.

Arin's hold tightened. He pushed her past Irex. "Don't you dare weep for him. If he weren't dead, I would kill him myself."

The sick were laid out on the ballroom floor. The smell was worse here: of vomit and the tang of human waste. Herrani moved among the pallets, wiping faces with wet cloths, carrying away bedpans, and it was strange to see them still acting like slaves, to see pity in their eyes, and to know that it was only pity that made them care for people they themselves had tried to destroy.

A Herrani glanced up, registered Kestrel's presence, and began asking Arin questions, but Kestrel didn't hear. She left his side. She stumbled in her haste, searching among the pallets, looking for wide brown eyes, a snub nose, a small mouth.

Kestrel almost didn't recognize her. Jess's lips were violet, her eyelids swollen shut. She was still wearing her ball gown, an airy green confection that looked horribly wrong on her now.

"Jess," Kestrel said. "Jess."

The girl's breath hitched, then changed to a wheeze. It was the only sign she gave of consciousness.

Kestrel sought Arin. He was standing against the far wall. He wouldn't meet her gaze.

She strode to him. Grabbed him. Pulled him toward her friend.

"What is this?" she demanded. "What poison did you use?"

"*I* didn't—"

"It was something you'd have easy access to, in the countryside, maybe. A plant?"

"Kestrel—"

"You could have harvested it months ago, let it dry, then powdered it. It had to be colorless, to mix with the iced wine." Kestrel raced through memories of everything Enai had ever told her about local plants. "Simberry? No, it couldn't have worked so quickly—"

"It was nightlock."

"I don't know what that is."

"A spring root, sun-dried, then ground."

"So there's an antidote," Kestrel insisted, though Arin had indicated nothing of the kind.

He took some time to answer. "No."

"Yes, there is! The Herrani were the best doctors in the world. You would never have let a poison exist without finding a cure for it."

"There's no antidote . . . only something that might help."

"Then you should be *giving* it to them!"

He turned her shoulders so that she couldn't see the rows of pallets. "We don't have it. No one planned for survivors. The herb we'd need should have been gathered in the fall. It's winter. There will be none left."

"Yes, there will. There's been no snow yet. No frost. Most plants don't die until the first frost. Enai said so."

"True, but—"

"You will find it."

Arin was silent.

"Help her." Kestrel's voice broke. "Please."

"It's a delicate plant. They might have all died in the cold, and I'm not sure I'll be able—"

"Promise me you'll look," Kestrel said, as if she had not sworn that his promises were worth nothing.

"I will," he said. "I promise."

He insisted on taking her to his house first.

"I can go with you into the mountains," she said. "I can search, too."

His smile was dry. "You're not the one who spent hours as a child poring over botany books, wondering why one species of tree had four-fingered leaves, and another, six."

The swaying of the carriage made Kestrel drowsy. Hours of lost sleep weighted her eyelids. She struggled to keep them open. Outside the window, dusk had given in to the night.

"You have less than three days," she murmured.

"What?"

"Before the reinforcements arrive."

When he said nothing, Kestrel voiced what he must be thinking. "I suppose it's not the time for you to be hunting in the mountains for a plant."

"I promised I would go. So I will."

Kestrel's eyes slipped shut. She faded in and out of sleep. When Arin spoke again, she wasn't sure whether he expected her to hear him.

"I remember sitting with my mother in a carriage." There was a long pause. Then Arin's voice came again in that slow, fluid way that showed the singer in him. "In my memory, I am small and sleepy, and she is doing something strange. Every time the carriage turns into the sun, she raises her hand as if reaching for something. The light lines her fingers with fire. Then the carriage passes through shadows, and her hand falls. Again sunlight beams through the window, and again her hand lifts. It becomes an eclipse."

Kestrel listened, and it was as if the story itself was an eclipse, drawing its darkness over her.

"Just before I fell asleep," he said, "I realized that she was shading my eyes from the sun."

She heard Arin shift, felt him look at her.

"Kestrel." She imagined how he would sit, lean forward. How he would look in the glow of the carriage lantern. "Survival isn't wrong. You can sell your honor in small ways, so long as you guard *yourself.* You can pour a glass of wine like it's meant to be poured, and watch a man drink, and plot your revenge." Perhaps his head tilted slightly at this. "You probably plot even in your sleep."

There was a silence as long as a smile.

"Plot away, Kestrel. Survive. If I hadn't lived, no one would remember my mother, not like I do."

Kestrel could no longer deny sleep. It pulled her under.

"And I would never have met you."

Kestrel was dimly aware of being lifted. She wound her arms around someone's neck, buried her head against his shoulder. She heard a sigh, and wasn't sure if it was hers or his.

There was the rocking motion of being carried upstairs. She was settled onto something soft. Shoes were pulled from her feet. A thick blanket drew up to her chin, and someone murmured the Herrani blessing for dreams. Enai? Kestrel frowned. No, the voice was all wrong for Enai, but who would say those words, if not her nurse?

Then the palm on her forehead was gone. Kestrel decided she would solve the puzzle later.

She slept.

The horse slipped on a scree of small rocks. Arin kept his seat as the animal floundered, then splayed its hooves and caught its balance.

Things would be even worse, Arin thought grimly, when he had to ride down instead of up the path. He had been searching for almost a full day. The little hope he'd had of finding the plant dwindled.

Finally, he dismounted. The mountain was a barren gray-brown, no trees, and he could see, up ahead, the treacherous gash the Valorians had poured through ten years ago. He saw a shimmer of metal. The weapon of a Herrani, clothes camouflaged as he or she—along with several others— guarded the pass.

Arin slipped behind an outcropping of rock, pulling his horse after him. He wedged the reins in a crack between two boulders. Arin shouldn't be seen—and neither should his horse.

He ought to be up there, guarding the pass, or at least striving in some way to keep his country.

His. The thought never failed to thrill him. It was worth death. Worth almost anything to become again the person he had been before the Herran War. Yet here he was, gambling the frail odds of success.

Looking for a *plant.*

He imagined Cheat's reaction if he could see him now, scouring the ground for a wrinkle of faded green. There would be mockery, which Arin could shrug off, and rage, which Arin could withstand—even understand. But he couldn't bear what he saw in his mind.

Cheat's eyes cutting to Kestrel. Targeting her, stoking his hatred with one more reason.

And the more Arin tried to shield her, the more Cheat's dislike grew.

Arin's hands clenched in the cold. He blew on them, tucked his fingers under his arms, and began to walk.

He should let her go. Let her slip into the countryside, to the isolated farmlands that had no idea of the revolution.

If so, what then? Kestrel would alert her father. She'd find a way. Then the full force of the empire's military would fall on the peninsula, when Arin doubted that the Herrani could deal even with the battalion that would come through the pass in less than two days.

If he let Kestrel go, it was the same as murdering his people.

Arin nudged a rock with his boot and wanted to kick it. He didn't. He walked.

Thoughts chipped at his sanity, proposing solutions only to reveal problems, taunting him with the certainty that he would lose everything he sought to keep.

Until he found it.

Arin found the herb threading up through a patch of dirt. It was a pitiful amount, and withered, but he tore it from the ground with a fierce hope.

He lifted his eyes from his dirty hands to see that he had again come into view of the mountain pass. An idea robbed his breath.

The idea was as small as the leaves in Arin's hand. But it grew, put down roots, and Arin began to see how the Valorian reinforcements might be beaten.

He saw how he might win.

22

WHEN KESTREL AWOKE IN THE BED, SHE DIDN'T want to think about how she had gotten there.

Then the day was swallowed whole. Cold crept into the house, the dusk seemed to weigh on Kestrel's shoulders, and her mind filled with Arin, and Jess.

She heard a key turn in a lock. Kestrel sprang to her feet, realizing only then that she had been sitting and staring at nothing. She wound through the rooms of the suite until she was before the last door, and it opened.

Sarsine. "Where is Arin?" she said.

Better to reveal nothing. "I don't know."

"That's a problem."

Silence.

"It's a problem for *you*," Sarsine clarified, "because Cheat's here, demanding to see Arin, and since my feckless cousin is nowhere to be found, Cheat wants to speak with you instead."

Kestrel's pulse slowed, the way it used to when Rax was readying some kind of swift assault, or when her father asked a question and she didn't know the answer. "Tell him no."

Sarsine laughed.

"This is your family home," Kestrel said. "He is your guest. Who is he to command you?"

Sarsine shook her head, though the rueful set of her mouth said that she didn't blame Kestrel for trying. When she spoke, her words weren't meant as a threat, but Kestrel heard the echo of one—whatever Cheat had originally said. "If you don't come with me to see him, he will come here to see you."

Kestrel glanced at the walls, thinking of the suite's pattern of rooms, how they turned inward like a snail shell, giving the impression that one was secreted away from the world, tucked into an intimate, lovely space.

Or trapped.

"I'll go," she said.

Sarsine brought her to the atrium, where Cheat sat on a marble bench before the fountain. Torchlight cast itself around the room, and the fountain's water tumbled with red and orange streaks.

"I want to speak with her alone," Cheat told Sarsine.

She said, "Arin—"

"—is not the leader of the Herrani. *I* am."

"We'll see how long that lasts," said Kestrel, then bit her lip. He saw her do it, and they both knew what it meant.

A mistake.

"It's fine," Kestrel told Sarsine. "Go ahead. Go."

Sarsine gave her a dubious look, then left.

Cheat propped his elbows on his knees and gazed up at Kestrel. He scrutinized her: the long, loosely clasped hands, the folds of her dress. Kestrel's clothes had mysteriously appeared in the suite's wardrobe, probably while she had slept, and she was glad. The dueling ensemble had served well enough, but wearing a dress fit for society made Kestrel feel ready for different kinds of battle.

"Where is Arin?" Cheat said.

"In the mountains."

"Doing what?"

"I don't know. I imagine that, since the Valorian reinforcements will come through the mountain pass, he is analyzing its values and drawbacks as a battleground."

Cheat gave her a gleeful smirk. "Does it bother you, being a traitor?"

"I don't see how I am."

"You just confirmed that the reinforcements *will* come through the pass. Thank you."

"It's hardly worth thanking me," she said. "Almost every useful ship in the empire has been sent east, which means there is no other way into the city. Anyone with brains could figure that out, which is why Arin is in the mountains, and you are here."

A flush began to build under Cheat's skin. He said, "My feet are dusty."

Kestrel had no idea how to respond to that.

"Wash them," he said.

"What?"

He took off his boots, stretched out his legs, and leaned back against the bench.

Kestrel, who had been quite still, became stone.

"It's Herrani custom for the lady of the house to wash the feet of special guests," said Cheat.

"Even *if* such a custom existed, it died ten years ago. And I'm not the lady of the house."

"No, you're a slave. You'll do as I command."

Kestrel remembered Arin saying that she could sell herself in small ways. But had he meant this?

"Use the fountain," Cheat said.

Anger spread through Kestrel, but she knew better than to show it. She sat at the edge of the fountain, dunked his feet in, and washed briskly, the way she had seen slaves work at the laundry. If she had been a slave, she might have been able to pretend that she was washing something else, but she had never washed anything other than herself, so there was no denying that she held skin and flesh and bone.

She hated it.

She lifted the feet out of the fountain and set them on the tiles.

Cheat's eyes were half-lowered, the blacks of them very bright. "Dry them."

Kestrel stood.

"You're not leaving," he said.

"I must fetch a towel." She was grateful for the excuse to get away, to go anywhere, and not come back.

"Your skirt will do."

It was harder, now, to keep her face from flickering with

what she felt inside. She stooped, using the hem of her skirt, and wiped his feet.

"Now oil them."

"I have no oil."

"You'll find some underneath a tile decorated with the god of hospitality." Cheat pointed at the floor. "Press its edge. It will spring open."

And there were the vials, covered with ten years' worth of dust.

"They're in every Herrani house," Cheat said. "Your villa, too. Or rather, *mine*. You know, there's no need for you to stay here against your will. You could come home."

Kestrel splattered oil onto Cheat's feet and smeared it into the rough skin. "No. There's nothing there I want."

She felt his gaze on her bowed head, on her hands moving over his feet. "Do you do this for Arin?"

"No."

"What *do* you do for him?"

Kestrel straightened. Her palms were greasy. She rubbed them into her skirts, not caring that disgust was at least one of the things Cheat wanted to see.

Why, why would he want that?

She turned to leave.

"We're not done," he said.

"We are," said Kestrel, "unless you'd like to see how much my father taught me about unarmed combat. I'll drown you in that fountain. If I can't, I'll scream loud enough to bring every Herrani in this house running, and make them wonder what kind of man their leader is, that a Valorian girl so easily snapped his self-control."

She walked away, and he didn't follow, though she felt his eyes on her until she turned a corner. She found the kitchens, the most populated place in the house, and stood by a fire, listening to the metal clatter of kettles. She ignored the strange looks.

Then she was shaking, as much with fury as anything else.

Tell Arin.

Kestrel waved that thought away. What good would telling Arin do?

Arin was a black box hidden below a smooth tile. A trap door opening beneath her. He wasn't what she'd thought he was.

Maybe Arin had known that this would happen, or something like it.

Maybe he wouldn't even mind.

ARIN BOUNDED ACROSS THE THRESHOLD OF his home. He raced through the lit hallways, then drew up short when he saw Cheat glaring into the atrium fountain.

Suddenly, Arin was a twelve-year-old boy again, hands caked with white dust from quarrying as much rock as he could to prove his strength to this man.

"I worried we'd miss each other," Arin said. "I went to your villa first, but was told you had come here."

"Where've you been?" Cheat was in an ugly mood.

"Scouting the mountain pass." When this deepened Cheat's frown, Arin added, "Since that's the path the rein-forcements will probably take."

"Of course. Obviously."

"And I know just what to do to them."

A glimmer stole into Cheat's face.

Arin sent for Sarsine, and when she came, he asked her to bring Kestrel. "I need her opinion."

Sarsine hesitated. "But—"

Cheat wagged a finger at her. "I'm sure you run this

house well, but can't you see that your cousin's bursting at the seams with a plan that might save our hides? Don't bore him with domestic details, like who's squabbling with whom . . . or whether your special charge isn't feeling social. Just get the girl."

She left.

Arin fetched a map from his library, then hurried to the dining room, where Cheat waited with Kestrel and Sarsine, who gave Arin an exasperated look that said she washed her hands of all three of them. She walked out the door.

Arin spread the map on the table and weighted its corners with rocks from his pockets.

Kestrel sat, armored in stubborn silence.

"Let's hear your plan, lad," Cheat said, and looked only at him.

Arin felt that surge of excitement he'd had long ago, when they first began plotting to seize the city. "We've already taken out the Valorian guards on our side of the mountain." He touched the map, ran a finger along the ribbon of the pass. "Now we send a small force through the pass to their side. We select men and women who can best pass as Valorian until the final moment. The imperial guards are removed. Some of our people take their place, others hide in the foothills, and a messenger is sent through the pass to alert our fighters, who have kegs of black powder stationed here"—Arin pointed to the middle of the pass—"on either side. We'll need people who know the mountains and can scramble far up enough to get good height on the Valorians. They'll also need to be willing to be crushed under any avalanche the explosions trigger. Four people, two for each side, will do."

"We don't have much black powder left," said Cheat. "We should save it for the real invasion."

"We won't be alive for the invasion if we don't use the black powder now." Arin flattened his palms on the table, leaning over the map. "Most of our forces, about two thousand strong, will be flanking our entry to the pass. A Valorian battalion always has roughly the same numbers, so—"

"Always?" said Cheat.

Kestrel's eyes, which had been steadily narrowing as Arin explained his plan, became slits.

"You've learned a lot as the general's slave," Cheat said approvingly.

That wasn't exactly how Arin knew details of the Valorian military, but all he said was, "The two forces, ours and theirs, will be roughly equal in numbers but not in experience or weaponry. We'll be the weaker of the two. And the Valorians will have archers and crossbows. They won't, however, haul heavy cannon when they're not planning for battle. That's where we will have the advantage."

"Arin, *we* don't have cannon either."

"We do. We just need to unload them from the ships we seized in the harbor and drag them up the mountainside."

Cheat stared, then thumped Arin on the shoulder. "Brilliant."

Kestrel sat back in her chair. She folded her arms.

"Once the entire battalion is in the pass," Arin said, "and they begin to emerge on our side, our cannons will fire into their front lines. A complete surprise."

"Surprise?" Cheat shook his head. "The Valorians will

send scouts ahead. Once someone sees the cannons, they're going to get suspicious fast."

"They *won't* see the cannons, because our weaponry and forces will be disguised under shrouds of cloth the color of these." He gestured at the pale rocks. "Hemp and burlap sacks taken from the dockyards will do, and we can strip linen from Valorian beds. We'll blend into the mountain-side."

Cheat grinned.

"So our cannons fire into the first lines," Arin said, "which will be cavalry. The horses, hopefully, will panic, and if not they'll still have a hard time keeping their foot-ing on that downward slope. Meanwhile, the black powder kegs go off in the middle of the pass and bring rock down, blocking one half of the battalion from the other. Then our force on the other side of the pass pours in and makes short work of one half of the Valorian battalion, which should be trapped and in chaos. We do the same to the other half. We win."

Cheat said nothing at first, though his expression spoke for itself. "Well?" he turned to Kestrel. "What do you think?"

She wouldn't look at him.

"Make her talk, Arin," Cheat complained. "You said you wanted to know her opinion."

Arin, who had been watching Kestrel's slight shifts in mood and body and had seen the resentment build, said, "She thinks the plan might work."

Cheat glanced between the two of them. His gaze lin-gered on Kestrel, probably trying to see what Arin saw. Then he shrugged in that showy style that had made him such a favorite as an auctioneer. "Well, it's better than anything I've got. I'll go tell everyone what to do."

Kestrel shot Arin a furtive glance. He couldn't read it.

Cheat embraced Arin with one arm and was gone.

Once alone with Kestrel, Arin drew the plant out of his pocket: a handful of green with a wirelike stem and slender-tipped leaves. He set it on the table before her. Her eyes flashed, became jewels of joy. It was treasure, the way she looked at him.

"Thank you," she breathed.

"I should have searched for it sooner," he said. "You shouldn't have had to ask." He touched three fingers to the back of her hand, the Herrani gesture that could acknowledge thanks for a gift, but could also be used to ask forgiveness.

Kestrel's hand was smooth. Glistening, as if it had been oiled.

She drew it back. She changed. Arin saw her change, saw the happiness bleed out of her. She said, "What do I owe you for this?"

"Nothing," he said quickly, confused. Didn't *he* owe *her*? Hadn't she fought for him once? Hadn't he used her trust to upend her world?

Arin studied Kestrel, and realized that it wasn't so much that she had changed but that she had slipped back into the same huddled anger that had tightened her shoulders the entire time she had been sitting next to Cheat.

Of course Kestrel was angry, having listened to a plot to destroy her people. But as soon as Arin assumed that this was it, his mind returned to that inscrutable look she had given him. He turned it over the way he might a seashell, wondering what kind of creature had lived inside.

He remembered that glance: the flick of brows, the tense line of her mouth.

"What is the matter?" he asked.

She seemed like she wouldn't reply. Then she said, "Cheat will claim your ideas for his own."

Arin had known that. "Do you care?"

A breath of disgust.

"We need a leader," Arin said. "We need to win. *How* doesn't matter."

"You've been studying," she said, and Arin realized he had quoted from one of her father's books on warfare. "You've been taking texts from my library, reading about Valorian battle formations and methods of attack."

"Wouldn't you?"

She flipped an impatient hand.

He said, "It's high time my people learned something from yours. You have, after all, conquered half of the known world. What do you think, Kestrel? Would I make a good Valorian?"

"No."

"No? Not even when I have such ingenious strategies that my general would steal them?"

"And what are *you*, that you would let him?" Kestrel stood, straight-shouldered and slender, like a sword.

"I am a liar," Arin slowly said the words for her. "Coward. I have no honor."

There it was again. That look, livid with hidden things. A secret.

"What is it, Kestrel? Tell me what's wrong."

Her face hardened in a way that told Arin he would get no answer. "I want to see Jess."

The plant lay scraggly and limp on the table.

Arin wondered what, exactly, he had hoped it would make better.

Snow sifted onto the walk leading to the carriage. Kestrel was grateful for the plant Sarsine carried with her, but the evening had soured her thoughts, twisted her insides with anxiety. She thought of Cheat. She considered Arin's plan—a cunning one, horribly likely to work.

It was more urgent than ever that she escape.

Yet how could she, in Arin's courtyard, surrounded by Herrani who looked increasingly less like ragtag rebels and more like members of an army?

If she *did* escape, what would happen to Jess?

Sarsine ducked into the carriage. Kestrel was about to follow when she glanced over her shoulder at the house. It shimmered darkly, glazed by the evening snow. Kestrel saw the architectural whorl that was her suite of rooms on the building's east side. The tall stone rectangle was her rooftop garden, though it seemed double its width.

The door.

Kestrel remembered the locked door in her garden and realized several things.

The door must lead to another garden that mirrored hers. This was why that high wall appeared twice as wide from the outside.

That other garden connected to the west wing, which glowed with windows as large as those in her suite, with the same diamond-pane details.

Most important, the roof of the west wing sloped downward. It ended over a room on the ground floor that might have been the library or parlor.

Kestrel smiled.

Arin wasn't the only one with a plan.

"Only for Jess," Kestrel told the Herrani healer, and didn't care that dozens of people were dying at her feet. She dogged the healer, unwilling to risk that one leaf might go to someone else, even though she saw other faces she recognized under the violet mask of the poison.

She chose Jess.

When the drink was prepared and tipped into Jess's mouth, the girl gagged. Liquid trickled down her chin. The healer calmly caught it with the rim of the bowl and tried again, but the same thing happened.

Kestrel took the bowl from the healer. "Drink this," she told her friend.

Jess moaned.

"Do it," Kestrel said, "or you'll be sorry."

"What a lovely bedside manner you have," Sarsine said.

"If you don't drink," Kestrel said to Jess, "you'll be sorry, because you'll never have the chance to tease me again, to see how I want too much and do such foolish things to get it. You'll never hear me say that I love you. I love you, little sister. Will you please drink?"

A click came from Jess's throat. Kestrel took it to be assent, and set the cup to her lips.

Jess drank.

Hours passed. The night deepened. Jess gave no hint of recovery, Sarsine fell asleep in a chair, and somewhere Arin was readying for a battle that could come as early as the dawn.

Then Jess inhaled: a thin, watery breath. But better. Her eyes cracked open, and when she saw Kestrel she rasped, "I want my mother."

It was what Kestrel had whispered to her once, when they were little girls sleeping in the same bed, their feet cold and soft and touching. Kestrel held her friend's hand now and did what Jess had done for her then, which was to murmur soothing things that were barely words and more like music.

Kestrel felt the feeble pressure of Jess's fingers against hers.

"Don't let go," Kestrel said.

Jess listened. Her eyes focused, and widened, and woke up to the world.

"You should tell Arin," Sarsine said later in the carriage.

Kestrel knew that she wasn't talking about Jess. "I won't. Neither will you." Disdainfully, she said, "You're afraid of Cheat."

Kestrel didn't add that she was, too.

That night, Kestrel tried the locked garden door again. She pulled against the knob with all her strength. The door was massive. It didn't even rattle.

She stood, shivering in the snow. Then she went back into her rooms and returned with a table, which she set against the wall in the far corner. She climbed onto the table, and was still nowhere tall enough to reach the top of the wall. She hoped the corner's angles would give her hands and feet leverage to push upward.

The wall was too smooth. She slid back down. Even with a chair on top of the table, the wall was too high for her, and putting anything on top of the chair would be precarious. She was likely to fall onto the stones.

Kestrel climbed down and studied the garden in the lamplight thrown from her sunroom. She chewed the inside of her cheek, and was wondering whether books stacked on the chair on top of the table would make a difference when she heard something.

The grate of a heel against pebbles. It came from beyond the door, on the other side of the wall.

Someone had been listening.

Was listening still.

As quietly as she could, Kestrel took the chair down from the table and went inside.

Before Arin left for the mountain pass, during the coldest hours of the night, he found time to order that every piece of furniture light enough for Kestrel to move be taken from her suite.

AS HIS PEOPLE POSITIONED THEMSELVES IN and around the pass, Arin thought that he might have misunderstood the Valorian addiction to war. He had assumed it was spurred by greed. By a savage sense of superiority. It had never occurred to him that Valorians also went to war because of love.

Arin loved those hours of waiting. The silent, brilliant tension, like scribbles of heat lightning. His city far below and behind him, his hand on a cannon's curve, ears open to the acoustics of the pass. He stared into it, and even though he smelled the reek of fear from men and women around him, he was caught in a kind of wonder. He felt so vibrant. As if his life was a fresh, translucent, thin-skinned fruit. It could be sliced apart and he wouldn't care. Nothing felt like this.

Nothing except—

And that was another thing war did. It helped Arin forget what he couldn't have.

There was a skittering sound. It rattled through the pass, growing louder until one of Cheat's messengers emerged and ran straight for the commander. Arin wasn't far from Cheat's side, but even if he had been he probably would have heard the boy's gasp. "Coming," he said. "They're coming."

After that, it was all buzz and haste. Checking that the cannons were properly packed, then checking again. Cutting fuses from long, thin coils of flammable cord. Huddling under the dun-colored cloth.

Arin peered through a hole cut into the sheet. His eyes burned from not blinking.

But of course he heard them before he saw them. The percussion of thousands of marching feet. Then the Valorian front lines emerged from the pass. Arin waited, and waited, for Cheat's first shot.

It came. The cannonball ripped through cloth, drove through the air, and smashed into the cavalry. It split horses and people into chunks. Arin heard screaming, but he blocked it out.

The stone-colored sheets were gone—no need for them now—and Arin was heaving a ball into the gut of a cannon, firing, doing it again, hands black with powder, when a woman appeared at his side. She yanked at his sleeve. "Cheat is hurt," she said.

The Valorians were firing back, arrows and crossbow quarrels piercing the air with terrifying accuracy. Arin sucked in a breath. He ran.

Arrows whistled past him.

He dove behind the boulders that partially shielded

Cheat's cannon. The man was stretched out on his back, face sprayed with black powder. Herrani clumped around him, staring down with shock.

"No!" Arin shouted at them. "Eyes on the Valorians, not him!" They startled, then returned to what they were doing, which was blowing as many holes as they could into the Valorian formations.

"Except you." Arin grabbed the nearest man by his shirt. "Tell me what happened." Arin crouched and patted Cheat's arms, chest, looking for blood. "No wounds. Why are there no wounds?"

"He just fell back," said the man. "When the cannon went off, the blast knocked Cheat off his feet. He must have hit his head."

Arin's laugh was wild. The first moment of battle, and the commander had gone unconscious. Hardly a good omen.

He dragged Cheat more securely behind the boulders and snatched a spyglass from the man's pocket. It had been taken from the general's villa. It was of fine quality.

A little too fine. Through it, Arin saw that the Valorian cavalry kept their seats and horses under control, even on a treacherously steep slope bombarded with cannon. They were advancing.

Then Arin saw worse. As he watched, some soldiers behind the front lines craned their necks to scan the sides of the pass. There was a bright flash of an arm guard as a Valorian drew an arrow, sighted a target above in the cliffs, and shot.

One of the four Herrani charged with setting off kegs of black powder fell from the cliff. Arin swore. He watched, and could do nothing, as the other three Herrani were spitted with crossbow quarrels.

That was it, Arin thought. That was the end of everything. If they couldn't split the Valorian battalion in two by bringing rocks down the pass, the Herrani would be quickly trampled under an experienced army that was already recovering from surprise.

But the last Herrani on the mountainside clung to the cliff, somehow still alive.

She fell. She flipped in the air and caught fire. That was when Arin noticed the small keg clutched in her arms. She hit the ground, and exploded. Fire raged through the Valorian army.

It was as much of a second chance as Arin would get.

"Target the archers," he ordered those manning Cheat's cannon. "The crossbows. Spread the word. Turn all fire on that squadron."

"But the Valorians are getting closer—"

"Do it!"

Arin poured a sack full of as much black powder as it could hold. He grabbed a coil of fuse, slung the sack over his shoulder, and ran to the base of the cliff.

It was insane, what he was doing. God-touched, as if someone had cursed him with the names of the gods of madness and death when he was a cradled baby. Because Arin was racing for a slim goat path scratched into the cliff. Then he was on the path, and he was going to break his ankles before he got as high as that loose-looking jumble of boulders netted by the black branches of winter bushes. And if he didn't break his bones first, he would be sighted and shot.

He was.

Pain blazed in his thigh. The shaft of an arrow jutted from his flesh. Another grazed his neck. He faltered, then forced a fresh burst of speed. Arin's heartbeat shuddered in his ears, loud as cannon fire.

A rise of rock to his left offered cover. He ran along it, high up into the pass. Then he crouched, shaking and swearing as he bled all over the sack of black powder. He jammed it into the base of a crumbling stony heap and fumbled with the fuse.

He lit a match and held it until his fingers burned and the fuse caught.

Then up. *Up*, as if his entire body was made of that word, scrambling to get above the coming blast.

It came. It ruptured the mountainside. It flung boulders off the cliff.

The ground slid out from under Arin's feet. He fell in a shower of rocks.

KESTREL HEARD THE CHEERING FROM FAR
away.

Her spirits sank. Valorian soldiers didn't cheer when
they won. They sang.

Arin's plan had worked.

Kestrel went to a diamond-paned window that overlooked the courtyard and, beyond it, the city. She flung it
open. Winter air rushed in, specks of snow pricked her cheeks.
She leaned past the windowsill.

A small group of horsemen were approaching the house,
their pace slow enough to match Javelin, whose rider slumped
over his neck.

Surely the Herrani wouldn't cheer if Arin was dead, or
dying?

Fool, Kestrel told herself. Dead men can't ride.

A storm of feeling confused her, and Kestrel didn't
know if her emotions were what they ought to be, because
she didn't know what she felt. She couldn't even think.

Then the horses stopped. Arin slipped off Javelin, and

there was a scuffle among the Herrani as each fought to get to him first. People supported him, nudged shoulders under his arms.

Arin's face was white with pain and blackened with patches of dirt and bruises. His torn clothes were stained crimson. Bright, bloody flags. One foot was bare.

He tipped his head back, caught Kestrel's gaze, and smiled.

Kestrel shut the window and shut her heart, for what she felt when she saw Arin limp up the path wasn't anything she had expected. She shouldn't feel this, not this:

A stark, shattering relief.

"A hero." Cheat stared down at Arin stretched on his bed.

Arin started to shake his head, then winced in pain. "Just lucky."

"Damned lucky. A tangle of bushes kept you from going over the cliff, you were practically buried under a pile of rocks, and still you didn't break anything."

"I feel as if I broke *everything*."

Cheat had an odd expression on his face.

Arin said, "You were lucky, too."

"To get knocked on my backside and miss the battle? I don't think so." But Cheat shrugged, sat on the edge of the bed, patted Arin's bruised shoulder, and chuckled when Arin swore. "There's always next time. Tell me what happened after you were fished out from under the rocks."

"The plan worked. The Valorian officers in the front and rear were cut off from each other by the landslide, which wiped out a good amount of their middle ranks. They surrendered. I think we managed to make sure no messengers escaped out the Valorian side of the pass. I sent the wounded to the governor's palace. Might as well turn that place into the hospital it's become."

"Our wounded, you mean."

Arin propped himself up on one elbow. "Both sides. I took prisoners."

"Arin, Arin. We don't need any more Valorian pets. We're already up to our eyeballs in aristocrats. At least their letters sow misinformation in the capital. And they provide some entertainment."

"What would you have had me do, kill them all?"

Cheat opened his hands as if the answer lay on his palms.

"That's shortsighted," Arin said, too weary to care about giving offense. "And beneath us."

Cheat's silence gained a hard edge.

"Look at it this way," Arin said more carefully. "One day we might be in a position to trade prisoners. This wasn't the last battle. Some of us might be captured during the next."

Cheat stood. "We can discuss this later. Who am I to keep our hero from his rest?"

"Please stop calling me that."

Cheat tsked. "People will love you for this," he said.

But he didn't sound as if that was a good thing.

The possibility of a future no longer felt frail to the Herrani. Before the battle, they had largely continued living where they had been slaves if they didn't have original homes to return to. Now empty Valorian houses were sized up. Cheat's permission was sought to move into one place or another, but sometimes people's eyes slid to Arin before they spoke. Then Cheat invariably said no.

Arin worked to construct their fighters into a proper army. He made a list of people who had distinguished themselves during the battle and suggested that they be made officers. The titles he wrote were the same as those used by the Herrani military before the conquest.

Cheat frowned at the list. "I suppose you want to bring the monarchy back, too."

"The royal family is dead," Arin said slowly.

"So what are you, the next best thing?"

"I never said that. And that has nothing to do with naming officers."

"Oh no? Look at this list. Half of them are former blue bloods, like you."

"Half of them aren't." Arin sighed. "It's just a list, Cheat. You decide."

Cheat gave him a measuring look, then scratched out some names and wrote in others. He signed with a flourish.

Arin said they should begin taking land outside the city, capturing farms and bringing in grain and other food-stuffs to prepare for a siege. "The Ethyra estate would be a good first choice."

"Fine, fine." Cheat waved a hand.

Arin hesitated, then offered him a small but full and heavy satchel. "You might find these books interesting. They're on Valorian wars and history."

"I'm too old for the schoolroom," Cheat said, and left Arin with his hand outstretched.

Kestrel began to hate her rooms. She wondered what kind of family Irex had had, that a lock workable only from the *outside* had been added to a suite so sumptuous that it must have belonged to his mother. The lock was Valorian brass, intricate and solid. Kestrel knew it intimately by now, since she'd spent enough time testing it to see if it could be picked or forced.

If she had to choose which aspect of the suite she despised most, it would have been a hard call between the lock and the garden, though these days she nursed a particular grudge against the curtains.

She hid behind them to watch Arin leave the house, and return—very often on her horse. Despite the way he had looked after the battle, his injuries weren't serious. His limp lessened, the bandage on his neck disappeared, and the raging bruises muted into ugly greens and violets.

Several days passed without any words between him and her, and that set Kestrel on edge.

It was hard to rub out the memory of his smile—exhausted, sweet.

And then that waterfall of relief.

Kestrel sent him a letter. Jess was likely to recover, she wrote. She asked to visit Ronan, who was being held in the city prison.

Arin's reply was a curt note: *No.*

She decided not to press the issue. Her request had been due to a sense of obligation. She dreaded seeing Ronan—even *if* he agreed to speak with her. Even *if* he did not loathe her now. Kestrel knew that to look upon Ronan would be to come face-to-face with her failure. She had done everything wrong . . . including not being able to love him.

She folded the one-word letter and set it aside.

Arin was leaving the general's villa, which had become the army's headquarters, when one of the new officers saluted him. Thrynne, a middle-aged man, was examining a batch of Valorian horses captured from the battle. "These will do well for our march on the Metrea estate," he said.

Arin frowned. "What?"

"Cheat's sending us to capture the Metrea estate."

Arin lost his patience. "That's idiotic. Metrea grows olives. Do *you* want to live on olives during a siege?"

"Er . . . no."

"Then go to *Ethyra*, where they will have stores of grain, plus livestock."

"Right now?"

"Yes."

"Should I ask Cheat first?"

"*No.*" Arin rubbed his brow, deeply tired of treading so cautiously around Cheat. "Just go."

Thrynne took his troops.

When Arin saw Cheat the next day, no mention was made of the commander's order or how it had been overturned. Arin's friend was cheerful and suggested Arin visit his "Valorian cattle," by which he meant the prisoners from the battle. "See if conditions are the way you'd like them," Cheat said. "Why don't you go there tomorrow afternoon?"

It had been a while since Cheat had asked him to do anything. Arin took the request as a good sign.

He brought Sarsine with him. She had a gift for organization, and had already shaped the governor's palace into something that began to look like a proper hospital. Arin thought she might know what to do about potential overcrowding in the prison.

Except that overcrowding turned out not to be a problem.

Blood slicked the prison floor. Bodies lay crumpled in cells. All the Valorian soldiers had been killed—shot through the prison bars or speared in their sleep.

Arin's stomach clenched. He heard Sarsine gasp. His boots stood in a dark puddle of blood.

Not all the prisoners were dead; those who had been captured the night the revolution began were still alive, staring at Arin with horror. They were silent . . . afraid, perhaps, that they would be next. But one of them stepped close to the bars of his cell, his body lean, face handsome, movements elegant in that way that Arin had hated. Envied.

Ronan didn't speak. He didn't need to. His scathing expression was worse than words. It blamed Arin. It called him an animal, rooting in blood.

Arin turned away. He strode down the long hall, trying not to feel as if he was fleeing, and confronted a guard. "What happened?" he demanded, though he knew the answer.

"Orders," the guard said.

"Cheat's?"

"Of course." She shrugged. "Should've been done long ago, he said."

"And you didn't think that there was anything wrong with this? With killing hundreds of people?"

"But we had orders," another guard spoke. "They're Valorians."

"You've turned this prison into a slaughterhouse!"

One of the Herrani hawked and spat. "Cheat said that you'd be like this."

Sarsine grabbed Arin's elbow and dragged him out of the prison before he did something stupid.

Arin blinked at the iron sky. He took huge, clean breaths of air.

"Cheat is a problem," Sarsine said.

Breathe, Arin commanded himself.

Sarsine twisted her fingers. Then, quickly, she said, "There's something I should have told you earlier."

He looked at her.

"Cheat hates Kestrel," she said.

"Of course he does. She's the general's daughter."

"No, it's more than that. It's the hatred of someone who is not getting what he wants."

Sarsine explained exactly what she thought Cheat wanted.

It scalded Arin. The knowledge bubbled up within him: a brew of anger and disgust. He had not seen. He had not understood. Why was it only now that he learned that Cheat had sought to be alone with Kestrel, and in such a way?

Arin lifted a hand to stop Sarsine's words, because on the heels of his last thought came another, even worse:

What if Cheat had meant the murders in the prison to be more than a show of power over Arin?

What if they were a distraction?

Kestrel rested her forehead against a window in her sitting room and gazed out at the empty courtyard. She willed the cold glass to freeze her brain, because she didn't think she could bear her own thoughts for much longer—or her own ineptitude. How was it that she was a prisoner *still*?

She was cursing herself when a hand stole up the nape of her neck.

Her body knew how to react before her mind did. Kestrel stamped her heel down on the man's instep, punched an elbow into the spot below the ribs, slipped under a thick arm—

—and was caught by the hair. Cheat dragged her to him. He used his whole body to push her away from the windows and up against a wall.

His hand pressed down on her mouth. She twisted her head to the side. Cheat's thumb dug in under her chin and jerked her face to meet his.

The other hand found her fingers and squeezed hard.

"Don't struggle," he said. "Soft things don't break."

HE TRIED TO PULL HER DOWN TO THE FLOOR. She wrenched a hand away and drove the heel of it into his nose. She felt it crunch. Blood spurted between her fingers.

Cheat grunted, gasped. His hands flew to the broken nose, muffling sounds, catching blood.

Freeing Kestrel.

She pushed past him. She was thinking, *Knife*. Her makeshift ceramic knife, hidden in the ivy. She had a weapon, she wasn't defenseless, this wouldn't happen, she wouldn't—

Cheat backhanded her across the face.

The blow knocked Kestrel off her feet. Then she was on the floor, cheek against carpet, blinking at the woven patterns. She forced herself up. She was shoved back down. She heard a dagger scrape out of its sheath, and Cheat was saying things she refused to understand.

Then there was a crash.

Kestrel couldn't wonder what that sound was, couldn't

even breathe under Cheat's weight. But he suddenly scrambled to his feet. He was no longer looking at her.

He was staring at Arin, who had slammed through the door.

Arin strode into the room. His sword was raised. His face was so pale and tight that it seemed to be made only of bones and fury.

"Arin," Cheat said soothingly. "Nothing happened."

Arin swung, and his blade would have cut Cheat's head from his neck if the other man hadn't ducked. Cheat began speaking as if they were arguing over a game whose rules had been forgotten. He said that it wasn't fair that Arin had the bigger weapon, and that old friends shouldn't fight. The Valorian girl had attacked *him*.

"Look at my face," Cheat said. "Just look at what she did to me."

Arin thrust his sword into Cheat's chest. There was the grind of metal on bone. A choking sound, a rush of blood. Arin pushed in up to the hilt. The sword's point pierced through Cheat's back and the man sagged, folding in on himself, pouring red onto Arin, but Arin's expression didn't change. It was all hard lines and murder.

Cheat's eyes went wide. Disbelieving. Then dull.

Arin let go. He knelt on the floor next to Kestrel. His bloody hand lifted to her bruising cheek, and she recoiled at the wet touch, then let herself be gathered into Arin's arms, held gently against his raging heart. She inhaled.

A gulp of air. Sharp. Shallow. Again.

She began to shake. Teeth rattled in her head. Arin was saying *Shh,* as if Kestrel was crying, which made her realize that she was. And she remembered that Arin wasn't shelter but a cage.

She pushed herself away. "Key," she whispered.

Arin's hands fell to his sides. "What?"

"You gave Cheat the *key to my rooms*!" Because how else, how else had Cheat crept in so quietly? Arin had invited him, opened his home, offered his possessions, offered her—

"No." Arin looked sick. "Never. You must believe that I would never do that."

Kestrel clenched her jaw.

"Think, Kestrel. Why would I give Cheat the key to your suite, only to kill him?"

She shook her head. She didn't know.

Arin passed a hand over his brow. The blood smeared. He tried to rub it away with his sleeve, but when he looked at her there was still a red streak above his gray eyes. The viciousness that had filled his face when he had entered the room was gone. Now he just looked young.

He stood, went to tug his sword out of the body, and felt the dead man's pockets. He pulled out a thick iron ring with dozens of keys. He turned it, staring as the keys slid and rang.

Arin shut them up inside his fist. "My house," he said thickly. He looked at Kestrel. "Keys can be copied." His eyes pleaded with her. "I have no idea how many sets Irex's family had. Cheat could have had this one, somehow, even before Firstwinter."

She saw how what he said might be true. She didn't think anyone could fake the horror on Arin's face when he first saw Kestrel on the floor. Or the way he looked now: as if what had happened to her was happening to him.

"Believe me, Kestrel."

She did . . . and she didn't.

Arin undid the ring, slipped off two keys, and set them in Kestrel's hand. "These are for your suite. Keep them."

She gazed at the dull metal on her palm. She recognized one key. The other . . . "Is this one for the garden door?"

"Yes, but"—Arin looked away—"you wouldn't want to use it."

Kestrel had guessed that Arin lived in the west wing suite, and that it had been his father's as hers had been his mother's. But it wasn't until then that she understood what the two gardens were for: a way for husband and wife to visit each other without the entire household knowing.

Kestrel stood, because Arin was standing and she had had enough of crouching on the floor.

"Kestrel . . ." Arin's question was something he clearly hated to ask. "How badly are you hurt?"

"As you see." Her eye was swelling shut, and the carpet had skinned her cheek raw. "My face. Nothing more."

"I could kill him a thousand times and still want to do it again."

She looked at Cheat's slumped body as it soaked the carpet with blood. "Somebody had better clean that up. It won't be me. I'm not your slave."

Quietly, he said, "You're really not."

"I might believe you if you gave me the whole set of keys."

The corner of his mouth twitched. "Ah, but would you have any respect for my intelligence?"

When night fell, Kestrel tried the garden door. Arin's garden was as bare as hers, the walls as smooth. His sunroom was dark, but the hallway that led from it to the rest of the suite was a glowing tunnel.

Somewhere in the layers and shapes of illuminated rooms, a long shadow moved.

Arin, awake.

She slipped back inside her garden and locked the door.

The shaking that had consumed her earlier—after—returned. It was deep inside this time. Even if she had stepped into the garden with the thought of escape, when she saw Arin's shadow she knew that she had really come for his company.

She couldn't bear to be alone.

Kestrel began to pace, pebbles scattering under her feet.

If she kept moving, maybe she could forget Cheat's weight. Her hot, stinging face. The moment when she understood that there was nothing she could do.

Arin had done it. Then he had shouldered the body and carried it away. He rolled up the gory rug and took that away, too. He probably would have repaired the door, which hung splintered on its hinges.

But Kestrel told him to leave. He did.

Arin was becoming the sort of person her father admired. Remorseless. Able to make a decision, walk through it, and close it behind him. Kestrel felt that Arin was a shadow of herself—or rather of who she was supposed to be.

General Trajan's daughter would not be in this position. She would not be frightened.

Her feet ground into the rocks.

Then she heard something, and stopped.

When the first note opened into the cold dark, Kestrel didn't understand what it was. A sound of pure, low, belled beauty. She waited, and it came again.

Song.

It welled like sap from a tree, golden beads on wood. Then a rich glide. A singer testing his range.

Loosening. Arin's voice lifted beyond the garden wall. It poured around her fear, and into it. The wordless warmth of music took a familiar shape.

A lullaby. Enai had sung it to Kestrel long ago, and Arin sang it to her now.

Maybe he had seen her in his garden, or heard her restless walk. Kestrel didn't know how he knew that she needed his comfort as much as she needed the stone wall between them. Yet when the song stopped and the night resonated with a silence that was itself a kind of music, Kestrel was no longer afraid.

And she believed Arin. She believed everything he had ever said to her.

She believed his silence on the other side of the wall, which said that he would stay there as long as she needed.

When Kestrel went inside, she carried his song with her.

It was a candle that lit her way and kept watch while she slept.

Arin woke. His throat still felt full of music.

Then he remembered that he had killed his friend and that the Herrani had no leader. He searched himself for regret. He found none. Only the cold echo of his own harrowed rage.

He rose and splashed water on his face, ran it through his hair. The face in the mirror didn't seem to be his, exactly.

Arin dressed with care and went to see what the world looked like.

In the hallways beyond his suite, he caught guarded glances from people, some who had been Irex's servants, some who had worked in this house during his parents' time. They had picked up where their lives had left off. When Arin, uncomfortable, had said that they didn't need to fill their old roles, they had told him that they'd rather clean and cook than fight. Payment could come later.

Other Herrani lived in Arin's house, fighters who were rapidly becoming soldiers. They, too, watched Arin pass, but said nothing about the body he had carried through the house yesterday and buried on the grounds.

The lack of questions made him edgy.

He passed the open library door, then stopped, returned. He pushed the door wider to see Kestrel more fully.

A fire burned in the grate. The room was warm, and Kestrel was browsing the shelves as if this were her home, which Arin wanted it to be. Her back to him, she slid a book from its row, a finger on top of its spine.

She seemed to sense his presence. She slid the book

back and turned. The graze on her cheek had scabbed over. Her blackened eye had sealed shut. The other eye studied him, almond-shaped, amber, perfect. The sight of her rattled Arin even more than he had expected.

"Don't tell people why you killed Cheat," she said. "It won't win you any favors."

"I don't care what they think of me. They need to know what happened."

"It's not your story to tell."

A charred log shifted on the fire. Its crackle and sift was loud. "You're right," Arin said slowly, "but I can't lie about this."

"Then say nothing."

"I'll be questioned. I'll be held accountable by our new leader, though I'm not sure who will take Cheat's place—"

"You. Obviously."

He shook his head.

Kestrel lifted one shoulder in a shrug. She turned back to the books.

"Kestrel, I didn't come in here to talk politics."

Her hand trembled slightly, then swept along the titles to hide it.

Arin didn't know how much last night had changed things between them, or in what way. "I'm sorry," he said. "Cheat should never have been a threat to you. You shouldn't even be in this house. You're in this position because I put you there. *Here*. Forgive me, please."

Her fingers paused: thin, strong, and still.

Arin dared to reach for her hand, and Kestrel did not pull away.

SHE HAD BEEN RIGHT. THE HERRANI QUICKLY
took Arin as their leader, either because they had always
admired him or because they had liked Cheat's flair for
savagery and assumed that if Arin had killed him he must
have been the better monster.

He was certainly the better strategist. Whole swaths of
the peninsula began to fall under Herrani control as squad-
rons were sent to capture farmlands. Food and water were
stockpiled, enough for a year of siege—or so Kestrel overheard from guards at the entrances of the house.

"How can you possibly hope to succeed against a siege?"
Kestrel asked Arin during one of the rare times he was home
and not leading an assault in the countryside. They sat at
the dining room table, where Kestrel wasn't allowed a knife
for the meal.

At night, Kestrel treasured the memory of Arin's song.
But by day, she could not ignore basic facts. The missing
knife. How any easy way out of Arin's home was guarded,

even ground-floor windows. Guards eyed her warily as she passed. Kestrel possessed two keys that did little more than prove that she remained under a privileged form of house arrest.

Was she to earn her freedom one key at a time?

And when her father returned with the imperial army—as he inevitably would—what then? Kestrel tried to imagine turning traitor and counseling the Herrani through the coming war. She couldn't. It didn't matter that Arin's cause was just, or that Kestrel now allowed herself to see that. She couldn't fight her own father.

"We can withstand a siege for some time," Arin said. "The city walls are strong. They're Valorian-built."

"Which means that we will know how to bring them down."

Arin swirled his glass, watching the water's clear spin. "Care to bet? I have matches. I hear they make very fine stakes." There was the quirk of a smile.

"We aren't playing at Bite and Sting."

"But if we were, and I kept raising the stakes higher to the point where you couldn't bear to lose, what would you do? Maybe you'd give up the game. Herran's only hope of winning against the empire is to become too painful to re-take. To mire the Valorians in an unending siege when they'd rather be fighting the east. To force them to conquer the countryside again, piece by piece, spending money and lives. Someday, the empire will decide we're not worth the fight."

Kestrel shook her head. "Herran will always be worth it."

Arin looked at her, his hands resting on the table. He,

too, had no knife. Kestrel knew that this was to make it less obvious that she wasn't to be trusted with one. Instead, it became more.

"You're missing a button," he said abruptly.

"What?"

He reached across the table and touched the cloth at her wrist, on the spot of an open seam. His fingertip brushed the frayed thread.

Kestrel forgot that she had been troubled. She had been thinking about knives, she remembered, and now they were talking about buttons, but what one had to do with the other, she couldn't say.

"Why don't you mend it?" he said.

She recovered herself. "That is a silly question."

"Kestrel, do you not know how to sew a button?"

She refused to answer.

"Wait here," he said.

Arin returned with a sewing kit and button. He threaded a needle, bit it between his teeth, and took her wrist with both hands.

Her blood turned to wine.

"This is how you do it," he said.

He took the needle from his mouth and pierced it through the cloth.

"This is how you build a fire."

"This is how you make tea."

Small lessons, sprinkled here and there, between days. Through them, Kestrel sensed the silent history of how

Arin had come to know what he did. She thought about it during the long stretches of time when she didn't see him.

Days passed after Arin had sewn the button tight to her sleeve. Then an empty week went by after he'd struck fire to kindling in the library fireplace, then even longer since he'd placed a hot cup of perfectly steeped tea in her hands. He was gone. He was fighting, Sarsine had said. She would not say where.

With her newfound—if limited—freedom, Kestrel often wandered through the wings where people worked. Some doors were barred to her. The kitchens were. They hadn't been before, on that horrible day with Cheat by the fountain, but they were now that everyone knew that Kestrel could roam the house. The kitchens had too many knives. Too many fires.

But there were fires lit regularly in the library and in her suite, and Kestrel had learned how to make one anywhere. Why not set fire to the house and hope to escape in the confusion?

One day, she studied the fringe on her sitting room curtains and clutched kindling hard enough to get splinters. Then her grip loosened. A fire was too dangerous. It could kill her. She told herself that this was why she returned the small sticks of wood to the hearth, and dropped them back into the kindling box. It wasn't because she couldn't bear the thought of destroying Arin's family home. It wasn't because a fire might also kill the Herrani who lived here.

If she escaped and sent the imperial army to the city, wasn't that the same as bringing death to every Herrani in this house? To Arin?

She was angry, then, at his foolishness for teaching her such an obviously dangerous skill as building a fire. She was angry at what the idea of his death did to her.

Kestrel slammed shut the lid on the kindling box, and on the sudden grief of her thoughts. She left her rooms.

She roamed the wing of servants' quarters: a corridor of small rooms set close together, with chalk-white, identical doors, at the back of the house. Today Herrani were emptying them out. Framed canvases went by. Kestrel watched a woman shift a large, iridescent oil lamp in her arms to rest on her hip like a child.

Like every other colonial family, Irex's had turned the servants' quarters into storage and had had an outbuilding constructed to house their slaves. Privacy was a luxury slaves didn't deserve, or so most Valorians had thought . . . to their undoing, since forcing their slaves to sleep and eat together in one collective space had helped them plot against their conquerors. It amazed Kestrel, how people set their own traps.

She remembered that kiss in the carriage on Firstwinter night. How her whole being had begged for it.

She had baited her own trap, too.

Kestrel moved on. She took the stairs down to the workrooms. The lower level was warmed throughout by the kitchens' constant fires. She passed the still room. The laundry, with its sails of hung sheets. She saw people busy in the scullery, where tubs were filled with pots and steaming water, and bare, copper-lined sinks waited for the washing of porcelain dining sets.

She walked past the scullery, then paused to feel a chill

breeze curl around her ankles. A draft. Which meant that somewhere nearby, a door had been left open to the outside.

Was this Kestrel's chance to leave?

Could she take it?

Would she?

She followed the current of cold air. It led her to a dry pantry, whose door was ajar. Grain sacks were stacked inside.

But this was not the source of the draft. Kestrel continued down the empty hallway. At its end, a pale blade of light cut across the floor. Cold flowed in.

The door to the kitchen yard was open. A few snowflakes swirled into the hallway and vanished.

Maybe *now*. Maybe *now* was the moment when she would flee.

Kestrel took another step. Her heartbeat trembled in her throat.

Then the door sang wide on its hinges, light flooded the hallway, and Arin walked in.

She bit back a gasp. He, too, was surprised to see her. He straightened suddenly under the weight of the grain sack over his shoulder. Quick as thought, his eyes went to the open door. He set down the sack and locked the door behind him.

"You're back," she said.

"I'm leaving again."

"To steal more grain from a captured country estate?"

His smile was perfectly mischievous. "Rebels must eat."

"And I suppose you use my horse in these battles and thefts of yours."

"He's happy to support a good cause."

Kestrel huffed and would have turned to wend her way back through the workrooms, but he said, "Would you like to see him? Javelin?"

She stood still.

"He misses you," said Arin.

She said yes. After Arin had stacked his final load of grain in the pantry and given her his coat, they walked out into the kitchen yard and crossed its slate flagstones to reach the grounds and the stables.

It was warm inside the stables. It smelled like hay, leather, grassy manure, and somehow sunshine, as if it had been stored here for the winter. Irex's horses were sleek beauties. High-spirited. Several of them stamped in their stalls as Kestrel and Arin entered, and another tossed its head. But Kestrel had eyes for only one horse.

She went straight to his stall. He towered over her, but lowered his head to push against her shoulder, breathe gustily over her uplifted hands, and lip the ends of her hair. Kestrel's throat tightened.

She had been lonely. She thought that loneliness shouldn't hurt so much—not when there was everything *else*. But here was a friend. Running a hand down Javelin's velvet nose reminded her of how few she had.

Arin had been hanging back, but now he came near. "I'm sorry," he said, "but I need to ready him to ride. Daylight's fading. I have to leave."

"Of course you do," she said, and was horrified to hear the choked sound of her voice. She felt Arin looking at her. She felt the question in his gaze, the way he saw her near tears, and this hurt, too, more than the loneliness, because it made her know that her loneliness had been for him, that it had sent her wandering through the house, looking for yet another little lesson.

"I could stay," he said. "I could leave tomorrow."

"No. I want you to go now."

"Do you?"

"Yes."

"Ah, but what about what *I* want?"

The softness in his voice made her lift her gaze. She would have answered him—how, she wasn't sure—if Javelin's attention hadn't turned to him. The stallion began nuzzling Arin as if he were the horse's favorite person in the world. Kestrel felt a pang of jealousy. Then she saw something that sent thoughts of jealousy and loneliness and want right out of her head, and just made her mad. Javelin was nibbling a certain part of Arin, whuffling around a pocket exactly the right size to hold a—

"Winter apple," Kestrel said. "Arin, you have been bribing my horse!"

"Me? No."

"You have! No wonder he likes you so much."

"Are you sure it's not because of my good looks and pleasing manners?" This was said lightly—not quite sarcastically, yet in a voice that nevertheless told Kestrel that he doubted he possessed either of these things.

But he *was* pleasing. He pleased her. And she could never forget his beauty. She had learned it all too well.

She blushed. "It's not fair," she said.

He took in her rising color. His mouth curved. And

although Kestrel wasn't sure that he could interpret what effect he was having on her simply by standing there and saying the word *pleasing*, she knew that he always knew when he had an advantage.

He pressed it. "Doesn't your father's theory of war include winning over the other side by offering sweets? No? An oversight, I think. I wonder . . . might I bribe *you*?"

Kestrel's fingers clenched. It probably looked like anger. It wasn't. It was the instinctive gesture of someone dangerously tempted.

"Open your hands, Little Fists," said Arin. "Open your eyes. I haven't stolen his love for you. Look." It was true that in the course of their conversation, Javelin had turned away from Arin, disappointed by the empty pocket. The horse nosed Kestrel's shoulder. "See?" Arin said. "He knows the difference between an easy mark and his mistress."

Arin *was* an easy mark. He had offered to bring her to the stables, and here was the result: from where Kestrel stood, she could see the open tack room, how it was organized, and everything she would need to saddle Javelin quickly. Speed would matter when she escaped. And she would, she *must*, it was just a matter of getting out of the house at the right time, the right way. Javelin would be the fastest means to reach the harbor and a boat.

When Arin and Kestrel left the stables, the snow had stopped and everything was crystalline. Kestrel wasn't sure if it had grown colder or only seemed that way. She shivered inside Arin's coat. It smelled like him. Like dark, summer earth. She would be glad to give the coat back. To see him

slip it on in preparation for whatever mission would carry
him away from here. He clouded her head.

She inhaled the cold air and willed herself to be like
that breath . . . a relentless, icy purity.

What would Kestrel's father think, to know how she wavered, how close she came sometimes to wanting to remain
a favored prisoner? He would disown her. No child of his
would choose surrender.

She went, under guard, to see Jess.

The girl's face was gray, but she could sit up and eat on
her own. "Have you heard anything about my parents?"
Jess asked.

Kestrel shook her head. A few Valorians—civilians,
socialites—had returned unexpectedly early from their stay
in the capital for the winter season. They had been stopped
in the mountain pass and imprisoned. Jess's parents hadn't
been among them.

"And Ronan?"

"I'm not allowed to see him," Kestrel said.

"You're allowed to see *me*."

Kestrel remembered Arin's one-word note. Carefully,
she said, "I think that Arin doesn't consider you to be a
threat."

"I wish I were," Jess muttered, and fell silent. Her face
seemed to sink in on itself. It was unbelievable to Kestrel
that Jess—*Jess*—could look so withered.

"Have you been sleeping?" Kestrel asked.

"Too many nightmares."

Kestrel had them, too. They began with Cheat's hand on the back of her neck and ended with her gasping awake in the dark, reminding herself that the man was dead. She dreamed about Irex's baby, dark eyes fixed on her, and sometimes he would speak like an adult. He accused her of making him an orphan. It was her fault, he said, for having been blind to Arin. *You cannot trust him,* the baby said.

"Forget your dreams," Kestrel told Jess, even though she couldn't follow her own advice. "I have something to cheer you up." She handed her friend a folded pile of dresses. Once, her clothes would have been too tight for Jess. Now they would hang on her. Kestrel thought about that. She thought about Ronan, in prison, and Benix and Captain Wensan and that dark-eyed baby.

"How do you have these?" Jess ran a hand over silk. "Never mind. I know. Arin." Her mouth twisted as if drinking the poison again. "Kestrel, tell me it isn't true what they say, that you are truly *his*, that you are on *their* side."

"It isn't."

With a glance to make certain no one overheard, Jess leaned forward and whispered, "Promise that you will make them pay."

It was what Kestrel had hoped Jess would say. It was why she had come. She looked into the eyes of her friend, who had come so close to death.

"I will," Kestrel said.

MARIE RUTKOSKI

316

Yet when she returned to the house, Sarsine had a smile on her face. "Go into the salon," she said.

Her piano. Its surface gleamed like wet ink. An emotion flooded through Kestrel, but she didn't want to name it. It wasn't right that she should feel it, simply because Arin had given back to her something that he had more or less taken.

Kestrel shouldn't play. She shouldn't sit on that familiar velvet bench or think about how transporting a piano across the city was no mean feat. It meant people. Pulleys. Horses straining to haul a cart. She shouldn't wonder how Arin had found the time and begged his people's goodwill to bring her piano here.

She shouldn't touch the cool keys, or feel that delicious tension between silence and sound.

She remembered that Arin had refused to sing for who knows how long.

Kestrel didn't have that particular kind of strength.

She sat and played.

In the end, it wasn't hard to guess which rooms had been Arin's before the war. They were silent and dusty. Any children's furniture had been removed, and the suite was fairly ordinary, its windows hung with deeply purple curtains. It looked as if for the past ten years it had served as a guest suite for the lesser sort of visitors. Its only unusual qualities were that its outer door was made of a different, lighter wood than those in the rest of the house . . . and that the sitting room had instruments mounted on the walls.

Decoration. Perhaps Irex's family had found the child-size instruments quaint. A wooden flute was tilted at an angle over the mantelpiece. On the far wall was a row of small violins, growing larger until the last, which was half the size of an adult violin.

Kestrel came often. One day, when she knew from Sarsine that Arin had returned home but she had not yet seen him, she went to the suite. She touched one of his violins, reaching furtively to pluck the highest string of the largest instrument. The sound was sour. The violin was ruined—no doubt all of them were. That is what happens when an instrument is left strung and uncased for ten years.

A floorboard creaked somewhere in one of the outer chambers.

Arin. He entered the room, and she realized that she had expected him. Why else had she come here so frequently, almost every day, if she hadn't hoped that someone would notice and tell him to find her there? But even though she admitted to wanting to be here with him in his old rooms, she hadn't imagined it would be like this.

With her caught touching his things.

Her gaze dropped. "I'm sorry," she murmured.

"It's all right," he said. "I don't mind." He lifted the violin off its nails and set it in her hands. It was light, but Kestrel's arms lowered as if the violin's hollowness were terribly heavy.

She cleared her throat. "Do you still play?"

He shook his head. "I've mostly forgotten how. I wasn't good at it anyway. I loved to sing. Before the war, I worried that gift would leave me, the way it often does with boys.

We grow, we change, our voices break. It doesn't matter how well you sing when you're nine years old, you know. Not when you're a boy. When the change comes you just have to hope for the best . . . that your voice settles into something you can love again. My voice broke two years after the invasion. Gods, how I squeaked. And when my voice finally settled, it seemed like a cruel joke. It was too good. I hardly knew what to do with it. I felt so grateful to have this gift . . . and so angry, for it to mean so little. And now . . ." He shrugged, a self-deprecating gesture. "Well, I know I'm rusty."

"No," Kestrel said. "You're not. Your voice is beautiful."

The silence after that was soft.

Her fingers curled around the violin. She wanted to ask Arin a question yet couldn't bear to do it, couldn't say that she didn't understand what had happened to him the night of the invasion. It didn't make sense. The death of his family was what her father would call a "waste of resources." The Valorian force had had no pity for the Herrani military, but it had tried to minimize civilian casualties. You can't make a dead body work.

"What is it, Kestrel?"

She shook her head. She set the violin back on the wall. "Ask me."

She remembered standing outside the governor's palace and refusing to hear his story, and was ashamed once more.

"You can ask me anything," he said.

Each question seemed the wrong one. Finally, she said, "How did you survive the invasion?"

He didn't speak at first. Then he said, "My parents and sister fought. I didn't."

Words were useless, pitifully useless—criminal, even, in how they could not account for Arin's grief, and could not excuse how her people had lived on the ruin of his. Yet again Kestrel said, "I'm sorry."

"It's not your fault."

It felt as if it was.

Arin led the way out of his old suite. When they came to the last room, the greeting room, he paused before the outermost door. It was the slightest of hesitations, no longer than if the second hand of a clock stayed a beat longer on its mark than it should. But in that fraction of time, Kestrel understood that the last door was not paler than the others because it had been made from a different wood.

It was newer.

Kestrel took Arin's battered hand in hers, the rough heat of it, the fingernails still ringed with carbon from the smith's coal fire. His skin was raw-looking: scrubbed clean and scrubbed often. But the black grime was too ingrained.

She twined her fingers with his. Kestrel and Arin walked together through the passageway and the ghost of its old door, which her people had smashed through ten years before.

After that, Kestrel sought him out. She used the excuse of those lessons he had given her. She said that she wanted more. She acquired a number of menial skills, like how to blacken boots.

Arin was easy to find. Although raids on the countryside continued, he increasingly relied on lieutenants to lead the sorties. He spent more time at home.

"I don't know what he thinks he's doing," Sarsine said.

"He's giving officers under his command the chance to prove their worth," Kestrel said. "He's showing his trust in them and letting them build their confidence. It's sound military strategy."

Sarsine gave her a hard look.

"He's delegating," Kestrel said.

"He's *shirking*. And for *what*, I'm sure you know."

This struck a bright match of pleasure within Kestrel.

Like a match, it burned out quickly. She recalled her promise to Jess to make the Herrani pay.

But she did not want to think about that.

It occurred to her that she had never thanked Arin for bringing her piano here. She found him in the library and meant to say what she had come to say, yet when she saw him studying a map near the fire, lit by an upward shower of sparks as one log fell on another, she remembered her promise precisely because of how she longed to forget it.

She blurted something that had nothing to do with anything. "Do you know how to make honeyed half-moons?"

"Do I . . . ?" He lowered the map. "Kestrel, I hate to disappoint you, but I was never a cook."

"You know how to make tea."

He laughed. "You *do* realize that boiling water is within the capabilities of anybody?"

"Oh." Kestrel moved to leave, feeling foolish. What had possessed her to ask such a ridiculous question anyway?

"I mean, yes," Arin said. "Yes, I know how to make half-moons."

"Really?"

"Ah . . . no. But we can try."

They went into the kitchens. A glance from Arin cleared the room, and then it was only the two of them, dumping flour onto the wooden worktable, Arin palming a jar of honey out of a cabinet.

Kestrel cracked an egg into a bowl and knew why she had asked for this.

So that she could pretend that there had been no war, there were no sides, and that this was her life.

The half-moons came out as hard as rocks.

"Hmm." Arin inspected one. "I could use these as weapons."

She laughed before she could tell herself it wasn't funny.

"Actually, they're about the size of *your* weapon of choice," he said. "Which reminds me that you've never said how you dueled at Needles against the city's finest fighter and won."

It would be a mistake to tell him. It would defy the simplest rule of warfare: to hide one's strengths and weaknesses for as long as possible. Yet Kestrel told Arin the story of how she had beaten Irex.

Arin covered his face with one floured hand and peeked at her between his fingers. "You are terrifying. Gods help me if I cross you, Kestrel."

"You already have," she pointed out.

"But *am* I your enemy?" Arin crossed the space between them. Softly, he repeated, "Am I?"

She didn't answer. She concentrated on the feel of the table's edge pressing into the small of her back. The table was simple and real, joined wood and nails and right corners. No wobble. No give.

"You're not mine," Arin said.

And kissed her.

Kestrel's lips parted. This was real, yet not simple at all. He smelled of woodsmoke and sugar. Sweet beneath the burn. He tasted like the honey he'd licked off his fingers minutes before. Her heartbeat skidded, and it was *she* who leaned greedily into the kiss, she who slid one knee between his legs. Then his breath went ragged and the kiss grew dark and deep. He lifted her up onto the table so that her face was level with his, and as they kissed it seemed that words were hiding in the air around them, that they were invisible creatures that feathered against her and Arin, then nudged, and buzzed, and tugged.

Speak, they said.

Speak, the kiss answered.

Love was on the tip of Kestrel's tongue. But she couldn't say that. How could she ever say that, after everything between them, after fifty keystones paid into the auctioneer's hand, after hours of Kestrel secretly wondering what it would sound like if Arin sang while she played, after wrists bound together and the crack of her knee under a boot and Arin confessing in the carriage on Firstwinter night.

It had *felt* like a confession. But it wasn't. He had said nothing of the plot. Even if he had, it still would have been too late, with everything to his advantage.

Kestrel remembered again her promise to Jess.

If she didn't leave this house now, she would betray

herself. She would give herself to someone whose Firstwinter kiss had led her to believe she was all that he wanted, when he had hoped to flip the world so that he was at its top and she was at its bottom.

Kestrel pulled away.

Arin was apologizing. He was asking what he had done wrong. His face was flushed, mouth swollen. He was saying something about how maybe it was too soon, but that they could have a life here. Together.

"My soul is yours," he said. "You know that it is."

She lifted a hand, as much to block his face from her sight as to stop those words.

She walked out of the kitchen.

It took all of her pride not to run.

She went to her rooms, yanked on her black dueling clothes and boots, and reeled in her makeshift knife out of the ivy. She bound the strip of cloth that held it around her waist. She went into the garden and waited for nightfall.

Kestrel had always thought that the rooftop garden was her best chance for escape. Yet she couldn't see how to take it.

She swept her gaze over the four stone walls. Again, she saw nothing. Kestrel stared hard at the door, but what good could that do her? The door led to Arin's suite, and Arin—

No. Kestrel was thinking that no, she would not go through that door, she could not, when it suddenly struck her that she had her answer.

It was little use considering the door as a way to pass *through* the wall. The door was a means to get *up* it.

Kestrel set her right hand on the doorknob and her left toes on the lower hinge. Her left hand braced against the stony line of the doorjamb, and she pushed herself up onto that hinge, balancing on such a small thing, just a strip and nub of metal. Then right foot up to meet her hand on the doorknob. She shifted her weight and stood to grasp the top hinge before she dug her fingers into the crack where the top of the door met stone.

Kestrel climbed up the door and onto the top of the wall that separated her garden from Arin's. She balanced along it until she reached the roof.

Then she was moving down its slope, running to reach the ground.

32

ARIN DREAMED OF KESTREL. HE WOKE, AND the dream faded like perfume. He didn't remember it, yet it changed the air around him. He blinked against the dark.

When he heard the sound, he realized he had been expecting something of this kind for a long time.

Light feet on the roof.

Arin scrambled out of bed.

Kestrel jumped onto the first floor, slid down its roof on her stomach, felt her toes nudge into a hollow. The gutter. She twisted to grasp it, then hung from the stone edge above the ground. She dropped.

The impact jarred and her bad knee twinged, but she caught her balance and sprinted for the stables.

Javelin whickered the instant she entered.

"Shh." She led him from his stall. "Quietly, now." There was no need for a lamp that might be seen from the house. Kestrel could feel her way in the dark to grab the tack that she needed. Easy. She had memorized the locations of bridle and bit and everything else on that day in the stables. She saddled Javelin quickly.

When they emerged into the night air, Kestrel glanced at the house. It slumbered. There was no cry of alarm, no soldiers pouring from its doors.

But there was a small light in the west wing.

It was nothing, she told herself. Arin had probably fallen asleep while a lamp burned.

Kestrel breathed in the scent of horse. It was how her father smelled when he came home from a campaign.

She could do this. She could make it to the harbor.

She mounted Javelin and dug her heels in.

Kestrel streaked through the Garden District, urging Javelin down horse paths to the city center. It wasn't until she had almost reached its lights that she heard another rider in the hills behind her.

Ice slid down Kestrel's spine. Fear, that the rider was Arin.

Fear, at her sudden hope that it was.

She pulled Javelin to a stop and swung to the ground. Better to go on foot through the narrow streets to the harbor. Stealth was more important now than speed.

Beating hooves echoed in the hills. Closer.

She hugged Javelin hard around the neck, then pushed him away while she still could bear to do it. She slapped his rump in an order to head home. Whether he'd go to her villa or Arin's, she couldn't say. But he left, and might draw the other rider after him if she was indeed being pursued.

She slipped into the city shadows.

And it was magic. It was as if the Herrani gods had turned on their own people. No one noticed Kestrel skulking along walls or heard her cracking the thin ice of a puddle. No late-night wanderer looked in her face and saw a Valorian. No one saw the general's daughter. Kestrel made it to the harbor, down to the docks.

Where Arin waited.

His breath heaved white clouds into the air. His hair was black with sweat. It hadn't mattered that Kestrel had been ahead of him on the horse path. Arin had been able to run openly through the city while she had crept through alleys.

Their eyes met, and Kestrel felt utterly defenseless.

But she had a weapon. He didn't, not that she could see. Her hand instinctively fell to her knife's jagged edge.

Arin saw. Kestrel wasn't sure what came first: his quick hurt, so plain and sharp, or her certainty—equally plain, equally sharp—that she could never draw a weapon on him.

He straightened from his runner's crouch. His expression changed. Until it did, Kestrel hadn't perceived the desperate set of his mouth. She hadn't recognized the wordless plea until it was gone, and his face aged with something sad. Resigned.

Arin glanced away. When he looked back it was as if Kestrel were part of the pier beneath her feet. A sail stitched to a ship. A black current of water.

As if she were not there at all.

He turned away, walked into the illuminated house of the new Herrani harbormaster, and shut the door behind him.

For a moment Kestrel couldn't move. Then she ran for a fishing boat docked far enough from its fellows that she might cast off from shore unnoticed by any sailors on the other vessels. She leaped onto the deck and took rapid stock of the boat. The tiny cabin was bare of supplies.

As she lifted the anchor and uncoiled the rope tethering the boat to its dock, she knew, even if she couldn't see, that Arin was talking with the harbormaster, distracting him while Kestrel prepared to set sail.

In winter. With no water or food, and surely very little sleep if she was to make a voyage that would take, at best, three days.

At least there was a strong wind.

She was lucky, Kestrel told herself. Lucky.

She cast off for the capital.

Once she'd sailed from the bay and the city lights had dimmed, then disappeared, Kestrel couldn't see the shore. But she knew her constellations, and the stars were as pure and bright as notes struck from high, white piano keys.

She sailed west. Kestrel moved constantly over the small deck, tacking the lines, letting the wind furl out the mainsail. There was no rest, and that was good. If she rested she would grow cold. She would allow herself to think. She might even fall asleep, and then risked dreaming of how Arin had let her go.

She memorized what she would say when she reached the capital's harbor. *I am Lady Kestrel, General Trajan's daughter. Herrani have taken the peninsula. You must recall my father from the east and send him to stamp out the rebellion.*

You must.

A bright, brittle dawn. Its colors were hallucinatory, and Kestrel found herself thinking that pink was colder than orange, and yellow not much better. Then she realized that this wasn't a rational thought and that she was shivering in her thin jacket. She forced herself to move.

Her hands chapped and bled in the freezing wind, ripped against the ropes. Her mouth became a dry cave. Thirst and cold were far more painful than hunger or fatigue. She knew that a few days without water could kill a person, even in the best conditions.

Yet hadn't Kestrel learned to steel herself against need?

She remembered Arin's face when she had reached for her knife.

She forced herself to forget it. She focused on the waves' swell and slam, steered past a bare, rocky island, and recited what she would say in two days' time if the wind held.

It didn't. The sails slackened during her second night. Her boat drifted. She tried not to look at the sky, because sometimes she saw glitter even though she knew the stars were hidden beneath clouds.

A dangerous sign. She was weakening.

Her body raged with thirst. She tore the cabin apart, thinking that a flask of fresh water must be somewhere. All she found was a tin cup and spoon.

Sleep, then. She'd sleep until the wind picked up. Kestrel tied the sails in the direction of the capital, then cut two pieces of twine. She rigged a chime out of the cup and spoon to wake her if the wind rose.

Kestrel slipped back into the cabin. Everything was still. No wind. No waves. No tilt and roll of the boat.

She focused on that nothingness, imagined it as ink spilling over everything she could possibly think or feel.

She slept.

It was a jagged, haunted sleep where her mind whirred through the words she was supposed to say when she reached the capital.

She struggled against images of Arin holding a plant, a bloody sword, her hand. She tried to wring the life out of the memory of her skin against his. Instead it beaded bright in her dark mind, strung itself out like liquid jewels, distilled down the way alcohol does, or a volatile chemical, growing stronger when forced to reduce.

Her half-asleep self said: *Arin let you go because a*

Valorian invasion was inevitable. At least this way, he knows when to expect it.

Kestrel heard music, and it called her a liar.

Liar, the bell rang.

And kept ringing, and ringing, until Kestrel wrenched awake and out of the cabin to see the cup and spoon clanging.

Against a vicious green sky.

Green storm.

Waves vomited over the deck. Kestrel had lashed herself to the tiller and could do little more than hang on, watch the wind shred the sails, and hope she was still pointed west as the boat sheered off crests of water and pitched down, and sideways, and down.

Arin let you go so that you would die, just like this.

But even dizzy, her mind saw no sense in that.

Kestrel worked again through the words she was supposed to say, spun them out from her like knitting she had seen slaves do. She tested the words' fabric, their fiber, and knew she couldn't speak them.

She would not.

Kestrel swore by Arin's gods that she would not.

No wind. She couldn't see much. Salt water had bleared her eyes. But she heard the boat scrape against something. Then came voices.

Valorian voices.

She stumbled off the boat. Hands caught her, and people

were asking questions she didn't fully comprehend. Then one made sense: "Who are you?"

"I am Lady Kestrel," she croaked. Unbidden—wretched, *wrong*—all the words she had memorized poured out before she could shut her mouth. "General Trajan's daughter. Herrani have taken the peninsula . . ."

SHE WOKE WHEN SOMEONE DRIBBLED WATER past her lips. She came instantly alive, begging for more as it was doled out in excruciatingly small sips. Kestrel drank, and thought of things whose beauty was raw and cool.

Rain on silver bowls. Lilies in snow. Gray eyes.

She had done something, she remembered. Something cruel. Unforgivable.

Kestrel forced herself up on her elbows. She lay on a large bed. She still saw badly, but well enough to observe that the softness cushioning her body was a fur so rare and valuable its animal had been hunted nearly to extinction, and that the man who held a cup of water wore the robes of the Valorian emperor's physician.

"Brave girl," he said. His smile was kind.

Kestrel saw it and understood that she had succeeded. She had reached the capital, had been recognized and believed.

No, she tried to say. *I didn't mean it.* But her mouth didn't work.

"You've been through an ordeal," the doctor said. "You need to rest."

There was an odd taste on her tongue, a faint bitterness whose taste turned into a numb feeling that prickled down her throat.

A drug.

The numbness held her down until sleep took over.

She dreamed of Enai.

Kestrel's sleeping self knew that this was not real, that the dead are gone. But she longed to sidle near Enai, to shrink into a small girl and not glance up, not search the woman's face for the blame that must be there.

Kestrel wondered how Arin's ghost would look at her.

He would stalk her dreams. He would show visions of himself killed in battle. He would make his mouth a mockery of the one she knew. His eyes would fill with hate.

That was how one looked at a traitor.

"You've come to curse me," Kestrel told Enai. "There is no need. I curse myself."

"Sly child," Enai said, as she had done when Kestrel had been naughty. But this was not the same thing, Kestrel wanted to say, as stuffing sheet music into the rafters of Rax's practice room and pulling them down to read when she was alone and supposed to be drilling herself in combat. It was not the same thing as a sharp word. A prank played.

Kestrel had bought a life, and loved it, and sold it.

Enai said, "A story, I think, to make you feel better."

"I'm not sick."

"Yes, you are."

"I don't need a story. I need to wake up."

"And do what?"

Kestrel didn't know.

Enai said, "Once there was a seamstress who could weave fabric from feeling. She sewed gowns of delight: sheer, sparkling, sleek. She cut cloth out of ambition and ardor, idyll and industry. And she grew so skilled at her trade that she caught the attention of a god. He decided to acquire her services."

"Which god is this?"

"Hush," Enai said. In that way of dreams, Kestrel found herself in her childhood bed, the one carved with hunting animals. Enai sat by her, shoulders elegant and straight in lines Kestrel had always tried to imitate. The woman continued her story. "The god came to the seamstress and said, 'I want a shirt made of solace.'

"'The gods have no need of such a thing,' said the seamstress. The god looked at her.

"The girl knew a threat when she saw it.

"She met his demand, and when the god tried on the shirt, it fit perfectly. Its colors changed him, made his face seem not quite as pale. The seamstress studied him and had thoughts she knew weren't wise to share.

"The god paid her in generous gold, though she hadn't named a price. He was pleased.

"Yet it was not enough. He returned, ordered a cloak of

company, and left even before the seamstress agreed to do it. They both knew that she would.

"She was putting the finishing touches on the cloak's hem when an old woman entered the shop and looked at all the things she couldn't afford to buy. The woman reached across the counter where the seamstress sat at her work. Wizened fingers wavered over the cloak of company. Faded eyes became so starred with longing that the seamstress gave her the cloak and asked nothing in return. She could make another one—and quickly.

"The god, however, was quicker still. He returned to her village sooner than he'd said. Who did he see but the elderly woman sleeping by her fire, wrapped in a cloak that was far too big for her? What did he feel but the grip of betrayal, the swift, deep dart of jealousy that should shame a god?

"He came to the seamstress's shop in that silent way of his, like ice forming in the night. 'Give me the cloak,' he demanded.

"The seamstress held her needle. It was no weapon against a god. 'It's not ready,' she said.

" 'Liar.' "

The word dropped with its own weight. Kestrel said, "Am I the seamstress in this story, or the god?"

Enai continued as if she hadn't heard. "He would have destroyed her then, but another path of vengeance occurred to him. A better means to wreak her misery. He knew that she had a nephew: a little boy, the only scrap of family remaining to her. She paid for his care out of her earnings, and he was sleeping now in a neighboring town, snug under the watchful gaze of a nurse the god could distract, and trick, and lull.

"He did. He left the seamstress's shop and slipped up to the slumbering boy. There was no pity for the small, rounded limbs, the cheeks flushed with sleep, the smudge of wild hair in the dark. The god had stolen children before."

Kestrel said, "This is the god of death."

"When the god drew back the blanket, his finger brushed against the child's nightshirt. He went still. Never, in all his immortal years, had he touched anything so beautiful.

"The shirt had been sewn from the cloth of love. He felt the plush of velvet, the skim of silk, the resilient woof and weft that would not fray. Yet there was one thing to it that didn't belong: a small, damp circle the size of a fingertip.

"Or a god's tear.

"It dried. The cloth smoothed once more. The god left.

"The seamstress, meanwhile, grew anxious. She hadn't heard from her best and worst customer for days. It didn't seem possible that she could have escaped him so lightly. One didn't defy the gods, and never *this* god. A fissure of thought began in the seamstress's mind. A suspicion. It widened into an earthquake that shattered her, for she suddenly saw, as the god had, the surest way to bring her to despair.

"She rushed to the neighboring town and the nurse's house. Her hand trembled against the door, for death was what she would find behind it.

"It flung open. The boy clambered into her arms, chiding her for being so long away this time, asking why she had to work so hard. The seamstress caught at him, held him until he complained. When she fluttered fingers over his face, certain that death had crept under his skin some-how and would burst forth in an hour, or a minute, if not now, she saw that the boy's forehead had been marked.

"Marked by the sign of the god's protection. His favor. It was a gift without price.

"The seamstress returned to her shop and waited. Her hands, for once, were not busy. They were calm strangers. They waited, too, but the god didn't come. So the seamstress did something frightening. She whispered his name.

"He came, and was silent. He wore nothing she had made, but his own clothes. They were impressively cut, an assured fit. Yet the seamstress didn't know how she had ever missed their threadbare state. The fabric had rubbed down to thin clouds.

"'I wish to thank you,' she said.

"'I do not deserve thanks,' said the god.

"'Nevertheless, I want to give it.'

"The god did not reply. Her hands did not move.

"He said, 'Then weave me the cloth of yourself.'

"The seamstress set her hands in his. She kissed him, and the god stole her away."

The story billowed through Kestrel, a fierce wind that smarted the eyes and bled tears down her cheeks.

"Oh, now," Enai said. "I thought the story was encour-aging."

"Encouraging? The seamstress *dies*."

"That's a grim interpretation. Let's say instead that she chose. The god let her choose, and she did. You, Kestrel, haven't made your choice."

"I have. Don't you know that I have? By now the

emperor has sent his messenger hawks to my father. War has already begun. It is too late."

"Is it?"

Kestrel woke. Her body was dim with hunger and shaken by dreams, but she got to her feet with a purpose. She dressed. Slaves came to her, their faces a map of the empire, of the northern tundra and southern isles, the Herran peninsula. She ignored that their number showed the emperor's respect for her. She ignored that the ceiling of her room was so high that she couldn't discern the color of the paint. She prepared herself to meet the emperor.

Kestrel was taken to a state room and left alone with the man who ruled half the world.

He was thinner than the statues of him, his silver hair cropped in the military style. He smiled. An emperor's smile is a gold-and-diamond thing, a fortress, a sword held out hilt first—at least when the smile is the kind he offered her then. "Have you come to claim your reward, Lady Kestrel? The attack on Herran began two days ago, while you slept."

"I'm here to ask you to stop the attack."

"Stop—?" The lines on his face sank deep. "Why would I do that?"

"Your Imperial Majesty, have you ever heard of the Winner's Curse?"

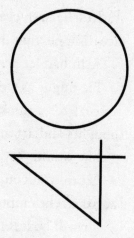

"THE EMPIRE SUFFERS FROM IT," KESTREL SAID. "It can no longer afford to keep what it has won. Our territories have grown too large. The barbarians know this. It is why they dare attack."

The emperor waved a dismissive hand. "They are mice nibbling at the grain."

"*You* know it, too. That is why you attack *them*, to make it seem as if the empire's resources are bottomless, our military unmatched, when really we are stretched as thin as old cloth. Holes have begun to appear."

The emperor's smile showed its sharp edge. "Careful, Kestrel."

"If you won't hear the truth, it's only a matter of time before the empire falls apart. The Herrani never should have been able to rise against us."

"That problem will be solved. As we speak, your father is crushing the rebellion. The city walls will fall." The emperor relaxed in his throne. "General Trajan isn't leading a war, but an extermination."

Kestrel saw every vulnerable part of Arin's body, his face disappearing in a welter of blood.

Arin had let her go.

He might as well have cut his own throat.

Fear rose, thick as bile. She swallowed it. She took her thoughts and arranged them like gaming tiles.

She would play, and she would win.

"Have you considered the cost of another Herran war?" she asked the emperor.

"It will be less than losing the territory."

"So long as the city walls hold, the Herrani can live through a long siege that will bleed your treasury."

The emperor's mouth pinched. "There is no other option."

"What if you could keep the territory without a war?"

He must have heard, as Kestrel did, her father's voice coming out of her mouth. That cadence of calculated certainty. The emperor's posture didn't change, and neither did his expression. But a finger lifted off the throne and tapped once against its marble, the way it might against a bell to hear the sound of its ring.

Kestrel said, "Give the Herrani their independence."

That finger slashed through the air to point at the door. "Leave."

"Please hear me out—"

"Your father's service to the empire will mean nothing to me—*your* service will mean nothing—if you speak another insolent, insane word."

"Herran would still be yours! You can keep the territory, so long as you let them govern it. Give them citizenship, yet make its leader swear an oath of fealty to you. Tax the people. Take their goods. Take their crops. They want their freedom, their lives, and their homes. The rest is negotiable."

The emperor was silent.

"Our governor is dead anyway," Kestrel said. "Let the Herrani supply a new one."

Still he said nothing.

"The new governor would, of course, answer to you," she added.

"And you think the Herrani would agree to this?"

Kestrel thought of the two keys Arin had set on her palm. A limited freedom. Yet better than none. "Yes."

The emperor shook his head.

"I haven't mentioned the best part about a swift end to the Herran revolution," she said. "Right now, the east thinks you have retreated. The barbarians congratulate themselves. They have heard, through spies or captured messenger hawks, of the difficulty that mires you in Herran." These were guesses, but they became belief when she saw the emperor's face. Kestrel pressed on. "The barbarians know that a siege against city walls well built will take time, so they pull back from the front lines where we fought them and return to their queen to share the good news. They leave a few token battalions to occupy land they think they won't have to defend. But if you were to send our forces *back*, and catch the barbarians by surprise . . ."

"I see." The emperor folded his hands and set the peaked knuckles against his chin. "But you overlook that Herran is a *colony*. The homes the Herrani want back belong to my senators."

"The barbarians have gold. Enrich the disappointed senators with plunder from the east."

"Even then. What you propose would not be popular."

"You are the emperor. What do you care for public opinion?"

His brows lifted. "A comment like that makes me wonder whether you're naïve or attempting to manipulate me." He studied her. "You are too clever to be naïve."

Kestrel knew better than to speak.

"You are the daughter of the most fabled general in Valorian history."

She didn't see what shape the emperor's thoughts were forming.

"You are also not unattractive."

Her eyes flew to his.

He said, "I have a son."

Yes, she knew, though what the heir to the empire had to do with—

"An imperial wedding," he said. "One that would make the military love me. One that would distract the senators and their families, so that their chief point of concern is how to receive an invitation. I like your plans for Herran and the east, Kestrel, but I'll like them even more if you marry my son."

One didn't stammer before an emperor. Kestrel drew her breath and held it until she could speak calmly. "Perhaps your son would prefer someone else."

"He wouldn't."

"We've never even met."

"So?"

The emperor's face became narrow with something Kestrel recognized as cruelty at the same moment she remembered that her father had always respected him. He said, "Is there some reason you do not seize the chance to become my daughter? Some reason that you argue so ardently for the Herrani? Rumors race around the capital, and I am not the only one to have heard of your duel with Lord Irex.

"No, Kestrel, a face of innocence will not work. We have already agreed that you are too intelligent for innocence. You may be glad that I don't require it in a daughter-in-law. I do, however, require a choice. Agree to marry my son, and I will lift the siege, send our forces back east, and cope with the political consequences. Refuse, and there will be a second Herran war, and different consequences.

"Choose."

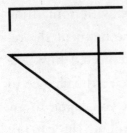

WHEN ARIN SAW THE VAST VALORIAN FLEET muscle into the harbor, he was relieved. When they destroyed the few ships taken on Firstwinter night, he was relieved, even as flaming wood scattered the water and the tindered wrecks sank.

The Herrani found courage in what they thought was Arin's fearlessness. He couldn't imagine their reaction if they knew that he had invited the war, and that the look on his face was joy.

He had felt more than seen the green storm that had ripped up the coast two days after Kestrel had left. The storm had barreled inside him, scoured out everything until he was a hollow space howling with the knowledge of what he had done, with the image of a small fishing boat tipped over, pushed under. He imagined a mouth filled with seawater, the way Kestrel would fight it. Her limbs loosening, then lost in a maze of waves.

The beginning of the siege probably meant Arin's death. But it also meant that Kestrel was alive.

So the Herrani thought his face held the mad delight of a warrior at the sight of battle. He let them believe it. *You are the god of lies,* Kestrel had said. He looked at his people and smiled, and the smile was a lie—but like writing in a mirror, whose reflection is the inverse of a truth.

After she had left, Arin ordered that the piers in the harbor be destroyed.

But when the Valorians arrived, they dropped anchor as close to shore as possible and sent engineers in small boats. Docks were swiftly rebuilt under guard, and the Herrani could do little but watch and wait behind the walls. Arin had set cannons along the battlements, but the harbor was out of range. Opening the gates and sending people to disrupt the reconstruction of the piers was suicide, so the Herrani watched the sun set and rise on the Valorian forces come ashore to unload siege engines. They hauled cannon. They wheeled kegs of black powder. They ranged horses and infantry. And they had somehow already sent soldiers around the city to the side that faced the mountains. Arin had reports of the insignias stitched on their jackets and knew that they represented the Rangers, an elite brigade who served as scouts and were skilled at subterfuge. They quickly melted into the rocks and bare trees.

A month before, Arin had ordered the digging of a trough around the city. When the days before the green storm had brought warm winds that made the winter ground soggy, the Herrani jammed debris into the muddy trough— furniture, chopped trees, broken bottles. The ground had frozen again.

Arin watched a man step to the edge of the deep,

littered rut. His face was obscured by a helmet, but Arin would have known, even without the imperial flag painted across the man's armor, who it was. He had seen the general's measured step before, the weight of the way he moved.

General Trajan inspected the trough. He glanced at the horses being unloaded from ships. Arin saw him see the difficulty of bringing his army across the trough—the disorder, the broken horse legs, glass wedged into hooves and stabbing through boots. He went to speak with a knot of engineers.

Planks of wood appeared. Foundations were laid. In a week, the Valorians crossed their makeshift bridges and came within reach of the wall.

They kept a wary distance after the Herrani lobbed flaming clumps of pitch taken from the shipyards and balled around paper and wood. There were casualties. A Valorian supply wagon was struck and burned. But other soldiers stepped forward to fill the gaps in ranks, and the remaining wagons were pulled to the rear lines.

The engineers began to build three mounds.

"Kill them," Arin told his best archers—few that they were, having only an innate knack for bows and crossbows and the little practice that seizing the countryside had brought.

The god of war favored them. The engineers dropped.

Yet soldiers took over the work. The mounds of earth and rock continued to rise, and were reinforced by wood from the disassembled bridges. They began to form towers.

Arin knew it was a matter of time before the towers reached the height of the wall, bridges were made to span the gap, and the Valorians crossed over.

"Tunnel under the wall," Arin told his soldiers. "Dig underground until you reach those towers. Then empty them from the bottom."

It took only a few days before the Valorians realized why the towers seemed to sink. Arin heard the general bark an order. Shovels drove into the ground around the towers. When they broke through to the tunnels, soldiers dropped down inside.

"Seal the tunnels!" Arin shouted.

He was obeyed. The Valorians didn't manage to enter the city that way. It was closed off to them, just as it was to the Herrani left to die in the tunnels.

The towers mounted. Arin had only a small arsenal of cannonballs and black powder, but he used most of it to explode the towers.

The Valorians pulled catapults forward. They shot fire into the city.

It began to burn.

A snowfall hissed down onto the fire, helped put it out. It was three weeks since Kestrel had left, and Arin—exhausted, sooty with smoke—remembered how confidently he had assured her that the Herrani could withstand a year of siege.

As if all that was necessary was a good stock of grain and water.

He used the last supply of cannon artillery to destroy the catapults. After that, the Herrani had only the wall and what they could throw off it to protect themselves.

There was a lull in enemy activity. Arin thought the snow had dampened their determination, or that the general was plotting his next move. But when something burst against the mountainside wall and it trembled like a living thing, Arin realized the lull had been part of the plot.

Rangers were blasting through the wall.

Herrani poured boiling water and tar down onto the Rangers. They screamed. They fell. But General Trajan had heard, as well as Arin, the sound of his success. He brought his troops, which Arin now realized had been positioned for this moment, around the city. Soon they would bring the brunt of their power to bear against the weakened wall. They'd ram through chunks of stone. They'd punch at the crumbling façade until a hole appeared and widened. They'd drag the hole open with grappling hooks cranked by siege engines. They would enter the city.

It would be a massacre.

Arin had taken position on the mountainside wall. He didn't see a ship enter the harbor.

But he saw a hawk—a small one, a kestrel—swoop over the city and dive toward the general.

The man pulled a tube from its leg and opened it. He went still.

He disappeared into the ranks of soldiers.

The Valorian army stopped its assault.

Then Arin's feet were moving along the wall, racing to face the sea, and although he couldn't have said that he knew what had happened, he knew that something had changed, and in his mind there was only one person who could change his world.

Another hawk was perched on the seaside battlements. It eyed him—head cocked, beak sharp, talons tight on stone. Snow laced its feathers.

The message it bore was short.

Arin,

Let me in.

Kestrel

KESTREL WATCHED THE GATE HEAVE OPEN.
Arin stepped through, and it slammed behind him so that
the closed wall was to his back as the sea was to hers. He
started toward her. Then his eyes flashed, as her father's had
when she'd met him moments before, to her forehead.
Arin's face whitened.

Across her brows was a glittering line of gold dust and
myrrh oil. It was the Valorian sign of an engaged woman.

She forced herself to smile. "You don't trust me enough
to let me inside the city, Arin? Well, I understand."

"What did you do?"

The brokenness of his voice broke Kestrel. Yet she held
the pieces of herself together.

"But Ronan . . ." Arin trailed off. "How, Kestrel?
Who?"

"Congratulate me. I am to marry the heir to the empire."

She saw him believe it. She saw betrayal wash across his
features, then understanding. She saw his thoughts.

Hadn't she pulled away from his embrace, escaped across his roof, and nearly drawn a weapon on him?

Who was he, to her?

And Kestrel liked to win. Wasn't the someday role of empress a tempting stake? Power might persuade where Ronan hadn't.

Arin's belief was cruel. Yet she said nothing to change it. If he knew the true conditions of the emperor's offer, he would never accept it.

"As pleasant as it would be to discuss the details of my upcoming wedding," she said, "more important matters are at hand. The emperor has a message for you."

Arin's eyes had darkened. His tone was biting. "Message?"

"Freedom, for you and your people. He appoints you governor. You are, of course, to swear loyalty to the emperor, receive his emissaries, and answer to him. But unless a matter doesn't directly concern the empire, you may govern your people as you see fit." Kestrel handed him a sheet of paper. "A list of Herran's expected taxes and tributes, to be paid for the honor of being part of the empire."

Arin crumpled it in his fist. "This is a trick."

"Surrender now, and accept his generous proposal, or surrender soon, when my father breaks down your wall, and see the end of the Herrani people. It could be a trick, but you will choose it."

"Why would the emperor do this?"

Kestrel hesitated. "Why?"

"If real, it *is* a generous offer. And it makes no sense."

"I advise you not to question the emperor's wisdom. If

you see a good opportunity, take it." Kestrel swept a hand to indicate her finery: the white furs, the gold, the jewels. "*I* certainly did."

There was an awful tension in Arin, one that reminded Kestrel of his childhood violin. He had been strung too hard for far too long. When he finally spoke, his reply came in a low growl. "I agree."

"Then give orders to open the gate. My father will enter and escort all Valorians in your city back to the capital."

"I agree," Arin said, "under one condition. You mentioned emissaries. There will be *one* emissary from the empire. It will be you."

"Me?"

"You, I understand. You, I know how to read."

Kestrel wasn't so sure of that. "I think that will be acceptable," she said, and wanted to turn away from how much she wanted this condition. How she would seize any chance to see him, even with the purpose of enforcing the emperor's will.

Since she could not turn away from her own wanting, she turned away from him.

"Please don't do this," he said. "Kestrel, you don't know. You don't understand."

"I see things quite clearly." She began to walk to meet her father, in whose eyes she had, at last, done something to make him proud.

"You don't," Arin said.

She pretended not to hear him. She watched the white sky dissolve into snow and shiver apart over the leaden sea. She felt icy sparks on her skin. The snow fell on her, it fell on him, but Kestrel knew that no single flake could ever touch them both.

She didn't look back when he spoke again.

"You don't, Kestrel, even though the god of lies loves you."

Author's Note

The idea for this novel came to me while sitting with my friend Vasiliki Skreta on a dark blue gym mat in the children's play-room of our apartment building. Vasiliki is an economist, and we were discussing auctions. She mentioned the concept of the "winner's curse." Quite simply, it describes how the winner of an auction has also lost, because he or she has won by paying more than what the majority of bidders have decided the item is worth. Of course, no one knows what something might be worth in the future. The winner's curse (at least, in economic theory) is about the very *moment* of winning, not its aftermath.

I was fascinated by this version of a Pyrrhic victory—to win and lose at the same time. I was tempted by the beauty of the term "winner's curse," which was first presented in a 1971 paper called "Competitive Bidding in High-Risk Situations," by E. C. Capen, R. V. Clapp, and W. M. Campbell. I tried to think of a novel in which someone would win an auction that exacts a steep *emotional* price. It occurred to me: What if the item at auction were not a thing but a person? What might winning cost then?

My first thanks for *The Winner's Curse* goes to Vasiliki. I must also acknowledge several texts that kept me company while writing. Although the world I've presented in these pages is my own and has no concrete connection to the real world, I was in-spired by antiquity, in particular the Greco-Roman period after Rome had conquered Greece and enslaved its population in the expected way of the time; slavery was a common consequence of war. Two books helped me think about the mentality of that period: Marguerite Yourcenar's novel *Memoirs of Hadrian* and Thucydides' *The History of the Peloponnesian War* (which I paraphrase at one point). The poem that Kestrel reads in her library is very close to Ezra Pound's opening of *Canto I* (which in turn echoes Homer's *The Odyssey*): "And then went down to the ship, / Set keel to breakers, forth on the godly sea."

So I give thanks to my reading . . . and to my readers. Many friends read and commented on *The Winner's Curse*. Some read a chapter, others whole sections, and others multiple drafts. Thank you: Genn Albin, Marianna Baer, Betsy Bird, Elise Broach, Donna Freitas, Daphne Grab, Mordicai Knode, Kekla Magoon, Caragh O'Brien, Jill Santopolo, Eliot Schrefer, Natalie Van Unen, and Robin Wasserman. Your advice has been indispensable.

Thanks also to those who have discussed this project with me, and offered ideas or moral support (often both!): Kristin Cashore, Jenny Knode, Thomas Philippon, and Robert Rutkoski (who came up with the phrase "the code of the call"). Nicole Cliffe, Denise Klein, Kate Moncrief, and Ivan Werning had really useful things to say about horses. David Verchere, as usual, was my go-to expert on ships and sailing. Tiffany Werth, Georgi McCarthy, and many Facebook friends chimed in on questions about language.

I have two small, sweet sons, and couldn't have written this book without help taking care of them. Thanks to my parents, in-laws, and babysitters: Monica Ciucurel, Shaida Khan, Georgi McCarthy, Nora Meguetaoui, Christiane and Jean-Claude Philippon, and Marilyn and Robert Rutkoski.

I'm very grateful to those who look out for me. My wise and warm agent, Charlotte Sheedy, and her team: Mackenzie Brady, Carly Croll, and Joan Rosen. My insightful editor, Janine O'Malley, who makes every book so much better. Simon Boughton, for valuing details. Joy Peskin, for being such a wonderful advocate. Everybody else at FSG and Macmillan, for their verve and delight in bringing books into this world, especially Elizabeth Clark, Gina Gagliano, Angus Killick, Kate Leid, Kathryn Little, Karen Ninnis, Karla Reganold, Caitlin Sweeny, Allison Verost, Ksenia Winnicki, and Jon Yaged. Thank you.

THE WINNER'S
CURSE

BONUS MATERIALS

DISCUSSION QUESTIONS

1. Kestrel lives in a colonized land her father conquered ten years ago. After the conquest, the territory's people—the Herrani—were enslaved. What happened wasn't Kestrel's fault, yet every day since has revolved around her advantages and power over others. If we profit from someone else's cruel actions, does that make us guilty, too? At what point do we become responsible for allowing an immoral situation to continue?

2. Arin says that Kestrel's old nurse, a former slave, could never have truly loved her. "If she loved you," he says, "it was because she had no choice." Is it impossible for love to exist between a slave and a free person?

3. From ceremonial military garb to elaborate ball gowns to a house slave's uniform, clothes play an important role in *The Winner's Curse*. How do clothes send messages in a society? What do you think people are trying to say or do when they dress a certain way? What do you want your clothes to say about you?

4. Kestrel thinks, "In the eyes of Valorian society, music was a pleasure to be taken, not made, and it didn't occur to many that the making and the taking could be the same." What's the difference between taking pleasure in something, and making your pleasure? Can you think of a situation where you must make something in order to take pleasure in it?

5. At first, Kestrel refuses to acknowledge her growing fascination with Arin. But other people see it, and vicious gossip begins. Can gossip be a weapon? How do you feel about the way society tries to make people conform to expectations by talking about them?

6. Arin despises Kestrel when she buys him, but gradually he comes to see her as a person he can respect and eventually love. At the same time, she's still part of a society that has taken everything from him. Is it possible to forgive an enemy?

7. If Kestrel's father lived in today's society, he could be tried for war crimes. But Kestrel loves him, and he loves her. What would you do if someone in your family committed a terrible crime? Would it change how you felt about that person?

8. Kestrel is a strategist. She could easily lead an army to victory by making the right military choices. But she doesn't want to go to war. Is there something that you are good at but also afraid of?

9. While Kestrel doesn't want to use her strategizing skills for military purposes, she's very happy to beat everyone at a game called Bite and Sting. How can playing games with others change how we feel about them?

An Interview with the Author

Photograph Stephen Grossman

This is an edited version of a PW KidsCast interview with author Marie Rutkoski and *Publishers Weekly* Children's Review editor, John Sellers.

John Sellers (JS): Well, maybe we should start off with the idea that gives the book its name, *The Winner's Curse*. Basically, I think it involves sort of biting off more than one can chew or more than one expected. Can you talk a bit about how that idea came your way and where it took you?

Marie Rutkoski (MR): Sure. "The winner's curse" is a term in economic theory that describes what happens at an auction when someone wins an item up for bid, but winning is predicated on paying too much for that item. Essentially, the winner of the auction has only acquired the object by bidding more than what everyone else thinks the object is worth.

This concept was explained to me by a friend who's an economist. We were sitting in the children's playroom of our building and I was really drawn to the phrase—to its beauty and to the idea that it is a bit like a Pyrrhic victory. You win but you also lose at the same time, or the winning comes at a very great cost. I tried to imagine a story that would fit with the title *The Winner's Curse* and when I began brainstorming, what I really wanted was to imagine a situation where someone wins something that exacts a steep emotional cost. I kept trying to think of what this item up for bid could be; what could cause something to be very emotionally costly? It occurred to me: What if the item up for auction was not a thing but a person? What, then, would be the ultimate cost of winning?

JS: In your afterword, I think you also mentioned taking inspiration in part from antiquity, especially from the relationship between the ancient Romans and Greeks. What sort of

research did you do and did you find anything surprising? W.
that how you got from this economic theory to the culture you
built in the books?

MR: Well, many years ago, I had taken a class in college on ancient art, and I remember my teacher commenting on how the Romans, after conquering Greece, felt culturally inferior to the people that they had subjugated militarily. The professor mentioned that in many Roman households there would be Greek slaves who would recite poetry and teach Roman children. Even at that time I was really fascinated by the inherent tension between the Romans, who had all the physical power, and the Greeks, who had a cultural caché but who had been captured and essentially transformed into objects for the Romans' bidding. So it was not that I actually did research on that topic but rather, that I had learned things that stayed with me for a very long time and came to the surface later when I was thinking about "the winner's curse"—the economic phrase. One of the most important things for me was to read Thucydides's *The History of the Peloponnesian War*. It was very useful in terms of thinking about how war is enacted and how, for example, a siege engine can be defeated.

Also important to me were the moments in the book that contemplated why people go to war and how people who want to go to war can pressure others to do so.

JS: One of the things I really enjoyed in the book was how roundly skilled both Kestrel and Arin are. Not only is Kestrel a talented fighter, but both she and Arin are incredible strategists, which I suppose is important when one of them is at war and conflict. Is it fair to say that as the series progresses maybe intellectual prowess will be as important as physical prowess in these books?

MR: Well, I would say intellectual prowess may be more important than physical prowess because Kestrel is *not* a skilled fighter. She has been forced to train in personal combat because her father is the highest-ranking general in the military. He very much wants Kestrel to be part of his world and she has tried for many years to please him and to be what he wants her to be, and she is basically up to snuff. She can defend herself; she's not a terrible fighter but fighting is certainly not something that she's good at. She fails at it quite frequently, much to her own and her father's dismay. But definitely in terms of military strategy, her mental skills are key. I would say also that although Arin is intellectually gifted and has a certain amount of physical prowess, his physical prowess is not uncomplicated. He was enslaved when he was nine years old and if he had been left to his own devices, if he had been allowed to grow up the way he had been growing up, he would have been someone who was bookish, maybe a little bit weedy, and not particularly athletic. Instead, he was forced to become physically strong, and someone he would not have wanted to become. Even though he has a certain natural gift for fighting and even though he is physically formidable, he is not at all comfortable with that. It is very hard for him to be in the type of body that he never would have wanted to have.

JS: So why do you think you ended up putting such an emphasis on intellectual prowess with these characters?

MR: For me, *The Winner's Curse* is fundamentally a love story, and I think that smart is very sexy. One thing I personally find appealing and that I hope readers will find appealing is seeing two people who are very attuned to the world around them—very observant, very strategic, and able to do a kind of mental dance with each other.

JS: This is set in a society where duels play a part and I feel like there's certainly an emphasis on honor in the book. Yet at the same time it's very hard to find anyone with a real concrete high ground. There are good and bad things being done on all sides. Does that play into the story you want to tell about war and how we go to war? Is that something you think is inherent in the nature of conflict and conquest?

MR: Absolutely. I also think this moral ambiguity is found in people who are not directly engaged in war. How do we contend with the legacy of violence that has happened in our culture's past? To what degree are we responsible for things we may not have directly participated in? These questions haunt me. And some of the novels that have had the greatest impact on me as a reader have been ones that have questioned ethics or show tricky moral situations. I've thought a lot about Henry James's novels and in particular *Washington Square*, where there's a doctor, the father of a girl who's fallen in love. He is certain that his daughter's suitor is only after her for her money.

Even though the doctor is right, the way he goes about trying to prove it is horribly wrong. I find a fascinating tension in stories when characters are both so right and so wrong. This is something that I tried to re-create for almost all of my characters in *The Winner's Curse*.

JS: Between the dueling scenes and the tile game that Kestrel plays, you include a lot of detail about the world itself in the book, and its customs and traditions. Thinking about this book but also *The Shadow Society* or your Kronos books, is that sort of very detail-oriented world building something that you love to dive into with your writing?

MR: Yes. In my non-author life I'm a professor of Renaissance literature, and I think what has long drawn me to studying a period of time and a culture so distant from us is imagining how things were and trying to create an image of what it would have been like to walk into a tavern during Shakespeare's time in London.

Something interesting about how I created the world of *The Winner's Curse* is that I began by writing a book that was more traditionally fantasy. I had been trying to figure out how to write a novel that had some kind of magical element to it, but I stopped early on within the first chapter because it felt superfluous. When I thought about it, what I really wanted was to tell a *human* story. And so in terms of genre this book is maybe a little weird or at least different, and not something that is typically seen. It's technically a fantasy because it's set in a made-up world that I've created, but aside from that there is no fantasy in it. There are no dragons, there's no magic; there's nothing like that. The focus is on people and why and how they do the things they do.

JS: And what is the planned scope of the series? Is it a trilogy? Will it be longer? Do you know where it's headed?

MR: I do know where it's headed, and it is a trilogy. The second book is called *The Winner's Crime* and I have a pretty clear vision of how I want the third book to go and how it will end. Its ending will be pretty definitive. I don't imagine that I will be writing a fourth one; the story will conclude with the third book.

JS: Have you been getting any feedback either from fans or other sources?

MR: I have gotten some feedback, from bloggers in particular, and it's been really exciting. It's especially thrilling to hear from them while they're in the process of reading. They'll post something on Twitter about where they are in the book and their reaction to something that's happened. Sometimes I'm surprised by the vehemence of their responses, by how excited or upset they get or when they find something really shocking. Of course nothing's shocking to me because I wrote it.

JS: Do you often hear from a lot of readers with questions about the Kronos Chronicles or your other work?

MR: I do! Though for the Kronos books I mostly hear from children—from kids who are in third to fifth grades, and I love that. It's really adorable when I get fan mail or questions from them. Sometimes I get e-mails from kids who really want me to write a fourth book and they will tell me how they think the story should go. They'll say "not only should you write a fourth book, but I have some ideas for you in case you don't have any. Let me tell you what I think should happen to Petra and all of her friends."

JS: So now is the Winner's Trilogy—and of course your work—basically what's consuming your time at the moment or are you working on other books? Do you have plans to return to the world of *The Shadow Society*?

MR: I don't have plans to return to the world of *The Shadow Society* and I don't know exactly what's in store for me after I finish book three of the Winner's Trilogy. Sometimes I think, well, if I still love this world and really want to stay in it, maybe I will write a prequel, and I have some ideas about that. But I actually don't know whether the next book I write will be middle grade, young adult, or adult. It depends on what I want to do with it but it will be about a young boy. And I really don't want to say anything more than that because it's such a zygotic idea at this point. It's just really unformed and I don't have time to think about it or plan it until I finish what I'm working on now.

JS: Sure. Well, congratulations again on the book of the moment, *The Winner's Curse*, and thank you again for making time to speak with me.

MR: Oh, it was completely my pleasure, thank you.

Following your heart can be a crime.

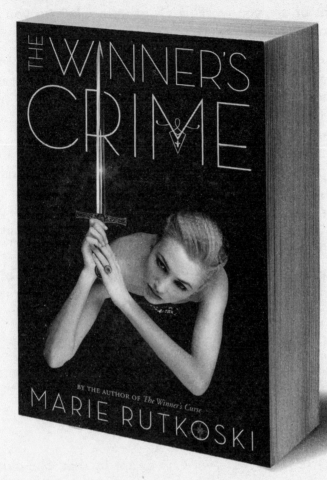

Keep reading for a sneak peek of

THE WINNER'S
CRIME

SHE CUT HERSELF OPENING THE ENVELOPE.

Kestrel had been eager, she'd been a fool, tearing into the letter simply because it had been addressed in Herrani script. The letter opener slipped. Seeds of blood hit the paper and bloomed bright.

It wasn't, of course, from him. The letter was from Herran's new minister of agriculture. He wrote to introduce himself, and to say he looked forward to when they would meet. *I believe you and I have much in common and much to discuss,* he wrote.

Kestrel wasn't sure what he meant by that. She didn't know him, or even of him. Although she supposed she would have to meet with the minister at some point—she was, after all, the imperial ambassador to the now independent territory of Herran—Kestrel didn't anticipate spending time with the minister of *agriculture*. She had nothing to say on crop rotation or fertilizer.

Kestrel caught the haughty tone of her thoughts. She

felt the way it thinned her mouth. She realized that she was furious at this letter.

At herself. At the way her heart had leaped to see her name scrawled in the Herrani alphabet on the envelope. She had hoped so hard that it was from Arin.

But she'd had no contact with him for nearly a month, not since she'd offered him his country's freedom. And the envelope hadn't even been addressed in his hand. She knew his writing. She knew the fingers that would hold the pen. Blunt-cut nails, silver scars from old burns, the calloused scrape of his palm, all very at odds with his elegant cursive. Kestrel should have known right away that the letter wasn't from him.

But still: the quick slice of paper. Still: the disappointment.

Kestrel set aside the letter. She pulled the silk sash from her waist, threading it out from under the dagger that she, like all Valorians, wore strapped to her hip. She wound the sash around her bleeding hand. She was ruining the sash's ivory silk. Her blood spotted it. But a ruined sash didn't matter, not to her. Kestrel was engaged to Prince Verex, heir to the Valorian empire. The proof of it was marked daily on her brow in an oiled, glittering line. She had sashes upon sashes, dresses upon dresses, a river of jewels. She was the future empress.

Yet when she stood from her carved ebony chair, she was unsteady. She looked around her study, one of many rooms in her suite, and was unsettled by the stone walls, the corners set insistently into perfect right angles, the way two wine. She could have asked why he had summoned her to dinner, and where the prince might be, but Kestrel had seen how the emperor loved to shape silence into a tool that pried open the anxieties of others. She let the silence grow until it was of her making as well as his, and only when the third course arrived did she speak. "I hear the campaign against the east goes well."

"So your father writes from the front. I must reward him for an excellently waged war. Or perhaps, Lady Kestrel, it's you I should reward."

She drank from her cup. "His success is none of my doing."

"No? *You* urged me to put an end to the Herrani rebellion by giving that territory self-governance under my law. *You* argued that this would free up troops and money to fuel my eastern war, and lo"—he flourished a hand—"it did. What clever advice from one so young."

His words made her nervous. If he knew the real reason she had argued for Herrani independence, she would pay for it. Kestrel tried the painstakingly prepared food. There were boats made from a meat terrine, their sails clear gelatin. She ate slowly.

"Don't you like it?" said the emperor.

"I'm not very hungry."

He rang a golden bell. "Dessert," he told the serving boy who instantly appeared. "We'll skip ahead to dessert. I know how young ladies enjoy sweet things." But when the boy returned bearing two small plates made from porcelain so fine Kestrel could see light sheer through the rims, the emperor said, "None for me," and one plate was set

narrow hallways cut into the room. It should have made
sense to Kestrel, who knew that the imperial palace was
also a fortress. Tight hallways were a way to bottleneck an
invading force. Yet it looked unfriendly and alien. It was so
different from her home.

Kestrel reminded herself that her home in Herran had
never really been hers. She may have been raised in that
colony, but she was Valorian. She was where she was supposed to be. Where she had chosen to be.

The cut had stopped bleeding.

Kestrel left the letter and went to change her day dress
for dinner. This was her life: rich fabric and watered silk
trim. A dinner with the emperor . . . and the prince.

Yes, this was her life.

She must get used to it.

The emperor was alone. He smiled when she entered his
stone-walled dining room. His gray hair was cropped in
the same military style as her father's, his eyes dark and
keen. He didn't stand from the long table to greet her.

"Your Imperial Majesty." She bowed her head.

"Daughter." His voice echoed in the vaulted chamber.
It rang against the empty plates and glasses. "Sit."

She moved to do so.

"No," he said. "Here, at my right hand."

"That's the prince's place."

"The prince, it seems, is not here."

She sat. Slaves served the first course. They poured white

MARIE RUTKOSKI

before Kestrel along with a strangely light and translucent fork.

She calmed herself. The emperor didn't know the truth about the day she had pushed for an end to the Herrani rebellion. No one did. Not even Arin knew that she had bought his freedom with a few strategic words . . . and the promise to wed the crown prince.

If Arin knew, he would fight it. He'd ruin himself.

If the emperor knew *why* she had done it, he would ruin her.

Kestrel looked at the pile of pink whipped cream on her plate, and at the clear fork, as if they composed the whole of her world. She must speak cautiously. "What need have I of a reward, when you have given me your only son?"

"And such a prize he is. Yet we've no date set for the wedding. When shall it be? You've been quiet on the subject."

"I thought Prince Verex should decide." If the choice were left to the prince, the wedding date would be never.

"Why don't *we* decide?"

"Without him?"

"My dear girl, if the prince's slippery mind cannot remember something so simple as the day and time of a dinner with his father and lady, how can we expect him to plan any part of the most important state event in decades?"

Kestrel said nothing.

"You're not eating," he said.

She sank the clear fork into the cream and lifted it to her mouth. The fork's tines dissolved against her tongue. "Sugar," she said with surprise. "The fork is made of hardened sugar."

"Do you like the dessert?"

"Yes."

"Then you must eat it all."

But how to finish the cream if the fork continued to dissolve each time she took a mouthful? Most of the fork remained in her hand, but it wouldn't last.

A game. The dessert was a game, the conversation a game. The emperor wanted to see how she would play.

He said, "I think the end of this month would be ideal for a wedding."

Kestrel ate more of the cream. The tines completely vanished, leaving something that resembled an aborted spoon. "A winter wedding? There will be no flowers."

"You don't need flowers."

"If you know that young ladies like dessert, you must also know that they like flowers."

"I suppose you'd prefer a spring wedding, then."

Kestrel lifted one shoulder in a shrug. "Summer would be best."

"Luckily my palace has hothouses. Even in winter, we could carpet the great hall with petals."

Kestrel silently ate more of the dessert. Her fork turned into a flat stick.

"Unless you want to postpone the wedding," said the emperor.

"I'm thinking of our guests. The empire is vast. People will come from every province. Winter is a terrible time to travel and spring little better. It rains. The roads become muddy."

The emperor leaned back in his chair, studying her with an amused expression.

"Also," she said, "I'd hate to waste an opportunity. You know that the nobles and governors will give you what they can—favors, information, gold—for the best seats at the wedding. The mystery of what I'll wear and what music will be played will distract the empire. No one would notice if you made a political decision that would otherwise outrage thousands. If I were you, I would enjoy my long engagement. Use it for all it's worth."

He laughed. "Oh, Kestrel. What an empress you will be." He raised his glass. "To your happy union, on the day of Firstsummer."

She would have had to drink to that, had not Prince Verex entered the dining room and stopped short, his large eyes showing every shift of emotion: surprise, hurt, anger.

"You're late," his father said.

"I am not." Verex's hands clenched.

"Kestrel managed to be here on time. Why couldn't you?"

"Because you told me the wrong hour."

The emperor tsked. "You misremember."

"You're making me look the fool!"

"*I* am making you look nothing of the kind."

Verex's mouth snapped shut. His head bobbed on his thin neck like something caught in a current.

"Come," Kestrel said gently. "Have dessert with us."

The look he shot her told Kestrel that he might hate his father's games, but he hated her pity more. He fled the room.

Kestrel toyed with her stub of a sugar fork. Even after the prince's noisy course down the hall had dwindled into silence, she knew better than to speak.

"Look at me," the emperor said.

She raised her eyes.

"You don't want a summer wedding for the sake of flowers, or guests, or political purchase," he said. "You want to postpone it for as long as possible."

Kestrel held the fork tightly.

"I'll give you what you want, within reason," he said, "and I will tell you why. Because I don't blame you, given your bridegroom. Because you don't whine for what you want, but seek to win it. Like I would. When you look at me, you see who you will become. A ruler. I have chosen you, Kestrel, and will make you into everything my son cannot be. Someone fit to take my place."

Kestrel looked, and her look became a stare that searched for her future in an old man capable of cruelty to his own child.

He smiled. "Tomorrow I'd like for you to meet with the captain of the imperial guard."

She had never met the captain before, but was familiar enough with his role. Officially, he was responsible for the emperor's personal safety. Unofficially, this duty spread to others that no one discussed. Surveillance. Assassinations. The captain was good at making people vanish.

"He has something to show you," the emperor said.

"What is it?"

"A surprise. Now look happy, Kestrel. I'm giving you everything that you could want."